Mark Antony Lower

**Wayside Notes in Scandinavia**

Mark Antony Lower

**Wayside Notes in Scandinavia**

ISBN/EAN: 9783337403164

Printed in Europe, USA, Canada, Australia, Japan

Cover: Foto ©Andreas Hilbeck / pixelio.de

More available books at **www.hansebooks.com**

# WAYSIDE NOTES

## IN SCANDINAVIA

By MARK ANTONY LOWER, M.A., F.S.A.

FELLOW OF THE SOCIETIES OF ANTIQUARIES OF NORMANDY, NEWCASTLE
UPON TYNE, AND AMERICA ; AND LATE F.S.A. OF LONDON ; MEMBER
OF THE ACADEMY OF SCIENCES OF CAEN, ETC. ETC.

HENRY S. KING & CO.

65 CORNHILL, AND 12 PATERNOSTER ROW, LONDON.

1874.

# TO CHARLES SCRASE-DICKINS, Esq.

## M.A., J.P., ETC. ETC.

### OF COOLHURST, SUSSEX,

(REPRESENTATIVE OF THE OLDEST DANISH FAMILY IN ENGLAND,)

THE FOLLOWING PAGES ARE RESPECTFULLY INSCRIBED

BY HIS MUCH OBLIGED, HUMBLE SERVANT,

## MARK ANTONY LOWER.

LONDON, *1st July* 1874

# Preface.

THOSE who have not carefully studied the complex character of our English nationality, are not aware how much we are indebted to the Scandinavian peoples, the Danes, the Norwegians, and the Swedes. Every intelligent reader of course knows that the earliest ascertained people of the land were the Celts, the Κελτοι of the classical writers, but I do not think that many have duly considered how much we are indebted to the Scandinavians, both in naval and military affairs, and in the formation of the manners and habits of the people, and of the language.

I hope these Notes will assist many who

*b*

have not visited those northern shores in a due recognition of that obligation.

I wish our modern tourists, instead of sticking to the old beaten tracks of travel, would sometimes go a little a-field, and visit less frequented highways. It appears that they find it necessary to follow in the same path that their fathers and friends have gone, like so many geese on a village green, and 'do' what others have 'done;' their principal object seeming to be, besides a holiday trip (which they may as well enjoy on British ground as elsewhere, without crossing the *narrow seas*), to 'hold up a corner' in a chit-chat in fashionable drawing-rooms.

Now, if my health and pecuniary means would permit, I would go into the byways instead of the highways of Europe, which not one in a hundred thousand Englishmen seems to care anything about. Just glance over a map, and see what a vast expanse of land is a *terra incognita,* almost untrodden by the English foot. How little is known of Lithuania, of Ukraine, of Wallachia, of the shores of the Dneiper, the Don, and the Volga, districts known only to the laborious few, but as little understood by the many as the 'Cannibal Islands' or the 'Mountains of the Moon.'

Let me entreat such to go to Scandinavia, and spend two or three months, say in May, June, and July, in those pleasant, hospitable countries, and I assure them they will not be less pleased than if they had been 'up the Rhine,' climbed the Alps (bringing home their *alpenstock* as a trophy[1]), or even to that Queen of Cities, Rome itself.

---

[1] I rather suspect that I have seen 'alpenstocks' in halls and drawing-rooms that have never crossed a mountain of any kind at all !

# WAYSIDE NOTES IN SCANDINAVIA

## *HISTORICAL, ARCHÆOLOGICAL, LEGENDARY, AND SOCIAL.*

On a fine Saturday evening in July 1873, my wife and I, departing from a suburb of London, went to the famous town of Wapping, and took state-rooms on board the 'Valdemar,' a large Danish steamer. She is a fine vessel, and on this occasion carried about 1200 tons of merchandise.

I had a threefold object in this tour: first, the restoration of my health, which had been very indifferent for several months; secondly, to show my wife the country of her ancestors, who by a credible tradition were of Danish descent, having settled in England about the

A

time of Canute the Great (she was *née* Scrase, in Danish 𝕾𝖐𝖗𝖆𝖆𝖌); thirdly, because I had long wished to visit the land of the Vikings, so much connected with our early ancestors, and who, robbers and pirates though they were, did more for the naval supremacy of England than all other influences put together.

Our good ship was of Newcastle build, and commanded by Captain Petersen. She is named after Valdemar II., surnamed *The Victorious*, King of Denmark in the thirteenth century.

We steamed out of port at ten o'clock on Sunday morning, and besides the pleasure of a passage down the Thames, had a delightful view of many familiar scenes on both sides of the river. After a few hours in the North Sea, we saw the most glorious sunset that eye could rest on.

> ' Sometimes we see a cloud that 's dragonish,
> A vapour sometimes like a bear or lion,'

and I distinctly saw a portrait of the head of

my little Chinese dog ' Ching.' The colours of the western sky varied from vermilion to carmine, and so on down to the deepest crimson. Even Turner in his wildest imaginings could never have touched that scene. It was the grandest spectacle of nature I ever beheld.[1]

We soon lost sight of land, but we felt quite at home. The passengers were ten gentlemen and three ladies—Danish, Swiss, and English. We were all soon as friendly and intimate as if we had known each other for years. A gentleman named Peckham, born in Kent, but long resident at Copenhagen, was unanimously elected our chief, as he was full of fun and humour, and kept us in a continual state of hilarity. During the days of our voyage we used to meet

---

[1] *Hamlet.* Do you see that cloud, that 's almost in shape like a camel?
*Polonius.* By the mass, and 'tis like a camel indeed!
*Ham.* Methinks it is like a weasel.
*Pol.* It is *backed* like a weasel.
*Ham.* Or like a whale?
*Pol. Very like a whale!*—*Hamlet*, Act III. Scene 2.

on deck about nine in the evening, and remain till midnight, relating anecdotes, cracking jokes, and singing songs, Danish, English, Irish, and Scotch. I never met with so merry a party before. They all sang the air of the tunes, except myself, and I was obliged to ' vamp in ' a little of my *bass*.

No incident of interest occurred, except the occasional meeting with a gallant steamer coming southward. We also saw what I had never seen before—a pair of black sea-ducks, swimming side by side, many leagues from the shore. In due time we reached the Skager Rack (called by our Jack Tars ' The Sleeve,' on account of its singular bend), and then the Cattegat. We arrived on the fourth day, after getting a peep of the shores of Jutland, at Elsinore, where we found vessels of many nations. It is the Land's End of Denmark. Some of us disembarked there, while others proceeded straight to Copenhagen.

Now, Elsinore disappointed us. True it is that Elsinore is a fine old town, with many historical associations, and many relics of by-gone ages. Kronborg Castle, now of no importance as a fortress, is an imposing structure of quadrangular form, with four towers, one of which serves as a lighthouse. The building dates from 1574 to 1585, and is a good specimen of the Renaissance style of the time of Frederik II. The view of it either from land or sea is extremely grand and romantic. The castle contains a good collection of pictures by modern Danish masters, and the prospect of the sea from the windows is delightful. The chapel, which has recently been restored, is worth a visit.

Northward of the town is Marienlyst, once a royal marine residence, but now belonging to a popular sea-bathing establishment—in short, a miniature Brighton. On a terrace behind they show you what they call the Grave of

Hamlet, a grove of trees within which some cunning genius, a good many years ago, placed a fragment of a column to indicate the grave. This has now been removed, and a kind of *cairn* of loose stones covers the spot. Nevertheless credulous Englishmen think they have seen Hamlet's grave, and bring away a stone from the heap as a trophy! Caroline-Mathilde inhabited apartments here before her removal to Hanover, and her rooms are still open to visitors.

I said we were disappointed with Elsinore; it was because we found no trace of Hamlet there. Indeed, many Danish *savans* treat that personage as a myth, and say that if ever he existed it was in Jutland about the ninth century. Shakspeare, with his usual anachronisms, makes him live since the introduction of gunpowder and cannon.

When the story of Hamlet's grave was pretty well established, curious visitors inquired for

Ophelia's fatal brook, and this was shown near the Marienlyst garden. It is a tiny stream, hardly large enough for a duck to swim in, and how our heroine managed to drown herself in it is a mystery. Altogether, Elsinore is 'the play of Hamlet, with the *part* of Hamlet left out!'

---

Now as we are safely landed in Scandinavia, I shall proceed to remind my 'gentle reader' of a few historical and geographical facts which may have escaped his recollection. Any one looking at a map of Europe will see that the peninsula of Scandinavia should form one political commonwealth, or rather kingdom, and this was originally the case. The severance of Sweden and Norway from Denmark took place long ago, and there seems to be no chance of their reunion, nor would it perhaps be desirable, for several reasons. Poor little Denmark, hemmed in on the east by Sweden, and by Norway on the west, and deprived of its adjuncts

Schleswig and Holstein by the tyranny of 'Pious
William' of Prussia, and his *master*, Bismarck, is
now one of the smallest states in Europe ; yet it
flourishes still, and God grant that it may always
do so ; though I was informed by some sound
Danish politicians that Bismarck could at any
time *annex* Denmark to the so-called 'Empire'
of Germany. Let England and France see to
that!  I will never acknowledge William as an
Emperor, nor Bismarck as a Prince, for neither
of them has a rightful claim to such a title.

More of the geography and history of Scandinavia hereafter.  Denmark is well governed,
and, so far as I could ascertain, King Christian IX.
is highly esteemed by all right-minded people,
though of course those of the ' baser sort ' sometimes exhibit disloyalty ; as was the case a few
days after we left Copenhagen, when all the
police of the city had to be called in to put
down a semi-revolutionary mob.

In Sweden and Norway King Oscar II. is

very popular. A correspondent of the English *Standard*, writing from Stockholm on August 11, 1873, says :—

' The Norwegian *Official Gazette* of yesterday gives the report of a remarkable speech which the King made at the festivities given in his honour a few days ago at Stafsskogen. The speech resumes in few words the political programme of Oscar II., and affords a worthy specimen of the manner in which a Scandinavian Sovereign understands his duties as his people's leader.

' His Majesty's words were these :—

' To-day is the last day of my long journey. I have visited the various parts of this kingdom, and the Queen has at the same time travelled through parts of the realm where no Queen ever set her foot before. Everywhere we came the people have greeted us with love, as we met them in love and in confidence, rejoicing in the feeling that the people look up to the Royal

House with loyal attachment and fidelity. My
family and I have been still more confirmed in
our love to this beautiful country, which from
my earliest childhood I have learnt to cherish
and esteem more and more.

' Norway is a happy country ; indeed, the two
sister countries are the happiest countries I
know. I would resume in three words the three
good things which I consider to constitute the
happiness of this country—they are Peace, the
Union, and Liberty.

' Peace is a precious thing, and Norway has,
thanks to God, been long enjoying its blessings ;
but it is necessary that we preserve our forces,
and that we do not in the good times when nature
showers her gifts upon us, allow ourselves to be
absorbed by our cares about them, and degraded
down to materialistic idolatry. In the days of
peace we ought to prepare ourselves for the time
when an enemy may threaten the independence
of our country, and it is the duty of every good

citizen to keep himself ready to defend his Fatherland.'

' In the union with Sweden, another free and independent country, Norway has a guarantee for a long and lasting peace. May the two peoples join hands without suspicion! They are now going on side by side in prosperity and increasing wealth, and while keeping their independence they will unite as brothers more and more closely together, and, if necessary, stand strong and united against any foe.

' Liberty is a blessing; but it ought not to be a Spanish liberty, but a Norwegian liberty, worthy of a community which above everything bows down in respect to God—not a lawless but a law-bound liberty. Obedience to the law has of old been characteristic of the Norwegian people, and it is the duty of every one, from the King down to the humblest citizen, to obey the laws rigorously. Most specially have we to defend the constitution of the realm, and protect it against one-sided party spirit. I drink to the health of our Fatherland—our old beloved Norway.

' It is too little to say that the King's words were received with respectful silence ; it was rather a solemn emotion that painted itself on the faces of the listening crowd while his Majesty was speaking in that clear and musical voice the peculiar charm of which will never be forgotten by those who have once heard it. The topics on which he dwelt are matters of vital interest for both countries. Reorganization of the army, and a closer union between Sweden and Norway are the two great reforms which must be made sooner or later if we wish to keep ourselves independent of the political commotions which shake so fatally the continent of Europe. Every true lover of his country looks forward to King Oscar's government to make those projects a reality, and to crush the opposition of so-called Liberals and patriots, whose sole aim it is to be able to boast before their constituents that they have succeeded in reducing public expenditure, thus proving their love of the " people," and their complete indifference to the welfare of the country. *Tout comme chez vous !'*

---

Nothing can be more affectionate than the feeling of the Danish people towards the Princess of Wales. They seem almost to worship her. The following verses, translated from the Danish, will go far to prove this :—

### TO THE PRINCE OF WALES.

*(Translated from the Danish at the Request of Royalty.)*

Amidst the flowers of Denmark grew
  A Rose of snowy whiteness :
In th' nation's heart it had taken root,
  And bloomed in fairy brightness.

Its grace in Britain's isle was known,—
  Fame o'er the waters bore it :—
' The Rose of Denmark stands alone !
  All beauty fades before it !'

Great Britain's Prince then sought a Bride,
  To share his regal brightness :
So he wooed the Danish Maid, and plucked
  The Rose of snowy whiteness !

She joyous smiled when Britain vowed,
  ' *This* Rose to me is dearest !'
While thousand hearts the choice approved—
  He chose of all the fairest !

*November,* 1862.                    R. S. E.

I have just alluded to the loyalty of the Norwegians, and I may perhaps be permitted to
quote a song of Denmark, showing the strong
attachment of the Danish people to their fine
old historical country. It was sung at the
Festival at Moen's Klint, July 6th, 1852, in
memory of the battle of Frederits, and has been
thus translated :—

      ' Denmark, fair Mother !
      Ocean out-risen,
      Loveliest flower on
          Mermaiden's breast !
      Pleasedly, even
      South-dwellers must
      Gaze on thy fertile and
          Bright-smiling coast.

Denmark, fair Mother !
—Destinies friendly,
Sang round thy cradle
    EVER THOU 'LT STAND !
Seasons roll onward,—
Oceans flow onward,—
Flourish thou shalt, whilst
    Waves wash thy strand !

Denmark, fair Mother !
—Aggression's hand shall
Wither, as oft as it
    Touches thy shore !
Soft through the greensward,
Forming thy throne-seat—
Firm shalt thou stand, till
    Time be no more !'

                R. S. E.

To return to personal narrative : we left Elsinore by rail on a fine summer evening for Copenhagen, a journey of about two hours. The route was principally through a kind of grove or avenue of trees, with an occasional glimpse of a heath or common. On reaching Copenhagen we repaired to the Jernbane (the Terminus Hotel), pleasantly situated, having in

front a spacious *place* paved with rough stone,
and full of life and bustle. Carriages and vehicles
of every description were constantly passing and
repassing. We saw multitudes of beautiful
horses—such horses as we never saw before.
Their necks are arched like those that we see
in Grecian sculpture, and they are usually in
pairs which would not disgrace any English
nobleman's carriage, though some of them are
employed in drawing waggons of the roughest
description, shaped somewhat like flat-bottomed
boats with the stem and stern cut off. No groups
of horses could surpass them. I don't know if
Rosa Bonheur ever saw them ; but if not, I
would advise her to go to Copenhagen for a
study. One peculiarity we specially noted,
namely, that the horses are accommodated with
a kind of rough camp-stool, whereon to rest their
nose-bags—a plan which ought to be adopted
by the 'cabbies' of England. In front of our
sitting-room we saw the Palace of Industry, a

fine spacious building, on each side of which is
a picturesque windmill, one of them curiously
built on the top of a house. We remained at
this hotel for two days, and then removed to the
Hôtel Royal, the principal inn in Copenhagen,
chiefly because it possesses an excellent table-
d'hôte, which the Jernbane does not boast of.
The arrangements of this establishment are of
the best and most comfortable kind, with reason-
able charges.

But now for Copenhagen. Well, I have seen
many great cities at home and abroad, but I
never saw one which so much impressed me as
did Copenhagen. Though not large, it is the
most interesting city I have ever seen. The
main streets are grand and imposing. The
houses are large, and have many windows, and
they are, every now and then, interspersed with
public buildings, which greatly add to the first
impression. Besides this, there are fine avenues
of trees everywhere, and summer walks beneath

them are truly delightful. Copenhagen may be called the 'City of Islands :' it is, indeed, an island itself, and is surrounded by numerous islets ; in fact, when you are in Scandinavia you hardly know whether you are on land or at sea.

The first Sunday morning after our arrival, we went to the English Church service, which is held in the place of worship belonging to the Moravian Brethren, Stormgade 21. We were some minutes too early, and waited in a kind of vestibule ; and I being weak and tired, a lady kindly brought me a chair. Shortly afterwards another lady entered, and inquired if I was ill. I told her that I was much indisposed, and she then informed us that she was wife of the Chaplain to the English Legation, and that she would direct the pew-opener to put us into a good place.

The Chaplain, the Rev. R. E. Ellis, M.A. of Cambridge, read the service excellently— his emphasis being, I think, the best I ever heard.

Soon after the commencement of the sermon I
was obliged to leave the church, my wife and
the pew-opener following me. Hereafter this
pew-opener shall be more fully described, as she
is a very remarkable person indeed.

As we were seated at the table-d'hôte, soon
after three o'clock, Mrs. Ellis came in, and
kindly invited us to spend a day at Rungsted,
on the Sound, where the Chaplain has a country
residence during the summer months—his principal abode being at Copenhagen. This we
accepted, and went, two days afterwards, to pass
what turned out to be a most pleasurable day.
We went up by a steamer, and the voyage was
of about an hour and a half's duration. The
banks of the Sound, with Denmark on the right
and Sweden on the left, are delightful; villas
and villages, interspersed with rich foliage, line
both shores, and the water of this narrow sea is
as clear as crystal. Opposite our entertainers'
house is the insulated spot known as Tycho

Brahe's Island, and it was there that that eminent astronomer lived.    Hveen is, I believe, the right name of the island, which was presented to Tycho by the King of Denmark.    He built an observatory upon it, and gave it the name of Uraniburg.    Part of the foundations of his observatory and his castle still remain.    Some distance inland is Horsholm, where a magnificent palace was built by King Christian VI., about a century since.    It was one of the finest of royal abodes, and was known as 'The Versailles of the North ;' but, unhappily, Frederik VI., though he was born within its walls, disliked it, and suffered it to go to decay.    In 1810 it was pulled down, and no remains of it now exist; but its site is marked by a little church, with no architectural pretensions.    So much for bad taste !

That singular personage, Tycho, a mixture of the soundly scientific and the superstitious, was perhaps, upon the whole, the greatest man that

Scandinavia has produced. He was much courted by royal and other personages, and James VI. of Scotland (afterwards our James I.) once paid a visit to his island. Tycho was a good Latin poet, and a man of general information, but the drawbacks of his mental character were his addiction to astrology, and his observance of omens. He died in 1601. But this is a digression, for which I crave the reader's pardon.

On arriving off the Chaplain's residence we were kindly met on a little jetty, of which there are many in the Sound, by Mrs. Ellis, who conducted us to her house. After a most friendly greeting by the Chaplain, we had luncheon, and Mrs. Ellis and a lady friend took my wife for a row on the Sound, while I remained ashore chatting with Miss Ellis, who gave me the latest English newspapers. From them I learned that my dear friend and patron, Bishop Wilberforce, had sustained a fatal injury on the very day that we had left our home, and this caused me many bitter tears. I found that Mr. Ellis was the nephew of my old and much esteemed friend Sir Henry Ellis, of antiquarian and British Museum celebrity. The Chaplain, though no courtier in the vulgar sense of the word, is evidently much esteemed at Court, and we heard that on a late occasion he had the honour of being seated at dinner between the Princess Dagmar, the probable future Empress of Russia, and Alexandra, now Princess of Wales. The latter, on the very day of her departure for England, presented him with an elegant gold watch and chain, with a souvenir inscription engraved on the case.

In the evening we returned, partly by an open omnibus, and partly by rail, to Copenhagen. The route was lovely,[1] through great masses of the finest foliage, such as we had never before

---

[1] The wild flowers, in close proximity to the salt water, are remarkably beautiful.

beheld—indeed, it was a kind of fairy-land. The Sound was delightfully calm, and I am sure we saw at least seven hundred vessels, of every sort, coming down or going up that narrow channel, sailing or steaming to the Baltic or back. We never saw so much marine activity before, and I doubt if it could be paralleled in the world.

Had we been an Earl and a Countess we could not have been received more courteously than we were, wherever we went. The Danish character is remarkable for frankness and hospitality, and as transparent as glass. As a rule, the ladies are not what we should deem beautiful, though some of them are eminently so. After an interview or two you become like old friends. I had an attack of illness which confined me to my bed for a day or two, and a lady, whom we had met, came to visit us. She sat by my bedside for half an hour, holding my hand in hers all the time, and talking in a manner calculated to cheer an invalid's heart. On another occasion my wife and myself visited several newly-made lady friends, and I kissed six of them without a single blush among the eight of us! I don't believe there is a coquette in all Scandinavia.

To return to our friendly pew-opener. She came to the hotel a day or two after our interview, to inquire after my health, and invited us to give her a call, which, of course, we did. She keeps a very pretty shop for the sale of what the Danes call *tobakker*. Passing through this apartment, we were ushered up-stairs into handsomely furnished rooms, and there found, *inter alia*, a piano, a harmonium, and an organ. She told us that she was of English birth, but had left this country with her parents at the tender age of six weeks. On arriving at woman's estate she married a Dane, and had by him ten children, all of whom, except her youngest daughter, have grown up and left her. She receives for her pew-opening duties fifty rix-dollars a year,[1] which, with much more, as we had reason to believe, she conscientiously devotes to the poor sick English sailor-boys who arrive in the port of Copenhagen. She told us, with much emotion, that it was her habit to go and pray with the poor lads, and that she had closed the eyes of many of them. She is a most intelligent woman, of unaffected manners, and is well educated ; and besides translating the Scandinavian languages into English, writes elegant verses. Her name is Blichfeldt—and God bless her for her benevolent exertions !

Social status is much less attended to in Scandinavia than in England, and as there are few distinctions of creed — nearly the entire population being Lutherans—a more friendly feeling seems to exist than in many other parts of Europe.

---

[1] A rix-dollar is 2s. 3d. of our money.

The shops in the principal streets are excellent, and many of them offer an assortment of elegant merchandise. In some parts of Copenhagen, however, the shops are underground, and you have to go down steps as to cellars, to make a purchase. Every third or fourth tradesman has a *handel* to his name, or rather trade. Thus a bookseller is a bog-handel ; a merchant, a handelsmand ; a tea-dealer, a thee-handel ; a cheesemonger, an ostehandel, or ostehandler, etc. etc.—the word signifying trade, commerce, or a dealer.

Most of the better class of tradesmen speak English, as also do the waiters at the principal hotels. Mr. Macgregor, of ' Rob Roy' celebrity, informed me that the English language would answer our purpose well, without resorting either to French, or to Latin *pronounced in the continental mode*—an expedient to which I have had occasion to resort before now. Mr. Macgregor especially remarked that the Swedes were most desirous of acquiring some English, and that even children would get behind one's chair for the purpose of picking up our conversational phrases. I can, truly say that several educated Norwegian ladies whom we met spoke our language with the greatest purity and the best accent, though some of them had never been in England.

With respect to the furnishing of the houses (I speak principally of Denmark), there is much *ideal* comfort. The absence of carpets in summer, and the great want of open fireplaces or hearths, make us feel that we are not at home, and that at least some English comforts are wanting. The rooms are mostly heated by upright cylindrical iron stoves, surmounted with imitation bronze statues; and at night, man and wife are *divorced* into two little beds, like those used by the pupils in boarding schools. Everything reminds one of the French style in furnishing.

A table-d'hôte is a famous institution, and I wish it could be fairly said that we possessed it in England; but we insular folks are so *select* and exclusive that most people prefer dining in private rooms, thereby losing a great deal of social enjoyment. At the table-d'hôte, at the Copenhagen Hôtel-Royal, where nearly a hundred guests of many nations sat down daily, we met with some very interesting people. Close to me on several occasions sat the well-known Rev. Dr. Aitken of Edinburgh (D.D.), now seventy-five years of age, who, in his younger days, had been well acquainted with Sir Walter Scott, and in later times with the celebrated Danish sculptor Thorvaldsen, during the period when he was pursuing his studies at Rome. Of Thorvaldsen more hereafter. My *vis-à-vis* was a well-known English county member; and there were many other persons of distinction (some Americans), whose names I omitted to note down; but all were polite and friendly, and the dinners passed off with much hilarity and good-will. A table-d'hôte is pretty much the same everywhere, but we noticed one peculiarity here, namely, that mutton and beef succeeded the soup, and preceded the fish. The dessert was very good, and so were the ales and wines. As a rule the northern mutton is not to be compared with that of our famed South Downs or Leicesters. The sheep are small, and wear the long tails which were born with them. They are curiously marked on their backs with red and crimson ochre. The beef is better, and great numbers of cattle are exported to England. Agriculture and cattle-breeding receive much attention in Denmark, and there is scarcely a rood of ground that is not in some way utilized where such a thing is practicable. The farms are small, and are often cultivated by their own proprietors. Such persons as we call 'gentlemen farmers' are scarcely known.

A word on the peasantry and the other working classes. They are mostly clean and decently
habited. When they meet a superior they salute
him by raising their caps, and they do the
same to persons of their own position, if known
to them. The little peasant boys have their
light hair cropped close to their heads, and
look like small convicts lately come out of
prison.

Now for a few words on the history of the
three countries, taking each separately; and
first of Denmark.

Denmark, as Sir John Lubbock well observes,
in his *Prehistoric Times*, occupies a larger space
in history than it does on the map of Europe.
Not only, as he truly remarks, that many a more
important nation may well envy the Danes the
position they hold in science and art, but it is
besides undoubtedly true that the *antiquity* of
Denmark, as of Scandinavia generally, was its

most splendid period, and that to which even now the greatest interest attaches. Certainly the memorials of prehistoric Scandinavia are among the most curious in Europe; and happily there have arisen in our later days men of diligent research and great learning, who have, so to speak, *edited* the historical relics of unknown ages. The earliest ascertained historical fact in the history of Denmark, to which a considerable portion of Jutland and South Schleswig then belonged, is a war with Germany in the days of Charlemagne. A treaty concluded in 810 made the river Eyder the boundary between the two contending powers, and so continued till 1864. In the days of Charlemagne, the Danes, Norwegians, and Swedes remained in pagandom, but shortly afterwards, in 827, the gospel was introduced into Denmark by Ansgarius, a monk from Westphalia. It took no deep root till after the conquest of England by Sweyn and Cnut. At the death of Cnut, his large territory, comprising Denmark, Norway, England, the south of Scotland, and large tracts on the Baltic coast, was broken up, and Denmark was long divided by internal feuds.

Then comes what is called the Valdemarian period, during which kings Valdemar I., Cnut VI., and Valdemar II. bore successful rule. The Danes now turned propagandists of Christianity, and waged war against the pagan countries on the south and east of the Baltic. During a battle fought near Revel in Russia, in 1219, a great miracle occurred. The Danes having discarded the old pagan flag of the Raven, a new one was vouchsafed them by Heaven, and sent down to them. Under this new banner they became victorious. It was a red flag with a white cross, still the national ensign by sea and land, and is called the *Dannebrog*.

In the *Danish Ditties done into English,*

by the Rev. R. S. E., there is a national war-song, which includes the following stanza :—

> ' The Dannébrog 'tis known,
> The Dannébrog 'tis known,
> It fell from heaven down,
> Yes, it fell from heaven down ;
> It floats upon the mast,
> The soldier grasps it fast,
> And no Flag in the world besides like ours from Heaven
> was ever cast.'

Truly there is no nation under the sun that is prouder of its national ensign than is Denmark—not even England of its union-jack. Some sceptics of late times have been profane enough to say that the Dannebrog was sent to the Danish monarch by the Pope ; but I vastly prefer the legend !

Valdemar II. holds a position in the annals of Denmark similar to that assigned to our own Alfred. He was an eminent law-giver, and the oldest statute laws of the realm, both civil and ecclesiastical, date from his reign. 'He also caused the compilation of a most interesting account of the royal revenue derived from property in the whole of the kingdom—a kind of Domesday Book."[1]   His death in 1241 was followed by political discord from within and oppression from without.  A man, noble by birth and noble by disposition, came to the rescue.  This was Niels Ebbesen, a native of Jutland, who by his wisdom and daring courage put things once more into order.  The Danes, now thoroughly aroused, were led by a new sovereign, Valdemar III., and the integrity and independence of the kingdom were thoroughly restored.  That monarch's daughter, Queen Margaret, succeeded in securing the *rotundity* of Scandinavia, by adding to Denmark proper the realms of Norway and Sweden.  She was an able ruler, but unhappily, after her death, the united Scandinavian kingdoms passed to

---

[1] Murray, p. 11.

German magnates distantly related to the ancient royal family of Denmark. They lacked energy and ability, and after the lapse of upwards of a century, marked by many troubles, Sweden seceded from the union. Margaret's successor was Eric of Pomerania, who married Philippa, daughter of our Henry IV., whose gallant defence of Copenhagen (in the absence of her husband) against the fleets of the Hanseatic League, give her a great name in northern history.

The first of the Oldenburg dynasty, which still reigns in Denmark, was Christian I., and a younger branch of his family occupies the throne of Russia. King Christian acquired the duchy of Holstein. In the reign of Christian III. the Reformation took place, almost by common consent. Christian IV. (1588-1648) was a gallant soldier, a good political economist, and a man of exquisite taste—three qualities rarely combined in one sovereign. He erected numerous buildings, similar in style to what we call Elizabethan, and which is called in Denmark the Christian-the-Fourth style. Good specimens of his architectural taste are the Copenhagen Exchange, and the castles of Rosenborg and Fredriksborg. His son, Frederik iii., was less successful, and Charles x. of Sweden deprived Denmark of the provinces east of the Sound, which have ever since formed part of the Swedish dominions. For a long period the crown of Denmark had been elective, but after a time it became an absolute hereditary monarchy. Few of the kings of the Oldenburg dynasty cared much for the Danish nationality and language, their queens and ministers being chiefly Germans, and the natives of Denmark were possessed of very little influence.

Here I may remark that the names of Christian and Frederik have long been popular in Scandinavia, and numerous towns and minor places have these names as prefixes; thus we

have, in Denmark, Christiansborg, Christians-
havn, Christianso, Christianssæde; in Norway,
Christiania, Christiansand, Christiansund; and
in Sweden, Christenhamn and Christenstad.
Likewise with Frederic, we have in the three
nations Frederikborg, Fredericksal, Frederiks-
havn, Frederiksværk, Frederikstadt, Fre-
derickischort, Frediksgard, Frederikstad, and
numerous other minor places. It was the same
custom with our Anglo-Saxon ancestors, who
usually prefixed their own names or titles to
those of their estates. Hence we have, besides
Kingston and Queensborough, Milton, Arling-
ton, Michelham, Claverham, Peterborough, and
a thousand others.

Frederic v., who reigned from 1746 to
1766, married Louisa, a daughter of our George
ii., who was greatly beloved by the Danish
people. Their son, Christian vii., married
Caroline-Mathilde, daughter of our George iii.
The history of this queen of Denmark is very

painful. She was from an early age of a very sickly constitution, and her husband unfortunately gave himself up to a reckless life, which produced mental disease. Then Struensee, a famous German physician, an atheist and an admirer of Voltaire, became the virtual king of Denmark, and governed it for some time, no doubt with good intentions, but with very ill success, for by a court conspiracy his career was brought to a speedy conclusion, and he was beheaded in 1772. The Queen was suspected of an illicit *liaison* with Struensee, and was divorced from her husband and banished. She retired to Celle in Hanover, and died not long afterwards.

From the time of Struensee's fall, it has been observed, 'dates a strong and ever-increasing revival of Danish national feeling, of Danish literature, art, and science.' About the end of the eighteenth century the Danish commerce and its necessary shipping became very flourish-

ing, and, as the Danes observed the strictest
neutrality during that sanguinary period, they
were comparatively safe. But unhappily in
1802 the English Government commenced hostilities, with a view to compelling Denmark to
secede from the league formed by the neutral
states for the protection of their commerce—
one of the vilest acts ever perpetrated by an
English ministry. On the 2d of April 1802
a great sea-fight took place off Copenhagen
between Lord Nelson and the Danish ' Line of
Defence.' Nielsen is a common name in Denmark, and the Nielsens (etymologically the same
as Nelson) declare that our great naval hero
never conquered them, but that it was a ' drawn
battle,' which I partly believe.

Five years afterwards (1807) began a second
war with England. A fleet with twenty thousand
men left our shores, with a demand for the un-
conditional surrender of the Danish fleet. The
poor Danes expected no hostilities. Copenhagen

was unprepared for a naval attack, was without a garrison, and almost utterly defenceless. A three days' bombardment destroyed a considerable part of the city, and the Danish fleet was equipped and carried away by the English. I am almost ashamed to chronicle these things against my countrymen, but I can truly say that in our fathers' dealings with Denmark they behaved most dishonourably.

In 1814 Denmark was compelled to cede Norway to Sweden, but why I could never understand. I sometimes think that these diminutions of Danish power and authority may be regarded as a kind of retributive justice. The Danes of olden times were invaders and pirates, and they and their near neighbours conquered England, part of Scotland, Normandy, and other parts of Europe; but let that pass.

The Danish shipping and commerce were ruined, and the state was all but bankrupt; but by economical government, by the national resources of the country, and by circumstances of a fortunate character, Denmark held her own, and Frederik VI. was in a measure the happy instrument of saving his country from destruction : he died in 1839. In the meantime the so-called Schleswig-Holstein movement began to develop itself. ' It was an offshoot of the *unity* movement in Germany [Prussia], and had for its object to separate from Denmark and unite with Germany, not only the originally German duchy of Holstein, which had been acquired by Christian I. in 1460, but also the originally Danish duchy of Schleswig, which had never in any way been connected with Germany, but of which the southern part, by constant immigration, had become Germanized.'[1] The subsequent and recent history of Denmark will be in the recollection of most readers.

---

[1] Murray, p. 14.

With the exception of Switzerland, there is perhaps a no more picturesque country in the world than Norway, with its long range of mountains, the Dovrefjelds, its numerous *fiords* or arms of the sea, and its wonderfully beautiful waterfalls. There is so rugged a coast as cannot be found anywhere else, and the islands and islets are innumerable. Norway is about 1100 English miles in length, that is, half as long again as Great Britain, but in some places very narrow. The mountains at various points reach the vast elevation of 8000 feet.

Sportsmen, whether hunters or fishers, find such a fund of amusement as they could not enjoy in any other country. Draughtsmen in Norway most delight in the picturesque scenery of the land, and its wonderful *cloudage.* Altogether, there is nowhere so good a study for the geologist and the meteorologist as in the land of the Norsemen. The towns and houses are not very attractive, and the tourist should look out for the beauties of nature rather than for those of art. There are, however, some beautiful churches of early date. The costume of the Norwegians is very picturesque, especially that of the women. The old men cultivate long white hair, which flows down on each side of the face in truly patriarchal fashion. They wear red worsted caps, open shirt-collars, and jackets and waistcoats decked with silver buttons, as our English ancestors did three generations ago, when old men used to wear crown pieces on their coats, and shillings on their waistcoats,— an inoffensive mode of showing that they were not 'hard up' for money. As to the interiors of houses, it has been remarked that they are far more picturesque than cleanly, especially in the districts of Bergen and Tellemarken. In many cases the reception-room or Statssue is of a rich dark brown tint, caused by wood smoke; and this apartment generally contains all the family, and most of the family goods and family gods.

Norway is a truly sporting country, but as I can neither shoot nor fish, I cannot say much on that subject. Murray will tell you all about it. Game of all kinds is abundant, except partridges and pheasants. The capercailzie, the blackcock, and the ptarmigan may be found in their habitats to the sportsman's heart's content. Before I left England a friend told me that if I could pick up a pair of capercailzie and bring them to England alive, they would fetch ten pounds; but I was not fortunate enough to make the purchase.

The Danes call their great national meetings ' *things*,' and so I think they are. The Danish parliament (called the Rigsdag) consists of all sorts and conditions of men. It opens on the first Monday in October. A preliminary sermon is preached in the church adjoining the Castle of Christiansborg, and then the ministers of the Crown are present; cheers are given for the King whether he appears *in propriâ personâ* or not.

The next thing that the '*thing*' does is to elect a speaker, a deputy speaker, and other officers.

.The Danish House of Commons is a motley crowd ; and now it has as members, peasants, mechanics, little landed proprietors, clergymen, scholars, and in fact persons representing every grade of society. At this moment there are among what we call M.P.'s a shoemaker, a country schoolmaster, some retired butchers, and the like. This may suit Messrs. Odger, Bradlaugh, and Sir Charles Dilke, but it does not suit *my* ideas of a Parliament, which should be composed of men of high culture and refinement.

Since the foregoing was written, the following information has reached us. On the 19th of October 1873, the Danish House of Commons was dissolved by Royal direction, after only twelve days' existence. This *Folkething* consisted of 101 members, of whom 6 were cottagers or day-labourers, who receive 7s. 6d. a day for their services ; 49 peasants and small farmers of from 20 to 60 acres ; 19 miscellaneous, consisting of country schoolmasters, editors of small provincial newspapers, and tradesmen ; and finally of 27 members of high social position, independent means, and good education. One of the first class of M. P.'s is said to have filled up the hours he could spare from the *thing* in chopping up wood in the streets, his usual occupation !

Norway abounds in wild beasts and birds. In 1855 the bears killed amounted to 212, the wolves to 235, the lynxes to 125, the gluttons to 72, and the eagles to 2559! Between 700 and 800 mountain owls, and about the same number of hawks, are slain every year. Stags, elks, and reindeer are common, but beavers are almost extinct. The game-laws of Norway are extremely strict and severe.

One of the greatest natural curiosities in Norway is the mischievous leming, an animal of a brownish colour, about the size of our water-rat. These creatures do not appear year by year, but at intervals of three or four years. Their natural habitat is the mountains, from which they migrate when their numbers become too large for home-subsistence. Their water-passage is from east to west in a direct line, and they take boldly to broad rivers and large fiords till they arrive on the shores of the Atlantic. Should they encounter a heavy storm they are drowned in myriads, and float on the surface of the water. Many of them are supposed during their passage to be devoured by birds of prey. Their march is chiefly nocturnal, and they devour most of the corn or herbage in their route. 'Formerly the Norwegians believed them to have fallen from the clouds, and so great was the mischief caused by them, that they were solemnly *exorcised by the priests*, and a Leming Litany was appointed to be said with this object,'[1]—another instance of ancient Norse superstition.

---

[1] Murray.

Very little has been ascertained of the early history of Norway, and in this respect it resembles most of the countries of the west of Europe. The *Sagas*, as the most ancient compositions comprising the mythology and history of the northern races are called, can no more be relied on than the semi-fabulous history of Romulus and Remus and the subsequent kings of Rome, or even than the wild chronicles of the Chinese. Our best ethnographers, however, consider the aborigines to have been Lapps; but there is little doubt that the southern population of Scandinavia, comprising Denmark, most of Sweden, and all the south of Norway are of the Teutonic, German, or Gothic race, and in all probability came from Asia, in a nomadic manner, through the east and midland parts of Europe; but why, coming as they did from a warm climate, they should have settled in so bleak a district as Scandinavia is a puzzle not easily understood. Snorro Sturleson's celebrated chronicle, written in the twelfth and thirteenth centuries, is more trustworthy than the Sagas; but it is somewhat like the writings of our Geoffry of Monmouth, and must not be 'swallowed whole.' However, it is pretty certain that the settlement of these orientals was in petty communities, who continually waged war with each other. But at length there arose a leading spirit in the person of 'the fair-haired Harald' (Haarfager) who, in the latter part of the ninth century, made himself master of the whole country.

At the commencement of his career he was informed of the charms of one Gyda, daughter of the king of Hordaland, and he sent some of his retainers to offer her his heart, though he said nothing about his hand. She was proud and indignant, and would not submit to become his mistress, but said that on his becoming master of the whole country she would marry him. He admired her ambition, and vowed to all the Teutonic gods that he would neither cut

D

nor even comb his hair until he had subdued all Norway; which, as I have said, he eventually did, and then the fair Gyda consented to accept him, although he was already possessed of eight wives. This I think goes far to prove his Eastern extraction. From the time when Harald began to comb his fair hair again, about A.D. 885, down to about 1250, the history of Norway is full of stories of heroic warlike exploits.

The Vikings were in their glory, and probably brought home large spoils from their unfortunate neighbours, but there was not much peace in the country; for internal feuds and constant emigrations to other shores always prevailed. The Vikings, discontented with absolute rule, attempted settlements in other countries. As in Norway, so in Sweden and Denmark, the desire of a settlement in distant and more favoured climes became the ambition of the Scandinavian peoples. Thus the Norwegians obtained a footing in Scotland and Ireland, and the Danes in England and Normandy. Rollo, the first duke of Normandy, is said to have come to the south from Aalesund in Norway, and to have been called 'Hrolf Gangr' or *Rollo the Walker*, because he was so big and tall that no Norwegian horse could carry him! But contemporary chroniclers assert that he and his followers were Danes, and many of their descendants there still bear the name of *le Danois*. It must be remembered that Norwegians and Danes were indiscriminately called Northmen. The Vikings, with a spirit unequalled in those early times, made voyages to the shores of every country in Europe, even as far as Constantinople. In the tenth century they made mainprise of Iceland, and from thence some hardy adventurers made excursions across the Atlantic, and discovered North America some centuries before Christopher Columbus was thought of.

Hagen surnamed 'the Good' succeeded Haarfager in 933, and there is a *saga* concerning him. He was brought up in England under Athelstan. He tried to introduce Christianity into Norway, but it took no deep root until the twelfth century.

In 1016, Olaf II. became king of Norway, and he is known to later ages as Saint Olaf. His sanctity, however, may well be doubted, as he tried to enforce Christianity upon his subjects by fire and sword; and besides destroying the pagan temples, committed the most atrocious acts of bloodshed and robbery in the name of Christ! The people rose *en masse* against him, and he was obliged to seek refuge in Sweden.

He was succeeded in the government of Norway in 1028 by Cnut the Great, who was unanimously elected king. Olaf however tried to regain the monarchy and invaded the country. A tremendous battle was fought near Trondheim, in which he and most of his army were slain. This was in 1030. A few years later his body was found incorrupt; a belief in his sanctity was restored; his remains were conveyed to Trondheim for reinterment; and a chapel, built over them, at length reached the proportions of a Cathedral. Down to the Reformation, pilgrimages were made to his shrine. Churches were built in his honour in various parts of Scandinavia, and other countries, and even in London we have several churches dedicated to this sham saint.

Sweyn, the son of Cnut, was deputed by him to the government of Norway, with the title of king, but on the death of Cnut, A.D. 1035, he was dethroned by Magnus I., the illegitimate son of St. Olaf. He died in 1047, when his uncle Harald III., a mighty soldier who founded Osloe, now the city of Christiania, succeeded.

At the instigation of Tostig, brother of Harold II. of England, he made a raid upon our country. A great battle was fought at Stamford, in Lincolnshire, in 1066, and both Harald and Tostig were killed. The son of

Harald, called Olaf III., with the whole of the Norwegian fleet, fell into the hands of our Harold, who generously permitted Olaf to sail for the fatherland, with twenty ships. Poor Harold, the son of Earl Godwin, only three weeks later, was slain at the battle of Hastings by the followers of William the Conqueror. It is curious to note these feuds and tragedies among men of the same nationality and descent, for Harald of Norway, Harold of England, and William of Normandy were, as I have said, all of common origin.

Olaf III. was succeeded by his son Magnus III., surnamed ' Bare-foot," who became great in the roll of heroes and warriors of Norway. In 1098, provided with a strong fleet, he conquered the Isle of Man, the Shetlands, Orkneys, and the Western Isles of Scotland. He next tried his hand upon Ireland, where he was slain in 1098.

---

[1] Probably because he had gone on some pilgrimage without shoes.

Sigurd I., his son and successor, bore a surname, as most of the old Scandinavian monarchs
did, and his was *Jorsalalare*, which means a
'Traveller to Jerusalem.' He went thither
with an object partly religious and partly
warlike. He sailed in 1107 with a fleet of
sixty vessels, and was absent four years. He
passed the first winter in England, and received
the hospitality of Henry I. Passing on, he
engaged in divers battles with the Moors, both
in Portugal and at sea. When he landed in
Sicily, Roger, the Norman king of the island,
entertained him with great pomp and hospitality. On reaching Jerusalem, he offered his
military services to Baldwin, which the latter
gladly accepted. His last exploit in Pales-
tine was that of joining in the siege of Sidon,
and he received half the spoils. He returned
over land from Constantinople through central
Europe. 'The fame of this expedition still
lives in the memory of the peasants of the

Sogne Fiord, many of whose ancestors took part in it. Before leaving Constantinople, Sigurd placed the figure-head of his own ship —a dragon twelve feet long—on the Church of St. Sophia; but in 1204, after the capture of the city by the Crusaders, the new Emperor, Baldwin of Flanders, sent it as a present to the city of Bruges, from whence it was carried away in 1382 to Ghent; and there it still remains, on the great belfry, the pride of the citizens, and long a puzzle to antiquaries.' So states Murray's Handbook; but I cannot ascertain the source of the information, though it is probably correct.

After the death of Sigurd internal feuds and civil wars arose in Norway, but they were abated in 1152 by the kindly interference of the Pope's legate, Nicholas Breakspeare, an Englishman, afterwards Pope Adrian IV. This eminent man rectified the ecclesiastical condition of the country by obtaining for Trondheim a metropolitan see. The new archbishop's authority extended over all Norway, Iceland, Greenland, the Faroe Islands, the Shetlands, the Orkneys, the Hebrides, and the Isle of Man. The Norwegians distinguished the Hebrides as '*Syderöer*' (the southern islands), and hence the title of one of our bishops, '*Sodor* and Man.'

The Scots considering the Hebrides as part and parcel of their dominions sought to reannex them. Upon this Hagen IV. made war upon them, but died during the expedition, A.D. 1263. Norway now began again to decline by reason of intestine commotions, foreign wars, and loss of commerce, as also by a visitation of the ' Black Death,' which destroyed nearly half the population of England under Edward III., and is said to have been imported into Bergen by an empty English ship, whose crew had died on the passage. The archbishop of Trondheim and nearly all the cathedral authorities were stricken down, and the only bishop in the whole country who escaped was Solomon, bishop of Christiania. Thousands of the peasants fell victims, as also did the cattle and other domestic animals. Then followed a great famine ; navigation and commerce were almost destroyed, and for many generations Norway remained in a most abject condition.

Hagen VI. of Norway married the daughter of Valdemar IV. of Denmark, and died in 1380, and then his infant son Olaf III. became king of the two nations, which remained united until the beginning of the present century. This monarch died at an early age, and then his mother, Margaret, called the 'Northern Semiramis,' overcoming the king of Sweden, united the three Scandinavian nations under one crown.

Christian I. married a daughter of James III. of Scotland, and, in aid of her dowry, mortgaged the Orkney and Shetland islands ; but, not being able to raise money for their redemption, they fell back again to their proper owners, the Scots.

The next event of importance was the Reformation, which commenced in 1536, under Christian III., and was gradually carried on to a peaceful issue. In the reign of Christian IV. rich silver mines were discovered at Kongsberg, and copper mines at Roras. This distinguished monarch built Christiania on the site of the ancient Osloe, and founded the town of Christiansand. Long previously to this, Sweden had seceded from the Danish rule, though Norway still continued loyal. But it is not necessary here to give even an outline of the more recent historical events of this interesting country.

———

Geographically, Sweden is almost as flat as Norway is mountainous, though mountains of considerable height are scattered along its north-western border at the points most adjacent to Norway. At the upper part of the Gulf of Bothnia, the sea has long been receding. Sweden abounds in lakes, great or small, the principal being lakes Wener and Wetter, sometimes called Wenern and Wettern. The former is the larger, being upwards of 92 miles long. The forests are numerous and large, covering more than half the surface of the country. Pine and fir are the prevalent trees in the central district; the north abounds with birch, and the south with oak and beech; maple, lime, willow, ash, etc., are found in various districts. The mineral productions of Sweden are rich and varied, including copper, iron, gold (in small quantities), silver, zinc, lead, marble, and coal. The iron is the best in the world, and excels in the quality of toughness, as I have heard English blacksmiths say.

Like the other two Scandinavian countries, Sweden has little trustworthy early history—not even so much as the others. Snorro Sturleson, and Saxo Grammaticus, who flourished in the twelfth century, are its only trustworthy (?) historians. Scandinavia is spoken of in general terms by classical writers, such as Pliny and Tacitus, but there is no specific notice of Sweden.

The principal event mentioned by Snorro and Saxo in connexion with Sweden is the emigration northward of the Gothic tribes known as the *Sviar* under Odin ; they were afterwards designated Swedes. This event is thought to have taken place previously to the invasion of England by the Anglo-Saxons. Odin, so named after the great Scandinavian god, was an able man, and combined the characteristics of conqueror, king, and legislator : in his priestly capacity he was profound in the superstitious practices of the times. At length he himself was invested with the honours of a deity, and his *cultus* was widely spread throughout the north.

Freyer, the third in succession, made Upsala

his metropolis, and the temple which he built there became the most celebrated centre of pagan worship in Scandinavia. A succession of the subsequent kings were truly unfortunate : some fell in battle ; others committed suicide ; some were slain by their own people ; and, notably, one of them, called Domald, was sacrificed by his loyal subjects to appease the gods during a great famine, on the altar of Odin. A more unhappy dynasty was never known in the world, and it may well be said of it— 'Uneasy lies the head that wears a crown!' Foreign wars, internal revolutions, and piracy mark the traditions of that long and dismal period of northern history.

At length St. Ansgar laboured to establish Christianity during the reign of Bjorn in the ninth century, but without much success at first. At length Olaf, surnamed the ' Lap-king,' because he was baptized in infancy in his mother's lap, somewhat before the year 1000, succeeded.

During his reign three bishoprics were established and many churches were built. From his time Sweden was a nominally Christian state, but it was long after this that paganism really died out.

For three centuries after the introduction of the gospel into the country, continual wars were waged between the Goths and Swedes, each claiming the supreme authority. Sweden proved victorious, and to this day the title of her monarch is—' King of the Swedes and Goths,' just as in our own country down to the time of George III., the Sovereign was styled ' King of Great Britain, France, and Ireland.' In 1250 Stockholm was built and strongly fortified, the *leges scriptæ* were revised, and the internal administration underwent great improvement. The greatest monarch that Sweden had in mediæval times was Magnus I., whose reign commenced in 1275, and whose able administration reinstated order and tran-

quillity instead of the bloody career of ante-
cedent sovereigns.

I may here remark that *Magnus* was a very
common name for sovereigns in the Scandinavian
countries; and I may mention that, in 1839, I
had the pleasure of rescuing from destruction
the monumental inscription of a scion of Danish
royalty at Lewes, in Sussex, where I then resided. Affixed to the walls of the very ancient
church of St. John-sub-Castro there, there existed on two concentric arcs of a circle, and cut
on fifteen stones, an epitaph, which runs thus—

' CLAUDITUR HIC MILES, DANORUM REGIA PROLES ;
MANGNUS NOMEN EI ; MANGNÆ NOTA PROGENIEI :
DEPONENS MANGNUM, SE MORIBUS INDUIT AGNUM,
PREPETE PRO VITA FIT PARVULUS ARNACORITA.'

' Here is immured a Soldier of the Royal Family of Denmark, whose name *Magnus* bespeaks his distinguished
lineage. Relinquishing his greatness, he assumes the de-
portment of a lamb, and exchanges a life of ambition for
that of a lowly anchorite.'[1]

---

[1] I could never understand the reason why the *n* was introduced
into the name Magnus—but so it is.

Of this personage nothing is known in England. There have been many theories concerning him among local antiquaries, but I give no credit to any of them. He must therefore remain, I fear, 'a great unknown'—*Magnus Ignotus*, so far as English antiquarianism is concerned.

I made a very careful and elaborate drawing of this inscription at the time of its removal from the old church of St. John-sub-Castro to the new one; and I had the pleasure, when at Copenhagen, to present a faithful copy of it to the Museum of Northern Antiquities there, in the hope that some Danish archæologist may be able to throw light upon the princely recluse, his history, and his genealogical connexion with the kings of Denmark. I ought to have said that the epitaph is undoubtedly of the thirteenth century.

But to return from this digression. Thorkil, prime minister of Birger, the successor of Magnus, a man of high and noble character, promulgated a law for the suppression of slavery. 'What,' said he, 'is it not a monstrous sin that Christians should sell men whom Christ has redeemed by his blood?' Slavery never existed in Sweden from that period; and thus it will be seen that our Northern friends preceded us by several centuries in the knowledge of the true relation between man and man.

After the death of Magnus, Sweden was again in a state of anarchy, and, in the year 1389, King Albert having been defeated and captured, the crowns of the Swedes and Goths were united with those of Denmark and Norway by the illustrious Margaret, called, as we have seen, the Semiramis of the North. Not long afterwards arose the renowned Gustavus Vasa, or Wasa. The Scandinavians make scarcely any distinction between V and W, and thus resemble our Cockneys. Vasa was truly a 'man of the people,' a great statesman, and an adherent to the doctrines of Luther. In 1529 the Romish Church as the national faith was declared to be abolished, and Lutheranism became the recognised religion of Sweden. In 1544 the States decreed the sovereignty to be hereditary in his family.

Eric xiv., his eldest son and successor, was very unsuccessful in his wooing. He first tried his hand on our Queen Elizabeth; then upon Mary Queen of Scots, thirdly on a princess of Lorraine, and afterwards on a princess of Hesse; but these ladies all flouted him, and he was obliged to put up with the daughter of a peasant, who had been his mistress. His reign, which was marked by cruelty and confusion, ended in 1568, when he was deposed by his brother John, imprisoned for ten years, and then poisoned.

John tried to re-establish Romanism, but in vain, and his descendants were ultimately excluded from the crown. Gustavus Adolphus,

grandson of Gustavus Vasa, reinvigorated the
army, and raised the military glory of Sweden
to a pitch hitherto unknown in Scandinavia.
He was but eighteen when he ascended the
throne, but his precocity in military affairs and
his high principles attracted the attention of the
whole civilized world.    He shared the fate of
many of his predecessors, and was killed at the
battle of Lützen, in 1632.    After the celebrated
Thirty Years' War, Sweden was so raised in the
scale of nations that from an obscure state it
came to be considered one of the first of European powers.    War after war succeeded, and
Sweden was again reduced to its original and
normal condition.    There never was, since the
world began, so wretched a country as this, and
its history ought to be written in letters of blood.

After a long lapse of time, the celebrated
Bernadotte, a family connexion of Bonaparte,
was recognised as king of Norway and Sweden,
and assumed the title of Charles XIV.    He was

upon the whole a worthy monarch, and did his best to improve the lower classes, and to develop the commercial resources of the two countries. After a long and most active life, he departed this for a better, as I trust, in 1844.

To Bernadotte succeeded his son Oscar the First, 'worthy son of worthy sire.' A better king perhaps never existed. He died in 1859. Altogether there is no country under heaven. that has seen such vicissitudes as Sweden and Norway. Clouds have for the most part pervaded its political atmosphere, but they have been happily atoned for by the most glorious bursts of sunshine that this changeful world ever witnessed.

———

And now let us look over Copenhagen, my favourite city, and survey its glorious monuments and treasures of art and literature. And first, of the celebrated Round Tower, perhaps the most remarkable building in the world—the

Pyramids of Egypt not excepted. It is attached
to the Church of the Holy Trinity, and was
originally intended for an observatory, to
which use it was applied for upwards of two
centuries ; and it *is* an observatory still : not
in the sense of commanding a view of the
heavenly bodies, but in that of being the best
point from which to view the city, which lies
at your feet, and forms a very glorious spectacle.
It stands in a street with the very unpronounce-
able name of *Kjöbamagergade.*

It was erected by King Christian IV. The
tower consists of two hollow cylinders, and between them a spiral inclined plane winds from
the street to the summit, with an ascent sufficiently safe and easy for a carriage and four to
ascend. In 1716, Catherine of Russia actually
performed this feat, accompanied by Peter the
Great as outrider! When Nelson bombarded
Copenhagen in 1802, the treasures of the University Library were deposited in this tower.

Let us next visit the Thorvaldsen Museum—
a glorious sight, and worth a special pilgrimage
from any part of the civilized world. The building was erected about 1845, at the expense of
the city, to contain the great sculptor's works.
Thorvaldsen, besides being one of the best
sculptors—Phidias himself not excepted—that
ever existed, was a man of almost universal
genius in the fine arts. He was generous too,
and bequeathed to Copenhagen his fine collection of sculptures and pictures, many of which
latter he had bought at high prices in Italy and
elsewhere. His tomb is an ornament to the
grounds attached to the Museum—ornament, I
say, though it is neither grand nor imposing;
but to the eye of taste it has a peculiar charm
when we reflect on the greatness and goodness
of the man. The style of the building is excellent, and classical and Etruscan ornaments are
its most attractive features. The external
frescoes represent the grand reception given to

the great sculptor on his return from his travels to Copenhagen, which occurred on September 17th, 1838. They have suffered much from the climate of Denmark, where the weather is, in some winters, unusually severe. The building is quadrangular in plan, and consists of two stories, the lower of which contains only sculptures. The upper story is devoted to pictures and sculpture, for which there is no room below to spare. In each story there is a corridor fronting the courtyard, and a number of small rooms with *bas-reliefs*, and minor pieces of sculpture, including busts of Lord Byron and Sir Walter Scott.

To enumerate the various works of art in this wonderful collection would be beyond the scope of these pages; but I must mention a few of them. The famous ' Lion of Luzerne' is there; and in the Great Hall there are several colossal monuments, including Poniatowski, Schiller, Pope Pius vii., Copernicus, and, notably, the finely-executed frieze of Alexander entering Babylon, which was executed for the Quirinal at Rome. Afterwards we see St. John preaching in the Wilderness—a noble piece of art. Then there are statues of Ganymede, Amor and Psyche, Jason, the three Graces, Venus, Hebe, Mars and Cupid, Vulcan, Mercury, etc. There is also a statue of Jason, which, as Murray well observes, ' has a special interest for Englishmen, because it was an order given by one of our countrymen for the execution of this figure, which enabled Thorvaldsen to remain in Rome at a time when his means were exhausted. It was the first of his works that excited general attention, and from that time dates his success,' and his consequent fame. The ' Hall of Christ ' contains figures of our Saviour and the twelve apostles, executed for Vor Frue Kirke (Our Lady's Church—of which hereafter). Thorvaldsen, though not a scholar as to education, was thoroughly imbued with a classical taste, as is

evident from every work of his which we behold.
The 'Hall' is a most attractive place for both
the gentle and simple folk of Copenhagen, and
especially on Sunday afternoons, when soldiers,
shopkeepers, and the humblest peasants throng
this wonderful exhibition of art.    Beyond the
hall there is another row of cabinets, the most
attractive features of which are Ganymede with
Jupiter's eagle, Cupid in triumph, the Graces
with Cupid's arrow, Adonis, the Shepherd, and,
most noteworthy, *Thorvaldsen himself reclining
on Hope.*    On the staircase is a model of the
celebrated Hercules, which stands in front of
the Christianborg palace.    Among the pictures
in this noble collection are—

> Williams's Roman Girl.
> A Norwegian Cascade, by Dahl.
> Pictures of Roman Life, by Meier.
> Flowers and Fruits, by Jensen, the well-known Danish
>     painter.
> A Marine View by Melbye.
> The Burial of Our Lord, by Cornelius.
> Danish landscapes, by Buntzen and Libert.

A striking picture of Thorvaldsen and other artists at
    Rome, by Blunck.
Pictures by Kierschou and Boisen (landscapes).
Horace Vernet's portrait of Thorvaldsen.
Marstrand's Popular Rejoicings at Rome, etc. etc.

On the opposite side is a similar range of
cabinets, containing the great sculptor's books,
and many articles of *vertu*, such as vases, coins,
and cameos, as well as the furniture of his house.
It is worthy of notice, too, that the last two
works of the great artist, a bust of Luther, and
a sketch for a bas-relief, are to be seen here.

In the court-yard, which is ornamented in the
Pompeian style, the immortal artist lies, as I
have before said, in his quiet grave, ornamented
with evergreens and roses—emblematical, as I
suppose, of the beauty of the artist's works, and
of his undying fame.

Altogether, Thorvaldsen's Museum may be
considered one of the greatest educational esta-
blishments in the world. It gives a healthy
tone of thought to both rich and poor. I have

heard thousands of sermons in church and chapel, but there are sermons in Thorvaldsen's stones which are to my mind unequalled by the ablest preachers alive.

My wife was particularly struck with one object in the Museum—Cupid complaining to his mother of a sting from a bee ; a story which is well told by Anacreon, as follows :—

Ἔρως ποτ' ἐν ῥόδοισι
κοιμωμένην μέλιτταν
οὐκ εἶδεν, ἀλλ' ἐτρώθη·
τὸν δάκτυλον δὲ δαχθεὶς
τᾶς χειρὸς, ὠλόλυξε.
Δραμὼν δὲ καὶ πετασθεὶς
πρὸς τὴν καλὴν Κυθήρην,
ὄλωλα, μᾶτερ, εἶπεν,
ὄλωλα, κἀποθνήσκω.
Ὄφις μ' ἔτυψε μικρὸς,
πτερωτὸς, ὃν καλοῦσι
μέλιτταν οἱ γεωργοί.
Ἁ δ' εἶπεν, εἰ τὸ κεντρον
πονεῖ τὸ τᾶς μελίττας,
πόσον, δοκεῖς, πονοῦσιν,
Ἔρως, ὅσους σὺ βάλλεις.

This ode has been paraphrased in English, and

somewhat enlarged.   I can only remember the first portion of it, which runs thus :—

> ' Cupid once, in evil hour,
> Cropped the pride of Flora's bower :
> Cropped a rose, nor chanced to see
> Within its bud a sleeping bee,
> Until his finger felt the smart,
> Inflicted by its tiny dart ;
> Flying then, with ruffled mien,
> To the fair Idalian queen,
> " Oh, mama," he wildly cries,
> " Wounded, save ; your Cupid dies !
> Me a little serpent stung,
> Hid the rose-bud leaves among,
> 'Decked with curious wings like me,
> Ploughmen call the thing a Bee." '

The moral of the tale is, that Venus says to Cupid : ' You ought not to complain of the sting of a bee, when you have wounded so many hearts with your own winged arrows !'

The building which gave me more satisfaction than any in the capital of Denmark is the Museum of Northern Antiquities.   Of all the Museums I have visited—and they are by no means few—this is by far the best and most instructive. It is so excellently and scientifically arranged, that there is probably nothing like it elsewhere.

I was unfortunate in not meeting Professor Worsaae and Professor Stephens, two of the most celebrated antiquaries of Scandinavia, who were both out of town ; but I found an excellent substitute for them in Professor Engelhardt, author of the *Guide Illustré du Musée des Antiquités du Nord à Copenhague*, a most interesting little work, which treats ably of the subject. He may fairly take rank with the most eminent of living archæologists, and his courteous demeanour at once wins the esteem of the visitor. Here let me say that the letter-press of his little Catalogue, and its illustrations, are among the best that I ever saw. Thiele is the printer, and he may well be proud of his workmanship. If my volume should ever be reprinted in Scandinavia, I hope that it will issue from the 'Imprimerie de Thiele.'

Professor Engelhardt arranges his catalogue in five classes, as follows :—*A.* The Age of Rough Stones and Implements, and those which have been smoothed and polished, etc. *B.* The Age of Bronze. *C.* The Iron Age, from A.D. 250 to 450. *D.* The Middle Age, in the Roman style, down to about the year 1300. *E.* Modern or Renaissance style, to about 1660.

The Museum is divided into nineteen *salles* or apartments, and a detailed account of them is given by M. Engelhardt. I shall follow his arrangement. In the first apartment are the rudest implements. There is a fine collection of stone and bone implements which we English antiquaries (I know not why), call *celts.*[1] They

---

[1] There is a low Latin word *celtis*, meaning a chisel, and this may possibly be the origin of the name of the implement. I once believed, in common with most English antiquaries, that these implements derive their name from the Celts (κελτοί), who no doubt used them, and brought them into Europe.

may have been used either for the heads of battle-axes, or as chisels for more peaceful purposes. The workmanship is rude in the extreme. They are, as the Professor observes, cutting instruments in flint or bone. The ancient Scandinavians, as before remarked, lived on the products of the chase, and of fishing. The dog was the only domestic animal. The people knew how to procure fire, and used it to cook their provisions, and were sufficiently acquainted with the art of pottery to make rough culinary vessels. There are frequently found rude mounds of earth called Kiökkenmöddengs, which modern English antiquaries term 'Kitchen-middens.' There is a remarkable specimen of this kind of mounds on the heights of Newhaven, which I assisted, some years ago, in opening, with the aid of Mr. Henry Willett—just such a mound, which, though surrounded by Roman earthworks, was evidently of the prehistoric period, and might possibly be ascribed to the early Scandinavians, on their first visits to this country.

The first case contains a collection of relics procured from Meilgaard in Jutland, consisting of combs, oyster shells, and those of other shell-fish, fish, fish-bones, and bones evidently crushed for the extraction of the marrow, the remains of birds and fishes, and some utensils of truly primitive origin ; but no human bones. *Second*, Remains from the diggings at Meilgaard, including large pieces of stags' horns, pierced with a hole to receive a handle, others of a hammer-like form, and some intended for needles and bodkins, and a sort of combs, which the learned Professor thinks may have been used for the manufacture of thread ; flint implements, both jagged and polished. There are likewise fragments of pottery, calcined stones, broken bones of quadrupeds, and remains of birds[1]

---

[1] The ornithological remains are those of ducks, heath-cocks penguins, etc.

F

and fishes. *Third* and *Fourth*, Articles discovered in similar hillocks, on the shore of the Cattegat, above a hundred yards higher than the sea level. One of the places where they were principally exhumed is Havelse, in Seeland (Zealand), where these mounds extend over a distance of many hundred yards. Some of them are from fifteen to nineteen yards in length, and of considerable elevation. *Fifth*, Antiquities from the island of Magles, also in Zealand, consisting of flint implements and calcined stones. The greater part of these were found in pits, perhaps ancient forges, on the banks of a stream, and were mixed with charcoal and broken pottery. The remaining cases in this *salle* contain appliances which are supposed to have been used in some manufactory. There are 'piercers' and scrapers, and triangular hatchets. Most of these were exhumed at Korser and Hindsholm, and the whole are in flint.

The second *salle* is also rich in relics of the Stone Period, but of a more finished kind, the productions principally of an *atelier* at Anholt, an island in the Cattegat. There are many flint knives and other implements, including triangular hatchets and heads of arrows and spears. In consequence of the irregularity of oceanic movements in the northern regions, what was once the realm of Neptune is now firm ground, and the accumulation of sand has entirely changed the contour of the coast, so that things which would be supposed to have been close to the sea are found considerably inland. This, however, does not immediately apply to my present subject.

Some remains of another manufactory discovered at Hasselo, also in the Cattegat, are in this apartment. They include many flint celts and the refuse of their production. Besides these, there are many fragments of broken pottery, and many bones of the *phoca*, or seawolf, which seems to have been a considerable element in the food of the old Norsemen. A number of hatchets from the same quarter are here also. The date of these relics is of course prehistoric, and they indicate a state of barbarism lower than can now be found in any part of the world. The rest of this *salle* contains a great number of other rude antiquities from various parts of Scandinavia.

The third *salle* is principally occupied by polished or smooth celts, the second period of the Stone Age, comprising ends of flint arrows, with the appliances wherewith to affix them to the weapon. There are also some bone arrowheads, ornamented with rude incisions, one of which is intended for the portrait of a frog! Then there are the spears of harpoons, flint heads of lances, very nicely finished, specimens of scrapers in the forms of half-moons and crescents, and flint knives. Next we come to groups of objects in stone dug up from marshes and fields, principally in Jutland and Zealand. There are also remains of amber necklaces found in Jutland, at a place called Kaer (? castrum), which has furnished 1800 pieces deposited in a clay vessel. The richest depository of this kind is Læsten, near Randers in Jutland, where there were found nearly four thousand trinkets shut up in a little wooden coffer, and Professor Engelhardt supposes that they formed part of the stock-in-trade of an early amber merchant. Next we have the proceeds of *dolmens*, covered passages, or as they are called, the 'Chambers of Giants.' There we find artificial mounds, the centres of which are graves, formed of great blocks, covered with flagstones, encircled with hewn stones ; also some remarkable relics from Skovsgaard, where, at the base of a tumulus, were discovered, among other objects, three contiguous vaults constructed of rude stones, and containing nearly one hundred skeletons. In a bed higher up was discovered a polished stone supporting three vases filled with burnt bones, and some small objects in bronze.

Here let me remark, that in England, as well as in Scandinavia, urn-burial and the interment of the body, without cremation, existed contemporaneously from a very early period. A curious example of this practice was discovered by the late eminent geologist, Dr. Gideon Mantell, near the Caburn at Glynde, on the South Downs, where both skeletons and urns were found in juxtaposition.[1]

We have here, too, some relics from a 'giant's chamber' at Hielm, which contained about fifteen skeletons, and a great number of spear-heads, polished celts, hatchets, and chisels. Noteworthy are the remains of another giant's chamber from Uggerslev near Odense, consisting of fragments of hatchets, intentionally

[1] See an illustration in Horsfield's *History of Lewes*, vol. i.

broken,—but why, it is difficult to guess,—and a remarkable collection of little polished arrow-heads. Some of the objects are from Skovs-gaard.

I may here remark, that the tumulus referred to bears a strong resemblance, as to its ground-plan, to several relics in our own land, and I may specially mention two : one at Bosphrenes in Cornwall, and the other at Buxted in Sussex.

Next we see relics of amber necklaces, and the fragments of numerous earthen pots ; and afterwards the products of *dolmens* from Zealand. The diggings in a tumulus from a place near Borreby present some remarkable peculiarities. The cave was full of skeletons of men, women, and children, at least eighty in number ; whether a kind of family-vault or a general burying-place it is impossible to guess. There are also relics of human bones, partially burnt, found in a tumulus at Hammor. Then there are many sepulchral vases and goblets of small dimensions, made by hand, some with handles as if for suspension, and occasionally rather prettily ornamented, some of the crevices being filled with a white substance, probably zinc ; and specially, a large vase found in a marsh at Birkerod near Copenhagen. In Case 46 there are some very interesting relics, comprising hatchets, knives, and other implements in bone, the use of some of which can only be guessed at.

Next we see a number of bone implements looking like weapons, though they may have been intended for more harmless uses. There are also a number of free-stone implements, of which, as Professor Engelhardt observes, the uses are unknown. They are however beautifully finished, and show a vast amount of care and industry.

Now we come to the Bronze Period. In the fourth chamber there is an abundance of very interesting objects. Why bronze was used before iron I could never learn. Bronze is a compound metal, while iron ore is found on the surface, nearly all over the world.

This fourth hall contains cutting implements of bronze, which upon analysis is found to contain nine-tenths of copper and one-tenth of tin. It is curious to observe that, although many objects are ornamented with gold, neither silver nor iron turns up in those primeval days.

I daresay that gold was more plentiful in Scandinavia in those olden times than it is now. I never saw a piece of gold coin there, the currency being silver and copper. They have, of course, a currency of gold, but it rarely meets the eye, as almost all transactions are carried on in paper and silver.

The Professor thinks that the bronze used by the old Scandinavians was of foreign origin, and this opinion is probably correct. How and where the mixed metals came together nobody knows. Most of our manufactured articles are the result of what some call *accidents;* but I believe that they were given to us by the Providence of Almighty God.    Take glass for instance.

Cases 51 to 54 contain the remains found in wooden coffins formed from the trunks of oak trees, without the aid of a saw.    One remarkable instance of interment was at the bottom of a grave, where the remains of a man in his vestments, and with his arms, were found lying on a bullock's hide.    A tumulus at Treenhoi in Jutland had four of these wooden coffins, one of which contained clothing of manufactured wool almost perfectly preserved, consisting of a cap, a mantle, and a kind of *jupon.*    Several other relics, including bronze ornaments, were exhumed.    A similar tumulus, also containing four coffins and various bronze implements, was opened at Kongshoi, in the same neighbourhood.

At No. 55 we find remains from a tumulus

with vaults of unhewn stones, covered with flag-stones and planks of wood, containing skeletons, and covered with a kind of cairn. From a barrow of this kind in Jægersborg Wood near Copenhagen we see relics of a warrior's tomb with a circular shield, elaborately wrought, a sword, a hatchet, and other articles in bronze.

One of the most ancient tombs containing burnt human bones was opened at Hvidegaard, also near Copenhagen. In it were found fragments of flint, a woollen mantle covering the bones, with all the appearance of having been placed there with funeral ceremonies ; also a bronze sword in a scabbard of wood covered with leather, a fibula, fragments of a wooden vase, and two bronze knives, the head of a flint dart, the tail of a snake, the claw of a falcon, etc.

The learned Professor is of opinion that the person thus interred was both a magician and a warrior, which seems extremely probable.

I wonder what sort of a fellow he was, and when he lived and died.

In the fourth apartment there are some of the most remarkable bronze articles I ever saw; particularly a highly finished poignard from Flynder in Jutland, and a very curious trumpet in the form of a reversed letter S, with a chain attached, and highly ornamented. It is perhaps the greatest curiosity in the whole Museum. There are others, but of less elaborate workmanship. This one came from Maltbæck. I was told that the instrument could still be blown by a person possessed of great powers of lung.

At No. 58 there are the remains of burnt bones found at Voldtofte in a tomb, and covered with a flagstone. It also contained a large bronze vessel, three smaller ones, two knives, and a few minor objects in gold and bronze. In 59 there is a beautiful dagger from Breum in Jutland, which was discovered in a tumulus with two gold bracelets. But it would far exceed the limits of these sketches to give a detailed account of all the articles in this noble Museum; and therefore I must confine myself to the most striking and remarkable objects. Indeed, there are so many burnt human bones, relics in bronze and gold, votive swords, knives, awls, needles, buttons, rings, and such-like, together with handles of implements terminating in the heads of horses and swans, that it would require a catalogue larger than this book to describe or even to give an imperfect account of them all. The zealous antiquary must go himself to Copenhagen to realize the beauties and curiosities of this remarkable collection; and when there, I hope he will procure M. Engelhardt's valuable brochure as a guide.

In the fifth chamber are many curious relics of discoveries made in the open fields at some feet below the surface, either covered with a large stone, or enclosed in a vase. Many of these are presumed to be of religious origin;

and I am disposed to think that they are principally the graves of hermits or recluses. In the small island of Munko near Faaborg were disinterred, from a blackish soil, six small gold vessels, three above the other three, and covered with a stone. M. Engelhardt has strong reasons for thinking that most, if not all, of these articles are of Scandinavian manufacture.

In the sixth *salle* we come to the Iron Age, a very interesting period. M. Engelhardt observes that, 'vers le milieu du 3ème siècle de notre ère, le fer est d'un usage général en Danemark, pour la confection des armes et des instruments tranchants.' He adds that the use of iron brought with it a civilisation entirely different from that which existed in the age of bronze. Contemporaneously with iron, we find the introduction of silver and glass in Scandinavia. The manufacture of woollen cloth was also admirable. I am half inclined to believe that some new national element was introduced into the North at the period referred to. Rude art, which cannot have been derived from classical sources, seems also to have been contemporary. The representations of plants, animals, fantastic figures, and of men frequently occur. Well-constructed boats, and the use of horses, both for riding and draught, also appear to belong to this epoch, as do also the most ancient remains of alphabetic writing. The introduction of iron and of writing, as we have every reason to believe, have in all countries been the precursors of civilisation, and the amelioration of the condition of human life. The Iron Age, as described by some classical authors, is an error!

Of the religious opinions of the early Scandinavians we have no knowledge. The singular character of the remains found under great stones in the fields and sand-banks shows that the dead were buried with their treasures beside them. It would seem somehow that they had intercourse with the civilized inhabitants of '

southern Europe, for we find in their graves
Roman coins, ranging from A.D. 63 to 217;
with those of the Eastern Empire from 425 to
525; and even Cufic money of the ninth, tenth,
and eleventh centuries.    Empty graves sometimes occur, probably in honour of persons who
have died out of the country or on the sea, and
they may therefore be placed in the category
of cenotaphs or empty tombs.    A noticeable
feature in the Scandinavian graves is that many
of them contain classical or at least latinized
names, such as NIGELLIO F(ecit), DISAUGUS F. P.
CIPI POLIBI F. (Publius Cipius Polibius fecit),
etc.    One or two relics have even Greek characters upon them.    It may well be supposed that
at least some of the articles were brought from
the South and the East by Scandinavian pirates,
and were not manufactured in the north.

From 1859 to 1863 systematic 'diggings'
were carried on in Schleswig for the Museum of
Flensborg, and many curious things were dis-

covered, particularly in the turfy marsh at Nydam, which was once covered by an arm of the sea; and many boats, oars, etc., were exhumed, especially one boat, the remains of which have been put together. It is more than twenty yards long, and an excellent woodcut of it is given in M. Engelhardt's *Guide*. (Let me say here, that the art of wood-engraving is carried on in Copenhagen to great perfection, and that it is not surpassed in any part of the world.) The contents of these vessels were, among many other objects, fragments of shields, umbos, armour, knives, awls, etc. One of the most curious things in the Museum is a perfect helmet of bronze covered with a crown, indicating, no doubt, that it belonged to the armour of some eminent chieftain. It is curiously formed, and it covered all the head with the exception of openings for the mouth, nose, and eyes. It is in *repoussé* work, and ornamented with gold and silver.

G

In the seventh apartment are the results of a digging for the Museum at a sacred spot in the *Vimose*, near Odense. This marshy locality is surrounded by embankments, and it was found to contain fragments of coats-of-mail and ornaments. A number of combs were included in the *find*, one of which is inscribed with Runic characters. M. Engelhardt accounts for such remains being found in marshy spots by giving an analogous instance from classical history. I give it in his own words, as partly quoted from Tacitus : " Après la victoire qu'ils remportèrent sur les Romains près du Rhône, non loin d'Orange, (en 105 avant J. C.) les Cimbres restés maîtres des deux camps et d'un immense butin, anéantirent avec un anathème (execratio) nouveau et inusité, tout ce qui était tombé en leur pouvoir. Les vêtements furent lacérés et dispersés, l'or et l'argent jetés dans le fleuve, les cottes de mailles coupées en morceaux, les phalères mises en pièces, les chevaux eux-mêmes précipités dans le gouffre et les hommes pendus aux arbres par le cou, de sorte qu'il n'y eut pas plus de butin pour le vainqueur que de miséricorde pour le vaincu." I think this conjecture very probable, especially as Odin, the great Danish God (whose name appears in this connexion), was the Jack-Ketch of the Norsemen —the patron of hanging!

In the eighth *salle* are found blacksmith's tools, etc., dug up in natural hillocks, in Zealand. One of the most remarkable objects is a female skeleton found in the Island of Falster, accompanied by articles of the early iron period. It was dug up in a marshy spot, and the woman had probably been guilty of infidelity to her husband ; for Tacitus in his " Germania " informs us that, according to the law of some of the Northern nations, a woman who had deserted her husband ought to be thrown into a bog. In this department are seen traces of the early intercourse between Scandinavia and the East.

Byzantine coins, struck between the years 425 and 525, go far to prove this. Gold, at this epoch, seems to have been more abundant than in any other in Northern history. In the Museum (131) we find collars, bracelets, and rings, all of the precious metal. In excavating in a field at Broholm in Fionie, there were discovered articles in gold, the most valuable *find* ever made in Denmark : it was in weight more than four kilogrammes, and valued at from ten to twelve thousand francs. This treasure, probably dating from the fifth or sixth century, was accompanied by many curious articles.

Previously to about the year 1000, the Scandinavians carried on all their commercial transactions by means of exchange, and paid for their purchases bars of precious metal, rings, etc. ; but about the date mentioned they introduced a coinage of a very rude kind.

In the third and last epoch of iron—the epoch

of the Vikings—Roman and Byzantine relics introduced a general advancement in the arts of civilisation. The weapons of war began to be finished in a better style, and a particular alteration took place in their dimensions. Twisted dragons and *enchevêtrés* became common ornaments. Still Scandinavia as yet remained unchristianized, although western and central Europe had long previously accepted the gospel. This was the period of great conquests. Normandy fell into the hands of the northern nations, and that well-known pirate-chieftain, Rollo, made himself *dux* or chieftain of the province. In the words of the chronicler William de Jumiéges (lib. II. cap. 4), ' Nortmanni dicuntur quia, lingua eorum, Boreas *North* vocatur, homo vero *Man*; id est Homines Boreales, per denominationem nuncupantur.' I feel almost certain that Rollo was a Norwegian, and not a Dane, as is generally supposed.

Professor Engelhardt remarks that, towards

the end of this period of the Iron Age, the North is very rich in Cufic coins and Eastern ornaments, indicating the relations of Scandinavia (perhaps indirect) with Oriental nations.

No. 138 contains some curious relics found in the island of Falster, including a ploughshare, and a great number of articles in silver enclosed in a bronze vase—a strange association. There were also Arabic and European coins, which fix the date of the deposit not later than the year 990. On the same spot there were also brought to light bars of silver, diadems, collars, bracelets, either whole or broken, an 'ear-bob' in the form of a T, and some buckles. This collection appears to me more like a robber's hoard than a place of human interment, as it was only about a foot underground, and no skeleton was there.

No. 145 contains some most interesting remains from Sollested in Fionie, found under an artificial hillock. In it were discovered a funereal vault with walls and a pavement covered

with clay. Close by was an urn filled with
what are considered the burnt bones of a human
body, and near it remains of horse-harness, and
vessels in bronze. The character of these remains, as M. Engelhardt observes, shows them
to have been deposited in the latest period of
paganism in Denmark. 'We recall,' says the
Professor, 'the description given in one of our
*Sagas* of the funeral of Harald Hildeland, who
was slain at the battle of Braavalla, about the
middle of the eighth century. After the battle
Sigurd Ring caused search to be made for his
uncle's body, which when it had been washed
and placed on the funeral car, was carried to
his place of interment, which Ring had ordered
to be made. Then his horse was slaughtered
and placed in the tumulus, with Ring's saddle
upon him, so that the slain monarch might appear in the Valhalla [the Scandinavian heaven]
properly equipped! Ring then gave a great
funeral banquet, and recommended all the

grandees and the warriors present to cast into the grave some large rings and good weapons, in honour of King Harald.    After this had been done the grave was carefully covered up.'

In the ninth *salle* are many monumental stones with Runic inscriptions—but of these hereafter.

The tenth apartment, which is chiefly devoted to the mediæval period, contains some stones with Runic inscriptions, especially one which imports that Asur had placed it to the memory of his brother Aaskl, who died at Kurubielant (probably Carélie in Finland).    The upper part has an epitaph in Runic characters.    There are also two Runic stones, which M. Engelhardt thinks belong to the early age of Scandinavian Christianity.    Next we see a tombstone of a Danish bishop, who probably died in 1134 : this was found at Gjesenholm.    The effigy of the bishop is carved in relief.    At his feet we see a holy lamb holding a cross with one of his feet. The inscription is in runes, except one word, which is in Roman letters. A tombstone from Kierte in Fionie also deserves attention. It is roof-shaped, and is supposed to date from the eleventh century. The subjects represented on it in relief are a man, supposed to be intended for the deceased, fighting with a centaur, the emblem of evil. His weapon is a bow and arrow. Behind the centaur is an angel (perhaps St. Michael), with a tiny figure of the defunct, to represent his soul, which he evidently intends to carry to heaven. On the other side is a lion with a man's head in his mouth, alluding possibly to a verse in St. Peter : ' Your adversary the devil, as a roaring lion, walketh about seeking whom he may devour.' There is also a most hideous bowl-shaped font from Vendsyssel in Jutland, with the figure of a woman whom two lions are biting. This sculpture is no doubt emblematical of something— but of what I do not pretend to guess.

In the eleventh apartment we observe a sword,

the handle of which is carved from the tooth of a *morse* or sea-horse, and ornamented with interlaced serpents, recalling by their character the latest times of paganism. In 154-157 are objects designed for religious purposes, as censers, one of which is inscribed in Runic characters— 'Magister Jacobus Ruffus me fecit;' water vessels for the service of the altars, in the form of horsemen, rams, lions, and fabulous animals; reliquaries, one of which encloses a relic of St. Olaf, king of Norway, before mentioned; a piece of crystal with an incised cross and containing a relic; a cross in morse-tooth ivory with figures of Christ in his glory, with the just at his right hand and sinners on his left; the poor man in Abraham's bosom, and Dives in the torments of hell; and many other objects too numerous to be mentioned here.

The twelfth apartment contains articles of the second epoch of the middle ages—that is, from the thirteenth century to the period of the

Reformation in 1536. There are articles for religious uses, such as 'stational' crosses, wax candlesticks of painted wood, altars of painted and gilded wood, a 'tombeau du Christ,' etc. In *salle* thirteenth (181) there are papal bulls and other written documents, and numerous noteworthy articles, including painted glass and little portable chapels in which the Romish priests place the sacred elements when they visit the sick and dying. In *salle* fourteenth there are the basins of baptismal fonts, pyxes, chalices, and other sacramental objects, all from Danish churches. In the fifteenth, one of the most curious things is a chandelier in terra cotta for two candles. It is fashioned in the form of a barbican or entrance to a castle, with two towers and many windows, and Gothic archways.

Of the modern period there is little to be said, and so I must leave the sixteenth, seventeenth, eighteenth, and nineteenth *salles* with but few words. There are some fine tapestry, sculpture, clocks and watches (one of which belonged to Tycho Brahe, and bears his name and device, 'Quo fata me trahunt'), carvings in wood and other materials, pictures, armour, altars in silver and ebony, and various additional things very pleasant to look at, but hard to describe.

A very curious article is to be seen in this valuable Museum—Queen Dagmar's Cross. This lady was the wife of King Valdemar II., the 'Victorious,' and Professor Stephens, F.S.A., etc., has written a very interesting account of it in a brochure published in 1863.[1] I give a brief summary of it, partly in the Professor's own words :—

'In the year 1205, one of the noblest and

---

[1] Notwithstanding the great antiquarian knowledge of the learned Professor, I must protest against his orthography ; for he writes *soveran* for sovereign, *scull* for skull, *publisht* for published, *approcht* for approached, and such like ; and although he knows how Englishmen pronounce the name of the capital of Denmark, he chooses to call it *Cheapinghaven !*

most powerful monarchs then ruling in Europe, Waldemar II., or *the Victorious*, king of Denmark, sent a splendid embassy under the bold younker *Strangé* to Meissen, and begged the hand of the young and fair Dagmar Margareta, daughter of Premsyl Otakar I., king of Bohemia and Adela of Meissen.   She was not denied him, reached Denmark in the same year, and in the words of the ballad :

> " Silk along the earth was spread ;
>> So many gilded pennants ;
>> To land that lady was y-led,
> So sails the Younker Strangé to the Lady Dagmar.
>
>> His bride embraced he quick, I ween ;
>> So many gilded pennants ;
>> Gave her gold-crown and name of Queen,
> So sails the Younker Strangé to the Lady Dagmar."

' Wedded with great state at Ribe, her life was a dance on roses.   Beloved by her husband, she was the darling of his people.   Beauty, mildness, mercy, drew every heart.   Her first public act was one of grace and large-hearted sympathy.'

In the northern nations it was the custom for the bride, the day after the wedding, to ask the bridegroom a favour or two.   This Queen Dagmar did.   Her first request was that the King would release her uncle, Bishop Waldemar, from prison ; secondly, that he would give up all *plough-pennies* (a kind of feudal rents) ; and thirdly, release all those who sat in irons—meaning, I suppose, all the prisoners in the kingdom.

‘ As might be expected, she became, and she still remains, the idol of Denmark, worthily dividing the affection of the Commons with the redoubted Queen *Thyre*, “ Danmark's Bót,” who built the great wall against the Saxons, as afterwards with “ the Semiramis of the north,” Queen Margaret, that masculine heroine (a counterpart of our own Elizabeth) who, by the famous Calmar-union, first gave shape to that deep longing for a [united] Scandinavia.   Singularly enough, Dagmar's very name assumed a popular form, and a symbolical meaning.   It was originally *Dragomir* (the dear peacemaker), a Sclavic appellation long borne by the ladies of her house. But this meant nothing in her new country, and it speedily passed into *Dagmar* (the Day-may, the Maiden of the Dawn), whereby alone she is now known all the Northlands over.

'Thus, reigning in all men's hearts, year after year flitted away. And during this period she must have often accompanied her kingly partner to Ringsted, where stood a magnificent church, the resting-place of the patron saint of Denmark —*Holy Cnut, Martyr*, her husband's grandfather. This cloister church, originally dedicated to Our Lady and St. Benedict, was then one of the finest in Northern Europe, and, in spite of melancholy alterations and " restorations," is still a remarkable one. It had at this period become the royal mausoleum, the acknowledged death-home for the members of the royal dynasty, as well as their favourite resort when living. Hence " Ringsted will soon see him," said of any Danish prince at this time, signified that Ringsted church would soon see him deposited in one of its silent grave-kists. . . . . But Fortune's wheel stayeth not. Seven short summers are gone, and, the pains of a cruel childbed overtaking her—

> " Queen Dagmar lieth in Ribe sick,
>     Ringsted her soon will see ;
>   To leech-wives the wisest all Denmark through,
>     She sends in her agony.
>   *Queen Dagmar she resteth there in Ringsted.*"

She immediately sent, when her condition was hopeless, a messenger for King Valdemar, whom the young page found playing at " tables " in one of his palaces ; of course he was startled and grieved beyond expression.

> " Dan-king the tables shutteth quickly,
>     Clattered the dice and sung :—
>   ' God the Father forbid it now,
>     That Dagmar should die so young.'
>   *Queen Dagmar she resteth there in Ringsted.*"

' According to the legend, the King on his

arrival found his beloved Queen lifeless ; but at his approach her strong love called back her soul, and she took leave of her weeping husband, and prayed for outlaws and fettered prisoners.

· Then she died for ever.

> " Her eyes she stroketh yet once more,
>     Her cheeks they were so white :
> ' Heaven's Chimes, they are ringing for me,
>     No longer can I bide ! '
> *Queen Dagmar she resteth there in Ringsted.*"

This noble and virtuous Queen was of course buried at Ringsted, and probably, as Professor Stephens observes, some costly monument was placed over her ; but ' in later times the grave has been opened and rifled. It contains only trifling and dubious remains of Dagmar's body, and a couple of petty fragments of the old leaden coffin.' In addition thereto, there was exhibited in Ringsted church, in the last century, a skull, said to be that of the beautiful Queen. It was deposited in a cupboard in the church, as stated in a manuscript relating to that building (dated

1769), ' that *an ungodly fellow*, some fourteen or sixteen years ago, found a chance of stealing it away.'

It was probably in connexion with this barbarous sacrilege that Dagmar's Cross was brought to the light of day. ' Certain it is, that this precious work of art has always borne her name, and that ever since 1737 there has been a constant tradition that it was found in her grave.' The Danish antiquary Herbst has shown that it was added to the royal chamber of art·in the Palace Museum as early as 1695, so that some ' rifling' of the good Queen's grave, and even then with the addition to the protocol : ' this is said to have been worn by Queen Margareta Dagmar, King Waldemar II. his spouse.'   In that collection it remained until 1845, when it was transferred to the newly-founded Museum of Northern Antiquities, ' which has since become so famous for its matchless treasures.'

This relic is a constant attraction to all

visitors, 'for if there was ever a woman regarded for centuries as *holy*, it was Queen Dagmar.' Even less than a century ago, when a farmer or peasant went to Ringsted Church, he would approach the Queen's grave, and say, 'Dagmar, hail!'

That excellent and archæological monarch, King Frederik vii., who devoted so much of his time and learning to the conservation of national monuments, took this cross as a model for a wedding gift to our Princess Alexandra on her departure for England. He caused a facsimile of the cross to be made, arranged so as to open, and placed within it a fragment of silk, a small piece of wood, and a tiny slip of parchment. The silk was cut from the cushion on which the head of Cnut, king and patron-saint of Denmark, was found resting when his tomb was opened in 1833. This cushion is preserved in the Museum. The small fragment of wood was taken from a reliquary (now also in the Museum), in which it

lay, purporting to be a fragment of the Cross of
Christ, with the inscription 'De ligno D'ni.'
The slip of parchment has an inscription :
'Sericum de pulvinari, S$^{ti}$ Canuti, Regis et
Patroni Daniæ, manu Frederiki VII., regius
Daniæ, abscissum' (*silk from the pillow of St.
Cnut, king and patron of Denmark, cut off by
the hand of Frederik the Seventh, King of
Denmark*).

'Thus King Frederik endeavoured to make
the new cross a true copy of the original. Its
greatest value in the eyes of Dagmar doubtless
was that it contained costly relics.' On one side
of it is a rude figure of Christ on the cross, with
some unintelligible figures below. On the other
side are five small medallions, with Christ in
the centre, the Virgin Mary at his right, St.
John at his left, St. Basil above, and St. John
Chrysostom below, their names, contracted,
being in Greek characters. This most curious
relic of ancient art, which is less than two inches

in length, is evidently of Byzantine workmanship.

But one of the most striking features of this
great Museum is the Runic Hall, concerning
which Professor Stephens has printed a separate
and well-illustrated monograph. Professor and
State-Councillor Worsaae founded this hall in
March 1867, when, as Professor Stephens observes, it was high time that these old *lares*
should be taken care of and conveniently placed.
Some of them, for want of room, were lying in
out-of-the-way places in the Museum, some in
Trinity Churchyard, and others in the Round
Tower—all more or less liable to injury. They
bear the oldest remains of written language,
dating many hundreds of years before our
earliest parchments. ' They open up pictures
of the life, death, and exploits of our forefathers
that cannot be found elsewhere, and they offer a
striking proof of the oneness of all the Northern
*folkships.'*

The Professor remarks, that the most ancient pieces have inscriptions in an alphabet called 'Old Northern;' but this gradually became much modified and altered. It is greatly to be regretted that in Denmark, where stone is comparatively rare, these grand old memorials of ages long gone by should be ruthlessly broken up as soon as found. A Danish gentleman told the Professor that in 1867 he visited Jutland. When at Skive he heard that a Runic monument had been found a few days before. He drove to Haderup, about three Danish miles off, and talked with the finder, who informed him that the stone had been beaten into many pieces, and that all the fragments had been either used or thrown away. At least fifty of these blocks were destroyed within this century, in Denmark alone, and several of them were Old Northern. Alas! that the common people in every country —our own not excepted—should be so regardless of the relics of 'hoar antiquity.'

These stones are rude in the extreme, of irregular shape, and unhewn; still the runes are
for the most part readable by antiquaries skilled
in the subject. The Professor's monograph contains many illustrations of them on a large scale.
The first stone is supposed to have come from
a *how* or tumulus, discovered long ago near
Vordingborg, and its date is conjectured to be
about A.D. 600 or 700. It is of granite minne-
stone. It was first noticed by the famous chan-
cellor Christian Fris, about the middle of the
seventeenth century, when it was lying as a
paving stone under the excise-office at Vordin-
borg, and it was then transported to Copenhagen.
It was broken when first conveyed thither, but
it has been since mended : it is about 4 feet 5
inches long. The runes of the inscription are
from 3½ to 4 inches in length.

The next stone is of much ruder form and
execution, and is also of granite. It came from
Helnæs. The foolish workmen who found it

broke it into three pieces, and two of them were used as gate-posts! but they are now put together again. The carver's name is placed on this relic, thus : '*Æuæir* Fayed sculptured this stone and these runes.'

It may be remarked that the person here commemorated was drowned, and many other runic monuments mention death by drowning; which is not to be wondered at, when we consider that seafaring men, who constituted a large proportion of the population of Scandinavia, were constantly exposed to the disasters of a most dangerous ocean.

The next stone, 4 feet 2 inches broad, and 21 inches in thickness, was found at Snoldelev in Zealand, and is of the date of about A.D. 700 or 800. It is formed of a species of granite, and has upon it three horns, supposed to be an emblem of Thor, and a singularly shaped cross, which may be that of Woden. Its inscription runs thus : ' Kunuaet's stone,

son of Ruhalt Thyle (the Speaker) on the Sal-
hows.'

Next we come to a stone from Glenstrup in
North Jutland, supposed to belong to the ninth
or tenth century. This stone was formerly in
the south side of the parish church. It is said to
have been found on the top of a tumulus hard
by, not far from a spring called Thoro's Well.
Thoro was an early chieftain who had sacrificed
his son to the gods, and thereupon this healing
water had burst forth. After the introduction
of Christianity, the well, still retaining its cura-
tive powers, was dedicated to the Three Maries,
as was also the church. The block is of dark
granite, and measures about five feet by three.
The runes, though very much worn, inform us
that ' Thurir raised this for Kunar his father '
—but history gives no account of either father
or son.

The next memorial is of the dark igneous
stone called Dolerite. It was found in 1833,

in digging up the foundations of an old house at Kirkebo, formerly the see of the bishops of Færoe. The inscription seems to read : ' Uik set me up for Uniru.' The runes read from right to left.

Then we meet with another stone from Stenderup in Jutland. It is only a fragment, but the whole inscription is fortunately preserved. The legend is : 'May Jothin take Jothin !' Jothin is apparently the name of the Scandinavian god Woden, after whom the person commemorated was named. Perhaps the true reading of the runes is : ' O Woden, receive thy servant Woden !' Scandinavia has two stones bearing the name of the god Thor ; but this is the only one bearing that of Woden.

The next stone came, it is supposed, from Little Tarnby, in the parish of Harlov, hundred of Faxo, Præstoshire. It first attracted public attention so long ago as 1566, when Poul Vobis, governor of Tryggeraelde Castle had it removed to the castle yard. It is perforated with five holes, supposed by Mr. Stephens to have been made for the introduction of the ropes by which the oxen dragged it along. At a later date, about 1656, Christian Skeel, governor of the same castle, removed it to his seat at Vallo. In 1810 it was sent to Trinity Churchyard, Copenhagen, where it remained until it was removed to the Museum in 1867. It is hard 'greystone,' and about nine feet high, four broad, and one in thickness. Some of the runes are so much defaced, that it is difficult for the ablest runic scholar to decypher them. The inscription, however, is found to imply that 'Raknhilt, sister of Ulf, placed this stone, and Gared made the grave-mound. . . . Her husband was an eloquent (or illustrious) man, the son of Nairbi. . . . Few are now better born than he.—Let him be an outlaw who casts down this stone, or who drags it hence for other use, or for the grave of another man!'—reminding us somewhat of Shakspeare's epitaph in Stratford church :—

'Curst be the man who moves these stones,' etc.

One of the smallest stones in the Hall, and one of those nearest approaching a squared form, came from Asferg in North Jutland, and bears an inscription to this effect: 'Thurkir, the son of Tuki, raised this stone for Muli his brother, a very good Thane (soldier, hero, chief).' The date of this inscription is probably of the tenth century.

The next stone, supposed to be of about the same date, was brought from Bregningo in Lolland. The inscription is : 'These grave-marks (*i.e.* the stone and the barrow) were made in memory of Tuki, by Asa, his mother, and by his brothers, the sons of Tuki-Haklang.' After that, we see a stone of light granite. It is of the same style and period, and was discovered in 1814, at Ega in North Jutland. The legend runs thus : 'Alfkil and (?) his sons raised this stone for their friend (or kinsman) who was Landward (landwarden, governor, or bailiff) to Kitil the Norwegian.' Then we have a very small block, but a foot in thickness, from Kirkeby in Falster. It was formerly built into the wall of the church, from whence it was removed in 1811, by the Danish Antiquarian Commission, to the Round Tower. On it is a most rude representation of a ship or boat, and the inscription is to the effect that—'Osur set this stone for Oskitil, his brother, who was slain in Kuruli-Land (Carelia).' Thus this Danish mound was a cenotaph, as the Danish hero had fallen in Finland. Professor Stephens remarks that Wikin (or naval adventure) to Finland, is mentioned on several *Swedish* stones.

I have never visited Finland, but I have had the pleasure of making the acquaintance of a good many Finlanders. During the Crimean war, when Bomarsund was bombarded by our troops, and many of the Fins were captured, they were sent to the then disused old prison at Lewes, in which town I resided. The officers were of course on parole, and I used to open my house to them for soirées, etc. I am glad to say that my humble example was followed, but on a better scale, by some of my noble and gentle neighbours, and everybody was pleased with their polished manners and intelligent conversation. They nearly all spoke English fluently.

The great stone in the Museum is one from Torsted in Lolland. It is 7 feet high, and 6 feet 7 inches wide at its broadest point. That it was never squared is proved by the design, which is accommodated to its rude form when originally employed. The epitaph seems to read as follows: 'Æsrath and Hiltulf raised this stone for Frod, their wise (prudent or illustrious) kinsman; but he was the foeman (terror or scourge) of men. He fell in Sweden, and was then leader in Frikir's fleet (or forces) the hero of the war expedition.'

Next we have a fragment of a stone found in a highway pavement at Barse in Zealand. It contains only four runes, and is apparently of the eleventh century. There is also a small stone of about the same date from Frodebo, carved on the upper half with a double-lined 'cross pattée.' There is no inscription. Another stone, or rather a portion of one, was found built into the wall of the choir of Sandby church in Zealand. It has runes on both sides; but as the stone is only a fragment, no satisfactory reading of it has been achieved.

The sepulchral effigy of a northern bishop is among the most interesting relics in the whole of this wonderful Museum. It dates about the year 1135, and is really the earliest Christian memorial—properly so called—in the collection. The first engraving of it is in the voluminous work of Olaus Wormius, the eminent Danish antiquary, but the last and best is that in Professor Stephens's monograph. It was formerly in the chapel of Giesenholm Castle in North Jutland.   It is of dark granite, and measures about 5 feet 2 inches long, 18½ inches wide at top, and 16 at bottom, thus corresponding with the monumental stones of nearly every part of western and southern Europe.   In low relief it bears the figure of a bishop, standing, and about to bless—his episcopal staff firmly grasped in his left hand.   Below is a lamb, carrying on its left foot the holy *rood*, so frequently seen on our own ancient monuments and in painted glass —'*Agnus Dei qui tollis peccata Mundi.*'   The inscription on the sides and at the head of the tomb is in runes, and is thus rendered by Professor Stephens: 'Thurth raised this tomb over Thuro Æbeæson Lange.'   The right side may be read : ' Grant, we pray thee, O Mary, mercy : and may St. Nicholas guard him.'   The short edge of the stone at the head of the monument bears what is probably the name of the sculptor, ' Horderus.'   The bishop commemorated by this memorial was probably the bishop of Ribe, who fell in the battle of Fodvig in 1134; and his body appears to have been privately buried at Giesingholm.

There is a broken piece of red sandstone from Brattahlid in Greenland, the runes on which are much worn, and even the learned Professor cannot confidently decipher them.—The next object is a much more perfect and interesting one. It was formerly in the church wall of Brynderslev in North Jutland, the dedication of which it commemorates :—

'THIS IS NAMED CHRIST'S CHURCH FOR THE SALVATION OF MEN.'

The name of the founder or architect is also given :—' Suin, son of Karmunt.'

Runic letters were not always employed on stone only, but they are occasionally found on wood. Thus we have a specimen from Valthiofstad in Iceland, of the date of about 1100 or 1200. It is a beautiful door of pinewood, perhaps drift timber. It is 6 feet 7½ inches in Danish measure, and above 3 feet broad —'one of the finest specimens of old wood-carving in Europe.' It was formerly at the principal entrance of the parish church. This carving is supposed to represent King Diderik (or Theoderik) fighting with the winged Dragon, to rescue the perishing Lion ; but the inscription has never been read. 'The upper roundel in the lower compartment exhibits the victory of the champion over the dragon,' and there is a representation of Diderik on horse-back followed by the grateful lion. On the outside of the church, on a small slab, rests the same, or some other lion, with a small cross. The runic inscription on it is conjectured by the Professor to have been originally this :— 'Here see that mighty king sculptured, who slew the dragon.' One of the old Northern Sagas has the legend of this remarkable conflict, which is doubtless of Oriental origin. It has been remarked that the style and costume very much remind us of those of the Bayeux Tapestry.

The next articles in the Catalogue are two Icelandic chairs, supposed to date from about 1200 to 1300. They are rich and elegant articles in cornel-wood, carved with a knife. The seats form chests, and one of them has a lock and key; and they are both decorated with dragon and arabesque work, medallions, and foliage. The runes on the inscribed one convey no very intelligible meaning, but the Professor guesses that they signify that 'The *house-fru* (mistress) possesses this chair;' afterwards: 'But Benedict Narfson gave me to her'—whatever that may mean. On the front of the seat are the signs of the Zodiac, with inscriptions carved partly in runes, and partly in Latin-Gothic letters, signifying Sol in Tauro, Sol in Gemini, Sol in Cancro, and so on. The mixture of runes with Roman letters shows a curious phase in the history of Northern civilisation, and illustrates in *letters* what has been done in English in *words*. Our English tongue is probably the most 'composite' one in the world. There is scarcely a civilized nation that has not added to our vocabulary.

There are several other objects well worthy of attention from Iceland, etc., but I think the non-archæological reader will by this time have had a *quantum sufficit* of these runic matters. I will therefore conclude this portion of my sketches by a translation of an epitaph from Utskalar in South-west Iceland :—

'Here slumbers Bretiua, Orme's daughter : say a Pater-
    noster for her soul.
Light the loosened Soul that glideth
Far away from this poor earth !'

I do not pretend to Runic scholarship, and therefore I must acknowledge my obligations to Professor Stephens for the foregoing remarks, the substance of which is to be found in his account of the Runic Hall of the Museum, a monograph which I can conscientiously recommend to every English antiquary, not only for its literary merits, but for its beautiful illustrations, most of which are from drawings executed by the learned Professor himself.

———

We shall return to Copenhagen again; but in order to diversify these pages a little we will take a peep at higher latitudes. And first, of the Norwegian superstitions, once doubtless common to the whole of Scandinavia, but now principally limited to the inhabitants of the most northern portions of Norway, though not extinct perhaps in any part of Scandinavia.

I verily believe that Scandinavia is the true 'dream-land.' I never had so remarkable a 'vision of the night' as I had there. First I saw my father, who had been dead some years; then two of my brothers; then three of my sons; next the King of Denmark, who invited me to one of his palaces, and offered me knighthood (!!), which with many thanks I respectfully declined. After that I saw, with the greatest distinctness and apparent reality, One Whose holy name I am almost afraid to mention in this connexion. It was He who died for our sins on Mount Calvary. His gait and figure much resembled those represented by Gustave Doré. I knelt, and kissed the hem of his garment; but I can say no more, except that my dream was the most delightful one I ever experienced, or that any man could enjoy.

Perhaps it is owing to this mental phenomenon that much of the superstition of the northern parts of Scandinavia arises, especially in the extreme north of Norway. Mrs. Ellis [1]

---

[1] Great was our grief to learn, not many days after our return to England, that Mrs. Ellis, who was in excellent health when we left Denmark, had died after a short illness, from a severe attack of pleurisy. Truly we may say, 'In the midst of life we are in death,' and also that 'whom God loveth best He taketh soonest.'

kindly gave my wife a manuscript of her own translation from the Norwegian into English. It was written by Jonas Lie, and some extracts from it I take the liberty to insert.

It is entitled, *Second Sight, or Pictures of the North*. My first extract will give some idea of the stormy weather in the land of the Norsemen.

' I am acquainted with several people who, like myself, have a strong wish to wander out when the weather is stormy. They are generally such as have passed their youth in the country, and who have exchanged that freedom for a sedentary life in towns, and consequently feel almost suffocated by the narrow confinement of a room. Poets are also said to have the same inclination. . . . The roofs of the buildings shake, showering down tiles on the passers-by, turning streets into canals, and making corners of thoroughfares into most dangerous halting-places. . . . It sometimes occurs that a steady middle-aged official or man of business, who one would suppose would prefer sitting cosily by the fireside, resting after his day's work, suddenly informs his wife that unfortunately he is obliged to go out on business. Of course it *is* business! It would never do for a steady man, who may perhaps be chief magistrate or churchwarden, to acknowledge, even to himself, that he is so childish as to wish to go out in a storm, and that his only business is to walk on the pier, and see the foaming waves dash over the breakwater, and the ships swinging wildly about at their anchorage! Something, he makes himself believe, he has to do there, if only in a general way to see that the town, for whose prosperity he is in some way responsible, does not blow down. The fact is, there is a revolution in the streets —not political : defend him from being in any way mixed up with that,—but a revolution of the kind that has its attractions for him, because it awakens all his old feelings, and he manages to be there, not caring for the fact that this one, in its way, upsets all police arrangements,—breaks windows, extinguishes lamps, tears tiles from house-roofs, destroys bridges, knocks down out-houses, frightens policemen and watchmen home to their discomfort. Not a soul will take the trouble to go down and fasten the door; the porter is out, and till he returns nothing will be done.'

Another relation of a Norwegian storm is thus given in Mrs. Ellis's manuscript :—' It was in the afternoon, the day after Epiphany, the same day that the clergyman's family were to return home, that the dreadful storm began, which raged two days, and is still spoken of by many as the most fearful hurricane that had, in the memory of man, visited Lofoten. Happily the fishing season had not yet commenced. The storm, sleet, and immensely heavy seas came from the south-west, right

upon the West-bay, otherwise there would probably have been as many wrecks as during the
well-known storm in 1849, when many hundreds
of boats were lost in one day. Now there were
only a few boats, which were out fishing, lost;
and some sloops and larger ships stranded. The
storm increased towards night, the buildings
shook with every blast, and all of us remained
up, to keep watch through the night. Every
window, door, and hole was carefully closed.
The tiles rattled so that we were afraid that
parts of the roof would be blown off; and from
the chimney-tops there came a dismal, deep
rumbling sound, which one might almost fancy
to be cries of distress. We were all assembled
in one room, and a deep silence prevailed,
broken only by a remark about the storm, or
by one of the servants leaving the room to look
after things. My father was very uneasy about
his store and his sloop, which was lying in the
bay, and which had three anchors out to keep

it steady in the heavy seas, which, in spite of the good situation of the harbour, rolled in upon it. I saw him several times fold his hands, as if in prayer, and then he would walk up and down the room as though he felt comforted, until fear again seized him ; and he sat down pale and anxious as before.

'The storm still increased. Once we heard a dull crash, which might possibly come from the store. I saw drops of sweat start out on my father's forehead, and yet knowing I was utterly unable to bring him the slightest comfort. He took a light into the office, and returned with a large old Prayer-book, which he opened at "prayers and psalms" to be used in times of distress at sea. We all, without a word, arranged ourselves for prayer. My father sat at the table holding the book in his large rough hands, between the two candles. First he read the prayers, and then sang all the verses of the psalm, while those who knew the tune gradually joined in with him.  It was in every respect as prayers are held on board ship, when there is danger ; and my father had certainly taken his idea from some such scene in his youth.  During the service it seemed to us all as if there was a lull in the storm, and that it had increased again when we had finished.  It was said that the eldest Martinez (a shipwrecked Spanish captain) was on his knees in his room, and constantly crossing himself before his crucifix.  He had not much reason for anxiety, as his brig was anchored under the land in a small creek that was sheltered from the storm and heavy seas, but he repented not having gone on board to his son and his crew. . . .

'Towards morning there came somewhat of a lull, and, tired as we were, went to bed, with the exception of one or two, who were to keep watch.  When daylight came, we saw what destruction the storm had wrought ; many hundreds of tiles from the roof strewed the ground, the bindings of the wall exposed to the wind were torn loose, and the farther end of the pier lay under water, its supporters having been displaced by the waves.

'The warehouse had also suffered injury. Our sloop was in no little danger; two of its chain cables had already sprung, and its safety now depended on the last and longest, which was fastened to the ship's ring on the rock at the entrance of the bay. The only living thing on board was the dog, a large white poodle, which stood barking, with its fore legs on the taffrail, as we could see, though the wind rendered it impossible for us to hear. The sea was breaking over the fore part of the sloop; the danger was great; the long cable was strained so much that the middle of it hardly touched the water.

'The wind raged so fiercely that the seamen were obliged to creep along bent down, lest

they should be blown overboard. Help was
therefore out of the question. I crept up to
the hillock behind the house, and stood under
the shelter of a rock, whence I could over-
look the bay, and see outside. The appearance of West-bay was like a mass of silver-grey
smoke, which had been blown in from the
sea.    Under the land, green foam-topped
waves, mountains high, rushed forward with
roars like thunder, to be sucked back again,
leaving the sands bare and dry far out. At
one place, by a rock which extended far into
the ocean, the waves, every time they washed
against it, threw an immense jet of foam straight
upwards, which was caught by the wind and
driven like smoke in and over the land. At
another place the waves absolutely stormed a
sloping bank, now covering it with foam, and
then leaving it quite dry; and there was one
unfortunate sea-gull which had probably been
disturbed, fighting and struggling in the wind,

until its poor wings seemed almost turned inside out. I now bent my attention to the sloop in the bay. To my astonishment I saw a man on board, and recognised our strong servant Jens, who with another of our men adventured out to it in a six-oared boat. Immediately afterwards he went back alone to the boat, with a rope tied round him, and began the dangerous work of hauling it against the waves along the tightened rope out to the rock. I expected every moment that the boat would fill, and thought it took water several times. Whilst the boat went slowly on, my father and our people anxiously watched it from the beach. When Jens had climbed the rock, which the waves washed every moment, so that he stood up to his knees in water, he fastened the boat, and then began hauling the rope, and thus drew in another chain cable, which the man on the sloop had gradually let out. He had got the end of the cable in the ring, and

was in the act of fastening it, when we saw
three fearful waves coming, which would certainly dash over the rock.

' There was extreme danger now, both for the
life of Jens and for the safety of the sloop,
which would hardly hold on against the pressure with one cable.  I saw " French Martine,"
who was betrothed to Jens, wring her hands
over her head, and rush to the beach, as if she
intended to throw herself into the water after
him ; and I do not think that any of us who
were looking on dared to draw breath.  It
appeared as if Jens had also seen the danger :
he hurried down to the boat, where he still
might save himself, but it was only to take up
the rope, which he steadily wound several times
around his body, and then passed it through
the ring as if he no longer reckoned on his own
strength.  He had hardly finished when the
first wave, which struck him on the back, burst
over him and the rock.  The interval between

the first wave and the second he used in hauling the cable more in. Again came a wave, and again Jens stood safe ; and now he managed the last hitch on the rope, which saved the sloop. He had tried how hard a wave could press ; he had thrown the rope around him over his broad shoulders ; turned his pale face towards our house, as if he thought he was saying good-bye to it, and bent his head to receive the last, and, as usual, the heaviest wave of the three. When the foam had cleared away there was no Jens on the rock. In my anxiety I had dashed down to the others. When I arrived, they had saved not only the boat, which had broken away from the rock, but also the apparently lifeless Jens, whom they were carrying up to the house. The wave had taken him with it, for the rope had glided over his neck and deprived him of a part of his garments and some of his skin. He lay unconscious, with one arm bloody and torn by the

K

rope hanging by his side. At one place it was lacerated to the bone.

'My father, pale from anxiety, helped to carry him up to the house and lay him on the bed. When the poor fellow became conscious, he expectorated a quantity of blood, and had difficulty in speaking ; but my father, after examining his chest, joyfully declared that his life was in no danger. Jens became, for this act of saving the sloop, a man of wide-spread renown. From that day he was my father's trusted man, and the following summer he married French Martine.'

Many similar tales are told by old seafaring Northmen, but want of space will not permit me to recite them ; I must not omit to mention, however, that in the well-remembered storm of 1849 *many hundreds* of boats were lost in one day. I therefore pass on to a subject previously alluded to (on page 133), namely, the superstitions and legends of the northern Norwegians.

Jonas Lie's hero mentions a curious and very superstitious old woman who had the care of him after his mother's death. She was a small masculine-looking person, marked with small-pox, and had little brown eyes and grey hair; and to add to these charms she generally carried in her mouth a black clay pipe. Her name was Anne Kvœn. She was as sure that the brownie and the merman lived in the store and the boat-house of the elder M. Holst as she was that he lived in his own residence; and that elves and wizards held their invisible sports on the moun-tain tops! When a boat came in, she turned to the sea, spat, and mumbled words as a charm against the mermen. She saw every person's *double*, and therefore no door could be shut too quickly when any one came in or went out; and 'she had,' as David Holst informs us, 'always some mysterious warning of my father's return from a voyage. . . . In her charms the word *Jumala* was often used: it is the name of the old god of the Bjarmers, whose worship in the far north is not so entirely abolished as might be supposed.' Even to this day there are two altars, high up in the mountains in Finmark, which are dedicated to his *cultus*. Hence it appears that in the nineteenth century, even in civilized Europe, among the more ignorant, Christianity is made to shake hands with paganism.

David Holst describes his father's servants' hall in a somewhat graphic manner. He says that ' the *haunted* feeling that pervaded the house afforded much matter for conversation in the servants' hall, when the men, maid-servants, and journeymen-travellers, who were to have a night's lodging there, sat round the fire relating anecdotes of all sorts of wrecks and apparitions. In one corner sat our good strong Jens, with his carpenter's tools and work about him. He always attended to his work, listening to what others said. In front of the fire sat " furrier Nils," oiling his skins. He had got the title of "furrier" because he sewed the skins together. He was a small man with an uncombed head of yellow hair hanging down over his forehead, a face as round as the full moon, a nose like a small button, and, when he laughed, a thin-lipped wide mouth, and a large jaw that had much the expression of a skeleton's grin. His small milky eyes used to wink mysteriously, giving you the idea that he was clever. He was in reality the one who knew the greatest number of anecdotes, and had at the same time the knack of getting travellers to relate all that they knew of the invisible as well as the visible world. A third went by the name of Anders Tipler, because he sometimes got drunk.' This person was however, in his way, very clever and faithful, especially during a sea-storm. These honest men and maids amused themselves with ghost stories. One of them is said to have happened in the days of Erlandson's predecessors. It was as follows :—

'At that time an old store stood at a short distance from the parsonage. A party were sitting, talking and drinking, one Christmas Eve in the office, and about eleven o'clock, the beer-jug being empty, Rasmus the servant, a strong courageous man, was sent to the store, where the beer was kept, with orders to fill a large silver-topped jug. Arrived there, he placed his lantern on the barrel, and began to draw the beer. When the jug was full, and he was in the act of putting it to his mouth, he saw a monstrous figure in the dark background, where there were rows of beer-barrels, a frightfully large broad shape, from which issued an ice-cold draught, as if a door were open. It winked at him with with large dim eyes like two horn lanterns, and said " Christmas beer, thief!" But Rasmus did not lose his presence of mind ; he flung the heavy jug right at the merman's eyes, and ran away with all his might. Outside, the moon was shining brightly on the snow; screams and yells were heard from the beach, so that he knew that there were a great number of mermen pursuing him. When he got to the churchyard wall, they were close upon him, and he, hard pressed, cried out: "Help me, all ye dead!" The dead are great enemies of mermen. Rasmus heard the dead arise, and the noise and tumult of a battle followed. He in the mean-time was hotly pursued by one particular mer-man, who put out his hand to catch him, but he was just in time to reach the door, and was safe, though he fell upon the floor in a swoon. The day after, Christmas-day, the church-going people saw the churchyard strewn with lids of coffins, broken oars, and planks from wrecks. These were the weapons that had been used in the battle, and it was easy to see that the dead had been the victors. The jug was found to be flattened from striking against the monster's skull, and the lantern had been crushed when Rasmus fled.'

The Norsemen possess the faculty of 'second sight' in a wonderful degree, and they have visions sometimes of spirits and sometimes of realities. They have also premonitions of events about to happen. Sometimes they see large funeral processions with such distinctness that they can describe person, place, and look, the coffin, and the streets through which the cortège passes. Sometimes these foreshadowings turn out to be remarkably correct, and if one in twenty of them does so, the other nineteen are overlooked. According to a vulgar old English proverb :—

'What is hits is histories ;
What is missed is mysteries.'

———

To return to Copenhagen. One of the most interesting objects is the *Ethnographic Museum*. Its object is to illustrate the costumes and habits of the various nations of the world, in all the ages of barbarism. The collection was formed some years ago, and more recently it has been classified under the skilful management of Professor Worsaae. It occupies three stories. On the ground floor five apartments are devoted to prehistoric antiquities, and contain implements of the stone, bronze, and iron ages, from every part of the world. It would be difficult to give a detailed account of the contents of this interesting Museum; therefore I must content myself with observing that they principally relate to the following regions and countries :—

Europe, Asia, and South America and the Carribbean Islands, Central America, Mexico, and North America, Greenland.

The Esquimaux of Greenland, those of North America, and those of Northern Asia.

The North American Indians, and the Indians of Central and South America.

African Negroes, Hottentots, Bushmen, and Kaffirs.

Malays and other inhabitants of the Indian Archipelago.

The Papuas, and other natives of the Australian regions.

Natives of Siberia.

The Chinese, Hindoos, Persians, Arabs, Turks, Japanese, etc.

This is undoubtedly the finest ethnographical

collection in the world, and it would afford materials for the study of many days to the student of ethnology.

The largest and most prominent building of Copenhagen is the palace called Christiansborg. It stands on an island close to the harbour, but is approachable by bridges.   There was a castle on this spot as early as the twelfth century, but the edifice was several times destroyed and re-built.   When Copenhagen became the principal residence of royalty, King Christian I. and his son, King Hans, greatly added to its grandeur, size, and strength, and built a magnificent banqueting-hall.   In the entrance hall of the royal library are still to be seen in bas-relief effigies of King Hans and his Queen.   A larger building was erected in the early part of the eighteenth century ; but it was soon afterwards pulled down to make room for one of the handsomest palaces in Europe, built between 1733 and 1770.   This was unfortunately destroyed by fire in 1794 ; and it was not until 1828 that the present building, which is far inferior to the former one, was sufficiently finished for use. Even now it remains unfinished, and it has never been used as a permanent residence. Fêtes on a large scale are, however, carried on occasionally in its capacious halls. The façade is very grand, and ornamented with four colossal bronze statues, after designs by Thorvaldsen, representing Hercules, Minerva, Nemesis, and Æsculapius, to typify strength, wisdom, justice, and truth; but by an error Æsculapius is made to stand, not as the god of medicine, but as the emblem of truth! There is also a group designed by Thorvaldsen, representing Jupiter surrounded by the minor deities. The banqueting-hall (called the Riddersal)[1] is a gorgeous apartment 120 feet by 50,

---

[1] *Ridder, richter, rider*, etc., used in the northern languages of Europe, means a mounted soldier, in contradistinction to an infantry man. Our Knight-*rider* Street in London is consequently a tautologous expression.

and 44 feet high, decorated with white and gold.
The frieze, by the sculptor Bissen, represents
the procession of Ceres and Bacchus, emblematical of bread and wine.    In the ante-room of
this fine hall is Thorvaldsen's noble frieze,
Alexander's entry into Babylon.    Some of the
rooms contain pictures by Danish, Dutch,
French, and Italian masters.    Among other
halls for public use, are those for the *Things*, or
Chambers of Parliament.    Close to the palace
stands the chapel-royal (*Slotskirken*),[1] built in
the style of the castle, and arranged, as to the
interior, in excellent taste.    The only feeling
disparaging to the castle or palace of Christiansborg is, that it looks so wonderfully *new*.

One of the most charming places in the city
is the ' Tivoli Gardens,' a public promenade, and
attractive for its delicious evening concerts.    It
is approached by a fine avenue of trees, and
is altogether the most delightful spot in Copen-

---

[1] *Slot*, the Danish for palace or castle.

hagen. The music hall is built in a kind of
oriental style, and highly decorated. The
entrance fee being very small, all classes can
visit it. Thus, on our several visits, we saw
persons from the gentlest to the simplest present,
including little children not more than four years
old, who ran about the hall with the greatest
*sang froid.* My wife gave a little girl a ' sweet,'
which she happened to have in her pocket, and
she immediately kissed both my wife and myself,
as if she had known us long ago.

The conductor of the band is M. Dahl, a very
able musician and composer. The orchestra
contains violins, ' double-basses,' horns, etc., and
the whole performance cannot be surpassed in
any capital in Europe. When M. Dahl's own
compositions were played, he led off with an
enthusiasm quite glorious to behold. I sought
an introduction to him, and found him to be
a most well-informed and gentlemanly man.
Murray correctly calls the Tivoli a 'gigantic

Cremorne, but visited by better company;' and this is strictly true.

Copenhagen is rich in royal palaces, numbering no less than four. Besides Christiansborg, previously mentioned, there are Rosenborg, Amalienborg, and Frederiksborg, all possessing more or less of interest—but of these hereafter. The churches are not numerous, considering the size of the city. The principal one is *Vor Frue Kirke*, or the Church of Our Lady, a modern and most unchurchlike structure, after the fashion of a Roman *basilica*. It was built from a design by Hansen, the architect of the Christiansborg Palace, and is in no way remarkable, except for the Thorvaldsen sculptures. Behind the pulpit is a figure of the Saviour, and arranged on each side are the majestic statues of the twelve apostles, each with his conventional emblems— a glorious sight to behold. Surely such majestic sculpture is not elsewhere to be seen. Then there are noble carvings of St. John the Baptist in the Wilderness, Christ's Entry into Jerusalem, the Procession to Golgotha, the Institution of the two Sacraments, and over the alms-boxes, two figures representing Charity and the Guardian Angel. Outside of the church are two bronze statues, one of David by Jerichau, and another of Moses by Bissen.

This church stands on the site of a much older place of worship, dating from the twelfth century, which contained a great number of costly objects and valuable relics, and was connected with many important events in the history of Denmark; but alas! it was destroyed in the great conflagration of 1728. It was succeeded by a new edifice of imposing size and splendour, which was destroyed in 1807 by our bombardment. Shame to England, say I! The present church was finished in 1829. When we visited it we observed outside a funeral car with four pillars, and none of the black plumes which so disfigure the 'fashionable' English hearse, looking like

sable devils nodding in a friendly manner, as
much as to say, ' We 've got him at last !'   The
service was conducted in a solemn manner, with
musical accompaniments, and the coffin, on being
carried out, was covered with wreaths of white
flowers, such as in England we cast on the remains of the dear departed when they have been
deposited in the cold tomb.

The Church of Our Saviour (*Vor Frelsers*)
possesses a beautiful alabaster font, and a remarkable spire, with a singular winding staircase
outside, leading to a ball which it is affirmed
will hold a dozen people.   This I did not trouble
myself to go up to, though it is said that it commands an extensive prospect of the city and the
circumjacent country.   Helliggeist Kirke (the
Church of the Holy Ghost) is interesting for its
ancient, simple, and well-proportioned cemetery
chapel.   Holmen's Kirke is interesting as containing the mortal remains of some of the leading
naval heroes of Scandinavia, such as Tordens-

kjold, Niel Juul, and others. St. John's, in the northern suburb, is a sufficiently handsome edifice in the modern Gothic style, but objectionable on account of its being built of red brick, a material which should never, in my opinion, be used in ecclesiastical buildings; though it may perhaps be pardoned in such a country, where stone is scarce.

There is another ecclesiastical building called the Marble Church, which was commenced about 1746; but the undertaking, having been found to be too costly, was abandoned. There are also remains, consisting chiefly of an immense square tower of the church of St. Nicholas, which is noteworthy as the first in which the doctrines of the Reformation were enunciated. Altogether, Copenhagen cannot boast much either of the number or the grandeur of its churches. There are a Roman Catholic chapel, a Methodist church, a Greek chapel, and a ' Reformed ' church, none of which possess any features of interest.

L

Bombardments, fires, and other calamities have been most injurious to this fine city, and there are but few remains of 'hoar antiquitie' left, except in the Museums.

The *forum* of Copenhagen is Kongens Nytorv, near the centre of the city. It is a large and handsome square, in which stands the equestrian statue of King Christian v. This figure, with its allegorical accompaniments, possesses little artistic merit ; yet still, with its surroundings of flowers and turf, it produces a good effect. In the square itself are several public or semi-public buildings, including hotels, restaurants, coffee-houses, the Royal Theatre, Count Moltke's gallery, and the Academy of Arts. The principal streets run out of this square, especially Broad Street (*Bredgade*), which is considered the finest thoroughfare of the city. It leads to the explanade of the citadel, past the *Plads* or Place of St. Anne, where there is a sitting statue of Œhlenschläger, the celebrated Danish poet.

Here we also pass the residence of the British Legation or embassy, the Hôtel Phœnix, several great residences of the nobility, the Amalienborg, the Surgical Academy, the Frederik's Hospital, and several other noteworthy edifices.

Count Moltke's picture-gallery well deserves a visit. The pictures, chiefly of the Dutch school, are exhibited in the palace of the Baron Reedtz, and are the productions, among others, of Ruysdael, Rembrandt, Hobbima, Ostade, Teniers, Wouvermann, etc. etc.

Copenhagen of course possesses a University. It was founded in 1478, and it has at present about six hundred students, and the large number of forty Professors. Connected with the establishment is the University Library, one of the finest modern edifices of the city. It is built of stone and iron, elegantly finished, and contains more than 200,000 volumes, and about 4000 manuscripts.

Besides this library is the Grand Royal

Library, which is situated close to the Arsenal, a rich collection of the literature of all countries and ages. It contains nearly 561,000 printed volumes, and about 25,000 manuscripts, many of which are of great curiosity and value. The original hall of the library, which is 250 feet long, is supported by numerous columns, and very finely ornamented with white and gold. Since this grand hall was erected, eight other halls have been annexed for the deposit of augmentations. 'The collection of early printed books and block-books is very large and valuable; and the old Scandinavian and Oriental MSS. are specially so.' Many of these objects were formerly the property of eminent historical personages. Two striking figures of stone stand in the vestibule. They represent Hans, king of all Scandinavia, and his queen, Christina; and formerly stood at an entrance to the Palace. Their date is 1503.

One of the finest ornaments of Copenhagen

is the Exchange, built of brick in the renaissance style, commonly called Christian-the-
Fourth's style; and which, with the exception
of the material, strongly resembles what we
call Elizabethan. This edifice, however, is of
later date, and was not finished much before
1640. It has a very singular spire, rather
difficult to describe. It is fantastically formed
of four twisted dragons, with their heads downwards, and facing the cardinal points of the
compass.

To return to the royal palaces : Rosenborg
Castle is also in the Christian-the-Fourth style,
and is situated in the northern part of the city.
It is partly surrounded by a public garden of
considerable beauty. It was planned by the
monarch himself, and is known as the King's
Garden (*Kongen's Have*). The view of the
castle from some parts of these grounds is most
picturesque and pleasing. The design for the
building is attributed, I know not on what

grounds, to Inigo Jones, and it was begun in
1604. The garden was originally ornamented
with many fountains and statues; but all that
now remains of the *former* beauties of the
place are two most noble avenues of chestnut
trees, a bronze group, representing a horse
attacked by a lion, and two lions standing near
the bridge which leads from the '*have*' to the
castle. Here I may remark that the Lion and
the Dragon are two favourite animals which
were much in use, from early times, all over
Scandinavia. The lion is a 'familiar beast' in
Eastern climates, though not 'a friend to man;'
but of the origin of the dragon the naturalist
knows nothing, except that it may be the
crocodile in a greatly altered form. However
this may be, both the animals belong to Oriental
regions, and the ancient Scandinavians must
have imported their ideas of them from the
East long ages ago.

The grounds contain a School of gardening,

and there are extensive conservatories and hot-houses. Rosenborg is no longer a royal re-sidence, but is entirely devoted to collections of the kings of Denmark, chronologically arranged. It was founded after the death of Christian IV. in 1648. In 1858, Professor Worsaae increased and re-arranged this fine collection, which was begun soon after the year 1588, and has been brought down to the present time in illustration of the arts and customs of many ages. Either one *salle* or more is dedicated to the reign of each successive monarch, and decorated in the style of each reign. There is a great quantity of furniture, almost exclusively brought from the different royal residences, portraits of the royal family and of men distinguished in the arts of war and peace, with arms, vestments, jewelry, and the like, pertaining to each reign. As a collection of its kind, both for its variety and richness, and for its skilful arrangement by Professor

Worsaae, it is unsurpassed anywhere. In the beautifully decorated apartment called 'King Christian's Audience Hall,' are many curious objects, one of which attracts the attention of every visitor, namely, the 'Oldenborg Horn,' concerning which the following veritable legend is preserved :—

Once upon a time, say in the year of grace 989, Otto I. of Oldenborg was hunting in a lonely part of one of his forests, when he became athirst. He was hot and tired, but there was no water at hand, and he did not know what to do. By and by a friendly fairy came forward with this horn, and offered him drink. Otto put his lips to it, but finding it less pleasant to the taste than *otto* of roses is to the smell, he declined the draught. The fairy expostulated, and told him that, if he would only drink it off, great blessings would attend him and his family, but, if he refused, many misfortunes would befall him. The huntsman, however, declining the draught, threw it away, to the great displeasure of the kind-hearted fairy, who demanded the horn back again. But Otto thought it too valuable to be parted with, and so kept it, and handed it down to his descendants.

Now what a pity it is that the prying 'old fogies,' called antiquaries, will put such a matter-of-fact face upon things as they do. Why, they actually reject the legend *in toto*, and declare that the horn was made by some German artist for King Christian I., only comparatively the other day—that is, in 1479 ! They say that when the monarch visited Cologne for the purpose of making a treaty between the Emperor Frederik III. and Charles the Bold, Duke of Burgundy, he intended to dedicate the horn to their sacred majesties the Three Holy Kings of Cologne, and to deposit it in their well-known chapel there ; but, as his mission was fruitless, he retained it and brought it back

to Denmark.   For two centuries it was preserved at the palace of Oldenborg, and afterwards it was brought to Copenhagen.   The
material is silver, richly enamelled, gilt, and
decorated with the arms of Denmark, Germany,
and Burgundy, with numerous devices of
different kinds allusive to the before-mentioned
transaction.

Another evidence, I think, of the Oriental
origin of the Danes, is that their principal order
of knighthood is that of the Elephant, which
ranks with our own of the Garter.   In the
Rosenborg we observe the insignia of both
these orders, for many of the magnates of
Scandinavia have at different times been K.G.'s
of England.   Then we see the two gold vessels
called the Eyder Cup and the Homage Cup,
commemorative of the reunion of the whole of
Schleswig with Denmark, after its having been
for a long time separated from it.   The Eyder
was never again to be disrupted from Denmark.

This junction was effected in 1720; but the wretched affair of 1864 again sundered the duchy from the kingdom.

In this royal museum are preserved suits of regal costumes, including the coronation robes of Christian IV. in 1597, a remarkable feature.

Such another collection as that of Rosenborg could probably not be found in Europe; and the only others that can at all vie with it are those of the Hôtel de Clugni at Paris, and the celebrated 'Green Vaults' at Dresden. To describe all the remarkable objects here would require a large volume; and therefore I must confine myself to a slight account of the main features of interest. One of these is the bed-chamber of Christian IV., in which he died in 1648. It still retains its original handsome decorations, and contains many relics of that celebrated sovereign. The adjoining apartment was the king's study, and it still retains his chair and writing-table, with a variety of

elegant articles which belonged either to him
or to Anna-Kathrine, his queen, including the
king's 'knighting-sword,' with a gorgeously
enamelled golden hilt, a bridle and saddle
covered with hundreds of diamonds and pearls,
a splendid drinking-horn of silver, and a beautiful fountain in ebony and silver, six feet high,
to contain perfumed water. Many of these
articles are of Danish manufacture, and prove
the greatly advanced state of art in the North
more than two centuries ago.

The next rooms contain objects of Frederik III.
(son of Christian IV.), in what is called the
'Rococo' style. Here we behold the great
*crystal cup*, with figures in bas-relief, most
artistically wrought, and ten feet high, as also
a silver jewel-box presented by our Queen
Anne to Queen Sophia of Denmark, bespangled
with diamonds, glorious to behold. A curious
story is told of this object. When the de-
plorable fire at the Christiansborg took place in

1794, it stood in the Queen's toilet-room, and during the alarm was appropriated by a thief. The villain was however tracked by a loyal citizen, who bought it of him for a comparative trifle, and had it placed with the other royal relics in the Rosenborg. The Marble Hall next invites our attention. It is devoted to the reign of King Christian the Fifth, a man of splendid tastes, and to a great extent an imitator of his contemporary, Louis Quatorze. He used this *salle* himself, and had it decorated in the richest manner. There are numerous relics of his reign, including a very elegant and curiously formed cup, called the Wismar, for what reason I do not know ; but it is said to be one of the finest crystal works in Europe. On the first floor is a chamber called the ' Rose,' illustrative of the reigns of Christian v. and Frederik IV. It is hung with noble Italian tapestry, which is supposed to have been brought by the latter sovereign, with numerous other treasures, from

Italy in 1709. It was hung up at one or the other of the royal *borgs*, and at length reached Rosenborg, where little was known or cared about it, until the indefatigable Worsaae called attention to its excellence, and had it placed in its present position. It is a valuable piece of art, and supposed to be of Florentine workman-ship. The portraits and some of the furniture were saved from the disastrous fire at Fre-deriksborg in 1859. Art was under Frederik IV. in its highest position. He was rich, and un-encumbered with national debt; and as Den-mark had had its flint age, its bronze age, and its iron age, so this may be fairly styled the golden age of the country.

We Englishmen, who have been in our ignorance accustomed to think Denmark below the average of European civilisation, are very wide of the mark, probably from what we read in our schoolboy days of the barbarous Vikings and their doings in England, Scotland, and

Ireland, in the tenth and eleventh centuries.
But since that time the Scandinavians have,
for the most part, advanced *pari passu* with all
other civilized nations. Nay, more : I believe
that in the seventeenth century they surpassed
most of them, and certainly at that period the
monarchs and grandees patronized both the
fine arts and manufactures in a greater degree
than did those of any other country. And
now, in later times, the Northern nations have
not fallen off in this respect. Look at their
great system of railways, most admirably
conducted, and their street tramways in all the
larger towns. We praise our London tramways,
but they are nothing as compared with those
of Copenhagen. Let me add, that this most
useful invention is attributable to our Northern
friends; and even our cars are for the most
part imported into England from those regions.
We see, inscribed on the inside of numbers of
them, the words ' Copenhagen ' and ' Denmark.'

But to realize the actual state of civilisation in Scandinavia, Englishmen must go thither, and look for themselves.

Dean Swift, in his queer book, *The Tale of a Tub*, writes a ' digression in praise of digressions.' It is perhaps too much a fault of mine to digress; but when in a writing humour I cannot help myself. Now let us return to the Rosenborg.—One of the objects which attracts the notice of every visitor is the highly artistic font used for the baptisms of members of the royal family. When this sacrament is performed, a golden vessel is placed within the font.—Then there is the sword of that great warrior, Charles XII. of Sweden, which was presented by him to an officer in the Norwegian army who had bravely defended himself against a greatly superior force under the command of Charles, and at length was compelled to surrender when *hors de combat* from his numerous wounds. On the

same floor are various objects from the subsequent reigns, including the golden pistols of
Frederik v., one of the presents sent to him and
his Queen Louise, daughter of our George II.
—one of the most popular of the Queens of
Denmark. There are also many relics of the
unhappy Queen Caroline-Mathilde.

The 'Knight's Hall' (*Riddersal*) occupies
the whole of the second floor. It is a splendidly
decorated apartment, measuring 150 feet in
length, 28 in breadth, and about 20 in height.
Its present ornamentation is of the time of
Frederik IV., but the chimneys—all that remains
of the original structure, as far as this part of
the palace is concerned—belong to the days
of Christian IV. Until the beginning of the
eighteenth century this grand apartment had
a flat ceiling, with painted designs; but that
was removed, and the present vaulted ceiling, beautifully ornamented with carving, sub-
stituted. Twelve great pieces of tapestry adorn

M

the walls. They are said to be of Danish workmanship of the time of Christian v., from the
designs of Peter Andersen, and represent passages in the war between Sweden and Denmark
from 1675 to 1679. There are also candelabra,
lions in silver, and other things which are used
at coronations.

At the end of the hall are two chairs, the
larger of which is used as the coronation throne.
It is principally of the ivory of the *narwahl*
or sea-unicorn, and is very attractive and
magnificent. It may be remarked that this
ivory was once considered worth its weight in
silver. Near the top of the chair is a hollow
opening, in which at coronations is placed an
amethyst, said to be the largest and finest in
existence. This grand hall is connected with
small rooms in the towers, one of which contains the crown jewels, and is not open to the
public except by special favour. There is also
a splendid collection of Venetian glass, brought

hither by King Frederik on his return from Italy : it contains a rich treasure of what is called 'thread-glass' (*filigranglass*).  The other turret room is devoted to ceramic art, and contains, besides old Danish china, many excellent specimens of blue Sèvres and Dresden ware.

------

I am afraid that some of my readers will be tired of my rehearsal of the beautiful works of art at Copenhagen : so I will, for the present, relieve them and myself by another legend of Norway, which runs thus :—

On Kvalholm in Helgeland lived a poor fisherman called Elias, with his wife Karen, who had formerly been servant in a clergyman's family at Alstadhang.  Here they had a hut, and the husband went out to fish for the owners of boats, which he himself was too poor to purchase.  Ghosts were said to haunt Kvalholm.  In her husband's absence, Karen had often heard *uncanny* noises, which could not

bode any good.    One day when she was out
in the field, cutting grass as winter fodder for
a few sheep which they kept, she distinctly
heard talking on the beach hard by, but did
not venture to look that way, for she was sore
afraid of mermen. . . .  Each succeeding year
poor Karen added to the population, as the poor
almost uniformly do, and when she had had
seven years of matrimonial life she had six little
children to look after.    But both husband and
wife were frugal, sober, and industrious, so that
Elias had saved money enough, he thought, to
buy a six-oared boat, and start in the fishing
line on his own account.    One day while walking on the beach, carrying in his hand a large
staff with a barbed spike at the end, he found
unexpectedly a big seal, which was lying and
sunning itself below a rock, and which seemed
as unprepared to meet Elias as Elias was to
meet him.    Elias however thought him too good
a prize to lose, and accordingly dealt him a

couple of blows with his spike. The second
blow sent the spike into the back of the animal,
just below the neck. And now came a scene.
The seal—and he must have been a large one
—rose at once on his tail *as high as the mast
of a boat*, and looked at Elias with angry and
bloodshot eyes, grinning fiercely and showing
his big teeth, so that the poor fisherman was
almost out of his senses from sheer fright.
Then out it dashed into the sea, colouring
the foam of the waves with its blood. Elias
saw no more of it; but in the creek near his
hut there was found in the afternoon his staff,
with the iron spike broken off. Our good
fisherman thought no more of this occurrence,
and that same autumn bought the six-oared
boat, towards which he had been saving money
all the summer. One night, as he lay thinking
of his boat, it struck him that it might stand
better in the shed if he put an additional
support on each side. He was so delighted

with his new purchase, that it was a real pleasure for him to get up, light his lantern, and go down to look at it.   As he stood, with the light falling on the boat, he saw, resting in a dark corner, on some fishing nets, a face exactly like that of the seal.   It grinned at him a moment, its mouth getting larger and larger, until at last *a huge man rushed out of it*, and vanished through the door of the shed, yet not so quickly but that Elias could see, by the light of his lantern, a long iron spike protruding from his back.   Our fisherman of course became uneasy, but still his anxiety was more for his boat than for himself.   So he seated himself in the boat, and kept guard over it.   In the morning when his wife came down, she found him fast asleep, with the lantern burnt out by his side.

Going out one January morning, a fishing, with two men, in his new and highly-prized boat, Elias heard a voice from a rock at the entrance of the creek, shouting with a scornful laugh, 'When you get a ten-oared boat, then, Elias, beware!' But it was many years before our fisherman could get one—not before his eldest son Bernt was seventeen. In the autumn Elias and his whole family went in their six-oared boat to Ranen, in the hope of selling it, and with the addition of a little hard-earned money to buy a 'ten-oar' instead. A newly-confirmed Finn girl, whom they had adopted some years before, was the only person left at home.

Now there was a small ten-oared boat, which the best boat-builder in Ranen had constructed and tarred just before, and which exactly suited the notions of Elias. He well knew what a boat ought to be, and thought he had never seen one so well-built below the 'water-line.' Above that, in fact, it was only 'so-so,' and even to the inexperienced it looked heavy, and altogether wanting a smart appearance. The builder knew this as well as Elias did; but he said he thought she would be the best sailer in Ranen;

and that he should have her cheap if he would only promise one thing, and that was that he should change nothing in the boat, and not even touch the tarring.    And not until he had given a solemn promise to that effect did he get the boat.    But the sprite that had taught the builder this excellent form below the water-line, had left him to his own devices as to the arrangements above it, and they were very indifferent indeed.    The sprite had been with him beforehand and ordered him both to sell the boat to Elias at a cheap rate, and to insist on the promise of its being in no way altered. By this promise the boat was to have no cross painted on the stem and stern, as the custom is. It was not therefore to be a *Christian* boat.

Before sailing home, Elias went to a shop to provide some Christmas cheer, including a small keg of brandy.    In their pleasure over their purchase of the boat, his wife, himself, and even young Bernt, had taken a ' drop too much.'

They now set sail for home, their only ballast being themselves and the Christmas provisions. Bernt sat at the starboard; the wife with her second son had charge of the mainsail. Elias himself steered, and the two boys, aged fourteen and twelve, were to bail out the water from the boat with a scoop.

They had eight Danish sea-miles to sail (about thirty-six English miles), and as they got farther from land they found that the goodness of the boat would be tested before they reached home. A storm blew up, and the foaming waves began to dash angrily along the rising sea. Elias now saw what a good boat he had got. It flew along over the sea like a water-fowl, without shipping even so much as a spray; and he therefore thought he might take in one reef less than it would have been absolutely necessary to do with most ten-oared boats. Towards the afternoon he discovered a ten-oared boat, not far from him, with a full crew and a four-reefed sail exactly like his own. She was standing the same course, and he was sorry he had not seen her earlier. She seemed to be racing with him, and he could not resist the temptation of letting out a reef. The boat shot like an arrow past land-points, islands, and rocks. Elias had never seen such a grand sailing tour before ; and the boat proved to be really the best in Ranen. Meanwhile the storm increased and the waves dashed twice over the boat, coming in at the starboard, and sweeping out at the stern. As it grew darker the other boat kept closer, and so near were they that they could have thrown a scoop over to each other. On they sailed to-gether, the storm raging more furiously as night came on. The fourth reef ought now to have been taken in again ; but Elias did not like to lose the race, and thought he would wait until the other boat did the same, where it was quite as necessary. Now and then the brandy keg went round, as they had to keep out the cold.

The phosphorescent lights which played on the black wave near Elias's boat shone with such unusual strength round the other, that it looked as if she were ploughing through fire, and he could even see the ropes of the boat, and distinguish the crew with their sou'-westers ; but as they were to the windward, they were all with their backs to Elias, and almost hidden by the gunwale of the boat. Suddenly a very heavy sea, which Elias saw coming, washed over the boat. For a moment it seemed as if the boat stood still ; the planks shook and shivered under the strain ; and then the craft, which had nearly capsized, stood erect again, and continued her way.

While this was going on, Elias thought he heard a horrid screaming in the other boat. But when the squall had passed, his wife, who sat by the mainsail, said in a voice that pierced to his very soul : 'O God, Elias, that sea took Martha and Nils overboard !' They were the

two youngest children, and had been sitting
with Bernt.  Elias only replied : ' Do not let
go the sheet, Karen, or we shall lose more.'
Now, it was absolutely necessary to take the
fourth reef in ; and shortly afterwards the storm
raged with such fierceness, that Elias, though
afraid of making the sail too small on account
of the heavy waves, was forced to take in the
fifth also ; and still his sail became less and less.

The waves beat upon their faces, and Bernt
and his second brother Anton who had hitherto
helped his mother to hold the sheet, were obliged
to hold the yard, a measure resorted to when a
crew cannot even stand sailing with the last reef
in—in this case, the fifth.   The other boat, which
had been invisible a short time, now suddenly
reappeared close to them, and rigged precisely
like his own.  Elias began to feel a dislike to these
neighbours.   The two who held the yard seemed
to him from the glimpse that he caught of their
faces more like dead men than living people,

and they did not utter a word. Somewhat to
windward he saw another heavy sea—the crested
waves shining through the darkness—advancing
towards them, and he prepared himself to receive it. The boat was steered so as to head
it, and the sail let out as far as possible to give
the boat sufficient speed to cleave through the
wave. But the sea came upon them, again
laying the craft on one side; and when it righted
his wife had not hold of the sheet, nor Anton of
the yard-line : both, alas ! had been washed overboard. Elias thought he again heard the frightful screams in the air ; and he also heard his
wife anxiously calling his name. He knew that
she was overboard, and exclaimed : ' In the
name of Jesus !' and was then silent. He felt
that he would willingly have gone with her, but
at the same time he recollected that it was his
duty to endeavour to save the remainder of his
charge, namely Bernt and his other two remaining boys. At first they had been baling

out the water, but now they were obliged to
assist Bernt, which they did to the best of their
power.    Elias dared not let go his hold of the
helm, and he grasped it with an iron hand, which
had almost lost the sense of feeling from the
pressure put upon it.    A few minutes afterwards
the other boat, which had been invisible for a
short time, again made its appearance.    Elias
could now distinctly see the man who steered
it.   *Out of his back stuck a large iron spike,* which
he immediately recognised !  And now he quietly
made up his mind as to two things : first, that it
was the Merman who steered his boat alongside
of his own, and was working his destruction ;
and, secondly, that this night's sail was to be
his last.    He who sees a merman on the sea is
a doomed man !  He said nothing to his sons,
but silently commended his soul to God.
During the last hour the storm had compelled
him to change his course, and as a snow-storm
commenced he decided that he would not think

of landing until daybreak. The sail continued as before ; now and then the boys complained of the cold, but that could not be helped, and Elias sat too deep in thought to hear them. He felt such a terrible thirst for vengeance, that had it not been for his three boys, he would have run into the accursed boat, which still continued near him, and whose errand he too well knew.

If an iron spike could strike a merman, then a knife or hammer could also do so ; and he felt that he would sacrifice his life for one good stroke at him who had so cruelly taken his dear ones from him, and who even now wanted the rest. Between three and four o'clock in the morning, Elias saw something glimmering, of such a height that he at first thought he must be close under land, near some rocks. However, he soon found it to be a mountainous wave. Then he thought he heard a laugh in the other boat, followed by the words : ' Now, Elias, your " ten-oared " is to be upset.' Elias, who foresaw what was coming,

cried aloud : ' In the name of Jesus!' and told
his children to hold on to the boat with all their
might, and on no account to let go before the
boat was again fairly above the water.   He sent
the elder of the two young boys to Bernt, while
he kept the younger close by his side, stroked
his cheek, and assured himself that he held tight.
The  wave  came  thundering  on,  completely
burying the boat beneath it.   It next lifted its
stem, and then sank again.   When it again appeared keel uppermost, Elias, Bernt, and little
Martin still held on, but the youngest child was
lost.   It was now necessary to get the shrouds
cut to enable the  mast to float by the side, instead of, as now, pulling the boat down. . . .

Thus passed that dark and dismal night.   At
length poor Martin, whom his father had attempted to shelter, died and sank into the sea.
They had many times shouted for help, but now
they gave it up as useless.   There only remained poor Elias and Bernt, and the father

observed to his son that he thought he was
going 'to our mother,' but he felt sure that
Bernt would be saved if he would only hold
on like a brave lad.

Then he told him about the Merman whom
he had struck with the spike, and who was
now having his revenge, and that he would
not desist until he had killed him. About nine
in the morning day began to dawn, and then
Elias gave Bernt his silver watch and brass
chain, which latter he had broken in pulling it
out from under his tightly-buttoned coats. He
sat quiet for some time, but as it grew lighter
Bernt saw that his father was pale as death.
His hair had parted in several places, as it sometimes does when death is approaching, and the
skin was rubbed off his hands from holding on
to the boat. The son seemed aware that his
father's last hour had come, and got as near to
him as he could, in order to support him in his
dying moments; but Elias, seeing this, only

N

asked him to hold fast for his own safety, and said : ' *In the name of Jesus, I go to join our mother,*' and then threw himself backwards off the cabin top. When the sea had got its victim, it gradually grew calmer. It became more easy for Bernt to hold on, and as daylight was now come, hope and courage came also. Bernt knew where he was, for the boat drifted off his own village, Kvalholm. He now again shouted for help ; but he knew that his chief hope lay in the current which bore towards a place where a point of land broke the waves, and where there was smooth water. He drifted nearer and nearer, and came at last so close to one rock that the mast was rubbed by it, as the waves carried it backwards and forwards.

Stiff as poor Bernt was, from sitting and hold- ing on so long, he succeeded in getting a footing on the rocks, where he hauled the mast to land, and moored what was now his own ten-oared boat. The Finn maiden, who was alone at home, thought she heard shouts for help; and so she went to see from whence they proceeded. There she beheld Bernt on the rocks, and the boat beating against them. She rushed to the boat-shed, shoved an old boat off, and rowed out to his rescue.

Bernt lay sick all the rest of the winter, and the Finn girl was his only nurse. People thought he was rather queer afterwards; at any rate he never went to sea again, as he felt a great horror of the water. So he became a peasant-farmer, and as a matter of course in due time married the young *Finn-ess*, and 'lived happy ever after,' as the story-books say.

This weird legend is given nearly verbatim from Mrs. Ellis's MS. translation from the Norwegian. Of the date of it nothing seems to be known. The seals of the period must have been much larger than those of the present day; and I am sorry, as I have said, that this amphibious animal is gradually becoming extinct.   A great portion of the so-called seal-skin jackets and collars of which our ladies are so proud are nothing more than dyed Ostend and English rabbit-skins carefully put together !

The mermen of the north of Norway, let me add, were not of the same species as the traditionary mermaids of our nursery stories, 'human above and fishy below,' but had legs and feet like ordinary mortals; they were in fact a sort of ocean giants, always doing what they could to injure the poor Norsemen sailors. But now let us return again to Copenhagen.

———

This city contains four royal palaces, two of which I have attempted to describe.   The present King's abode is Amalienborg, which stands in the northern part of Copenhagen.   It is composed of four smaller palaces, formerly the residences of as many wealthy noblemen, but purchased by the King after the destruction of Christiansborg in 1794.   In the centre of the open space enclosed by these palaces stands a bronze statue of Frederik V. In one of these palaces the King himself resides, and in the others members of the royal family—except one, which is the Foreign Office.

The palace of Frederiksborg, surrounded by a noble park, is now the Military Academy. The park is a fashionable resort of the citizens, though indeed all classes are admitted. The tramway which traverses the whole city terminates at the principal gate. Within the entrance is a statue of Frederik VI., who was accustomed to spend the summer months here. He is in the posture of a sovereign giving audience to his subjects. The statue was cast in 1839.

Having spoken of the regal palaces of Copenhagen, I will say a few words concerning their royal occupants and their genealogy. The early part of the pedigree is like that of many others, and about as trustworthy as the story of the big seal just now related. It goes back to

Danus or Dangritha, who died 998 years before
Christ! His *sixty-first* successor was Gotric
or Godfrey, surnamed the Generous, who died
A.D. 809.

Here I may remark that nearly every northern king had a *surname* or nickname, similar
to our Cœur-de-Lion, Sans-Terre, etc. Fourth
in descent from Godfrey comes Siward III.,
called *Snake-eye* (A.D. 834). His son and
successor was Eric *The Child*, father of Cnut
*The Little*, whose son Frotho VI., about 921,
married an English princess called Emma. His
son and successor was Gormo *Angle*, father of
Harold V., called *The Niggard*, who married
Thyra, daughter of Ethelred, king of England.
His son Gormo *The Old* espoused another
Thyra, daughter of Edward the Elder, king of
England, and was grandfather of Sweyn II.,
surnamed *Forked-beard* (1041). Next comes
Cnut *The Great*, king of England, who married,
first, Alwine, countess of Northumberland, and

secondly, Emma, widow of Ethelred, king of England. By his first marriage he had Harold *Harefoot*,[1] king of England, Cnut III., or *Hardicanute*, and Sweyn, king of Norway. Cnut the Great had a sister, Estritha, who married, first, Richard III. duke of Normandy, and afterwards Ulpho, an English duke, and in her descendants the Danish monarchy afterwards vested. Her son by the duke, Sweyn III. (1047), was father of Eric III. *The Good*, and he had a son, Cnut *The Pious*, duke of Schleswig, grandfather of Valdemar *The Victorious* (1242).

His successor in the fifth generation was Margaret, Queen of Denmark, Norway, and Sweden, the Semiramis of the North, previously mentioned (1397). Her sister, Ingeburga, married Henry, duke of Mecklenburg, and had a daughter Mary, who married Wratislaus VII., duke of Pomerania. This match produced Eric or Henry x., king of Norway, who married

---

[1] Probably from his swiftness in running.

Philippa, daughter of our Henry IV. The next in succession was his grandson, Christian I., elected in 1448. His father was Theodorik *The Fortunate*, Count of Oldenburg. The sister of Eric X., whose name was either Catherine or Sophia, married the duke of Bavaria, and king of Denmark, Sweden, and Norway, who died in 1448, and was succeeded on the throne by his kinsman Christian I., just mentioned. He had several grandsons, of whom three, Christian II., Frederik I., and Christian III., reigned during the sixteenth century. The last-named monarch was ancestor by seven descents of Frederik V. (1766), who married Louisa, daughter of our George II., and was father of Christian VII., born in 1749, who married Caroline-Matilda, daughter of Frederick-Lewis, Prince of Wales, and was father of Frederik VI., who died without issue in 1839. Christian VII. was a man of learning and science—LL.D. and F.R.S. On the death of Frederik VI., his nephew, Christian VIII., succeeded, and died in 1848, leaving a son, Frederik, who died without issue in 1863. Thus the immediate line became extinct, and the next heir to the throne had to go back to the early part of the seventeenth century, ten descents, for the blood-connexion with the elder line, and he now rules Denmark with the title of Christian the Ninth. His Majesty has several children, including George, King of Greece, our own Alexandra - Caroline - Mary - Charlotte - Louisa, Princess of Wales, and Mary-Frederika-Sophia-Dagmar, married to the heir-apparent of the Empire of Russia.

———

Dry as the foregoing paragraphs may appear to some people, they may be interesting to others; and when we look at the number of matches between the royal house of Denmark and our own kings, princes, and other distinguished personages of Britain, we ought to be proud of our association with that ancient his-

torical country, and by all means to support it
by our friendship and to assist it with our arms.

Copenhagen has less than 200,000 inhabitants, but it is fast increasing in extent and
population.    Although it dates from before
the eleventh century, its aspect is comparatively modern, in consequence of the extensive
fires and sieges, bombardments, etc., which
have befallen it.    In the year 1728 a great
conflagration destroyed about 1650 houses, and
in another in 1795 more than three hundred
were reduced to ashes ; and our boasted Nelson
knocked down three hundred more.

It became a prosperous town in the days of
the celebrated Bishop Absalon, and was the
chief residence of the Danish kings about the
middle of the fifteenth century.    Previously to
that epoch it had become a royal fortress, and
even now its seaboard is defended by formidable
batteries.    The drainage of the city has always
been more or less unsatisfactory, on account of

the flatness of the surface. Hence it has been subject several times to the Plague. That disease in 1711 carried off more than 22,000 of the population, and in 1853 nearly 5000 died of cholera. The water is pure and good, and is copiously supplied from Artesian wells at a considerable distance.

Copenhagen has an Academy of Fine Arts, originally established in the royal palace, known as Charlottenborg or Kongensborg Nytorv. The various schools of art existing in the city have exercised great influence on the productions of the trades and manufactures of Denmark and the adjacent countries. The Academy contains an excellent collection of casts, etc., and in the early summer months there is an exhibition of sculpture, pictures, and other works of art. The charitable foundations, too, are numerous and well supported. The principal one is called the Vartou, a large brick building of the seventeenth century, near the

Westgate, and several sets of habitations for mechanics and labourers, which Murray likens to the Peabody buildings in London, which I have not yet seen. They are convenient and salubrious dwellings, and yet return a fair dividend to the owners. The Infant nurseries and the charities of the different trades are very numerous. An institution for the *blind* deserves special mention. There is a considerable number of places of amusement in the shape of theatres, ball-rooms, and such-like.

The isle of Zealand, which impinges on Copenhagen, is variously spelt Seeland, Sealand and Zealand. The last is that by which Englishmen know it, and the New Zealand of the southern hemisphere is named after it, just as the Boston and New York of North America are after two great towns in England. The part of Zealand nearest the capital is not impressive, being level and without many trees. The inhabitants are chiefly descendants of the

Dutch colonists who settled here in the early part of the sixteenth century. The costume of the common people is generally more like the Dutch than that of the Danes. The island has been described as 'an immense nursery garden,' and it supplies the capital with vegetables for the table. But on that part of the island north of Copenhagen there is much woodland, and to this district excursionists frequently go. The woods are partly on the coast, and partly around the little lakes inland. Thither many of the people of the capital resort during their short summer. This part of Zealand is spotted over with many hundreds—nay, thousands—of houses, mostly small, but some large, surrounded with picturesque gardens. The living in this part of the island is said to be very expensive, but we did not experience this.

Charlottenlund, five or six miles from Copenhagen, is a royal country-seat, generally occupied by some member of the Royal family, the present tenant being the Crown Prince. This is the great rendezvous of the Copenhageners on holidays and Sunday afternoons, when sometimes many thousands of them promenade the green lawns and the public walks, while music and dancing enliven the scene. The Danes are not great Sabbatarians, though but few improprieties occur. Somewhat late at night the excursionists for the most part travel homewards at the starting of the last train, car, or omnibus. Still those who are disposed for a more extended enjoyment or revel remain behind in great numbers, and walk home singing merry tunes and cracking jokes.

Near Charlottenlund is a large residence, built about a hundred years ago, by the celebrated Count Bernstorff, and bearing his name. It now, however, belongs to the Crown, and is used in summer by the Royal family. It is approached by a grand avenue of lime-trees. Further inland are the beautiful little

palace and grounds called Lyngby. The park
bears the poetical but singular nickname of
'beautiful roses.' The mansion is used as the
abode of the Queen-dowager. But one of the
most beautiful spots on the island is the deer-
park, which has been justly characterized as 'the
gem of the environs of Copenhagen;' it com-
prises more than four thousand acres, and is
divided into two parts by a narrow river. The
southern portion of the park abounds with fine
trees, including many of the noblest beeches in
the world. This is the Royal preserve for
thousands of red and fallow deer, and red and
*white* stags; the last-named being remarkable
for their size and noble proportions. Few
such fine deer-parks exist elsewhere—perhaps
nowhere. In the park are several large
inscribed stones commemorating the first meeting on the spot of students from all the
Scandinavian Universities. On the neck of
land between the sea and the park are many of

what may be called suburban villas of different grades of elegance and magnitude, one of which, called Skodsborg, was a favourite summer residence of Frederik VII.

I think Denmark contains, or has contained, more regal abodes than any other country in Europe. In the capital or the immediate environs there cannot have been less than nine or ten, while others stood in places more remote. Considering the smallness of the kingdom, the sovereigns must have had exceedingly large revenues, not perhaps so much from taxation of the people as from the possession both of crown and personal territory.

At Soborg there was once a great castle, which was, in early centuries, a place of confinement for state prisoners; and near it is Esrom, once a celebrated and well-endowed monastery; but few traces of even its foundation walls remain, so that we may say of it, '*Perierunt etiam Ruinæ.*' Gurre, on the same

route, was long ago a favourite retreat of some
of the kings, particularly of Valdemar the
Victorious, who kept a ' Fair Rosamond,' called
Tovelille, and there is a legend that he blas-
phemed his Maker by saying, that ' God might
keep heaven to himself, if he might hold on at
Gurre.' This profane expression was duly
punished at his death ; for, according to the
superstitious belief of the neighbourhood, he
may still be seen at night, with a weird and
demon-like troop of attendants, and a pack of
most unearthly hounds, breathing flames of
infernal fire !

Let us hope that when the king wooed and
won the fair Dagmar of Bohemia, he changed
his course of life, and finally ascended with
his queen to the Valhalla. I think there must
be some mistake in name and date, for Valdemar II. was, as we have seen, one of the wisest
and best of Danish monarchs, and I think the
legend must relate to some much earlier king.

o

Frederik II. built the castle of Frederiksborg about the year 1562, and some few traces of the original structure still remain. The greater part of the palace was pulled down by Christian IV., who replaced it at the beginning of the seventeenth century. In December 1859 a ' great conflagration destroyed the interior, and very numerous relics of royal and national interest were burnt. The exterior walls, however, were to a great extent saved, and they have subsequently been restored to nearly their earlier condition, at a cost of about £40,000 sterling.

The great banqueting-hall was utterly destroyed, and it has not been re-erected ; and the church was also so much damaged that it had to be rebuilt, and decorated in its former style, by the help of plans and drawings, made at different times, and which had fortunately been preserved. The palace occupies a peculiar position, standing, as it does, *on three islands*.

Among the few articles saved from the disastrous fire are the altar and pulpit of ebony, massively ornamented with solid silver, and the font. Charles IV. was an artist of no mean talent. He carved a great many subjects, which, with some exquisite paintings in the King's cabinet, were destroyed by the fire. An attempt is being made to build a facsimile of the cabinet from drawings executed previously to the fire, and is intended to be in the Renaissance style of Denmark. In the church are the armorial bearings of the Knights of the Elephant,—making it somewhat resemble our own St. George's Chapel at Windsor,—as also of many Knights of the Dannebrog, or the Grand Cross of Denmark. On the island next to the town stand two remarkable towers, erected by the founder of the castle.

The entrance to the next island is defended by a barbican or out-work, consisting of a massive tower ; and on the third island we come to the palace proper. It is composed of three wings, and has a gallery decorated with excellent sculptures. The building as we now behold it is not only a monument of one of the most accomplished of Scandinavian kings, but a proof of the national energy of the people of Denmark, who subscribed liberally to the reparations and restorations of the fabric, which could not have been carried out without their assistance.

This edifice might be designated, not indeed a 'Jackdaws' Parliament,' but a *Rooks' Court of Assembly*; for, in the evening, thousands of these birds from the large forest hard by assemble on the roofs, and after a few minutes' incessant cawing, depart. The meaning of this gathering is not understood. Can it be a kind of 'Convocation' among these black-robed gentry for the discussion of ecclesiastical affairs!

A book might be written entitled 'The Romance of the Danish Castles,' since every one of them abounds, not only in historical associations, but in the legendary lore with which they are connected.

Holy Wells, too, abound in this part of Scandinavia, and one may be particularly mentioned —St. Helen's Well, situated on the summit of a cliff near the ruinated castle of Asserbo. The tradition runs, that this holy woman was killed by some pagan Swedes, who cast her body into the sea, where it fell upon a stone, which immediately rose, floated on the surface, and conveyed the martyr to the shores of Denmark! Some Danish Christians resolved to bury St. Helen in a neighbouring church, but only reached this spot, when, *mirabile dictu!* the earth suddenly opened, and received the saintly remains. Thereupon sprang up fair water, forming a 'holy well.' This water soon became the resort of hundreds and thousands of people suffering from all kinds of diseases, under the firm belief that it was a universal medicine. The favourite time for a visit was St. John's Day, at night; and, till within the last half-century, many superstitious people came hither, still believing in the healing virtues of the well. The antiquary who visits these regions will find ample means of gratifying his conjectural powers by inspecting the various dolmens, barrows, and 'kitchen-middens' with which this district abounds. Denmark has been rich in historians and archæologists, from the days of the learned, though credulous, Saxo-Grammaticus (who flourished in the twelfth century) down to the present day; and this is perfectly natural, because few countries in Europe possess such 'strange eventful histories' as this does, neither can any region exhibit a greater number of primæval antiquities than this. In mediæval remains, however, it is not so rich; the churches are not, as a rule, very interesting, though some of them are very beautiful. The geology is worthy of attention; it has formed the subject of the well-known treatise of Sir Charles Lyell, as well as that of several works by native Scandinavian geologists.

Before visiting Denmark I was under the impression that Scandinavia was comparatively devoid of trees, except those of the pine tribe ; but was agreeably surprised to find vast forests, and almost every variety of tree found inhabiting British soil, and in much greater profusion. The scenery, too, everywhere abundantly exceeded my expectations, and for romantic beauty surpassed anything I had seen in England or elsewhere. I think that, on these grounds alone, many of us Southrons would like to take up our abode in those northern climes ; but the great drawback would be the long dark winters, though the brief summers are warm, not to say hot.

But to return : Roeskilde, in Zealand, was in the tenth century the residence of King Harald Blaatand, grandfather of Cnut the Great, and successive kings held it as one of the royal

palaces till the fifteenth.   Before Copenhagen
became the capital of Denmark, this was considered the metropolis, and was the see of one
of the earliest Bishops of the North.   Gradually
since that period, the city fell to decay, and its
present population, although now on the increase,
does not much exceed 5000.   The city formerly
had, besides the cathedral, fourteen churches
and six monasteries.   Only the cathedral and
the church of Our Lady are now in use for
devotional purposes.   There is also a holy well,
ascribed to King Hroe, a sovereign of the
mythical class.   Roeskilde Cathedral is the
largest ecclesiastical edifice of the kingdom, and
the bishop of Zealand, who resides in the capital,
is now considered the primate of the Danish
Church.   The Cathedral was the last resting-
place of a large number of the kings of Denmark.

The earliest churches in some of the countries
of Europe were built of wood.   In England, so

far as I am aware, there is only one, that of
Greensted in Essex, remaining. The original
church of St. Pancras at Lewes was of the same
material, until it was superseded by the once
magnificent priory-church, founded by Gun-
drada, daughter of William the Conqueror, and
her husband, William Earl of Warren. The
oldest church of Roeskilde was a wooden
one, built by Harald Blaatand in 975. In 1047
the present church was commenced in red brick,
under the directions of Bishop William (Vilhelm),
one of the many of our countrymen who, at the
time of Cnut the Great, emigrated under his
patronage, and carried with them the more
advanced civilisation of the south. The cathedral was finished about 1084, and some of its
original brickwork remains ; but, as was the case
with many great cathedrals, it suffered by fire
—notably in the years 1283 and 1443,—and
many alterations resulted. The arches before
the first fire were what we call Saxon or Roman-

esque, and many of them still remain.  After that, pointed arches occur, in what we designate as Early English.  The towers are also in the same style; but the spires, with which they are crowned, were erected by Christian IV., who also introduced a kind of Elizabethan western door, quite out of character with the building; as are the numerous chapels which have been erected round the structure at various periods.  For some years the work of restoration has been going on, under the direction of skilled architects, and some ornamental work, hidden from view for very many years, now appears in its original beauty.

This is by no means a large cathedral, though it is considered on the whole as one of the best in Scandinavia.  It consists of a nave, with north and south aisles, a choir with north and south transepts, and a clerestory.  The spires on the western towers are visible at a great distance, and present a fine aspect from every point of view. The nave is eighty feet high, and diminishes in width towards the choir, producing a very agreeable effect. I do not re-collect any other church with this arrangement.

To describe this fine edifice at length would occupy too many of these pages. There are fine mediæval paintings and sculptures in various parts; but the most interesting objects to the historical and archæological observer are the memorials of royal and other distinguished per-sonages. At the rear of the altar is the sarco-phagus of 'the Semiramis of the North,' Queen Margaret, who, as we have seen, united Den-mark, Sweden, and Norway under one sceptre. Dying in the year 1412, she was originally buried at Soro, but in the following year the Bishop of Roeskilde was determined to have her remains. These he took, *vi et armis*, and deposited them in his cathedral! The effigy on the sarcophagus is of life size. Bishops everywhere were sturdy fellows in those days;

and fought not only the 'good fight of faith,' but understood the use of carnal weapons also.

On the floor there are many slabs indicating the graves of illustrious persons, though some of the oldest ones have been sacrilegiously removed. The organ, which is said to have been set up in 1555, is of great size and of excellent quality: it contains no less than thirty-six stops. One of the most interesting objects in the church are the stalls in the choir, twenty-one on each side. They are ornately carved, and date from 1420. In the last-named year considerable alterations were made in the choir, which contains the sarcophagi of Frederik IV., Christian V., and their consorts, and in the vaults beneath are deposited the remains of several children of the royal family. The skull of St. Lucius, Pope, and patron saint of the cathedral, the oldest seal of the establishment, and other objects of curiosity, are preserved in the Museum of Northern Antiquities at Copenhagen.

At the time of the alterations just alluded to the bones of several distinguished persons were disturbed, and immured within the columns. Among these were the skeletons of King Harald, A.D. 985, Queen Margaret-Fredkulla, 1130, Svend Estridson, 1076, and the English Bishop Vilhelm, 1076—a strange way of disposing of the relics of the illustrious dead! In the north aisle of the choir are portraits of famous dignitaries of the cathedral, and of all the bishops of Zealand subsequently to the Reformation ; and in the south aisle, or rather in the sepulchral chapel built by Frederik v., are the sarcophagi of Frederik himself, and his consort, and many subsequent sovereigns. That of Frederik vii. is of polished oak, with a rich wreath of oak leaves in solid gold. That of Frederik v. is of marble, executed by Wiedewelt, the celebrated Danish sculptor. The next chapel is that of the three Holy Kings of Cologne. The monument of Christian iii.,

by Cornelius Floris of Antwerp, is highly
artistic and beautiful.   In the crypt below lie
the remains of Christian I., who built the chapel
before 1464, as a mausoleum for himself and
his family.   Some years ago, when this
monarch's grave was examined, his body was
found to be less than 6 feet 2 English, though
tradition had made him of gigantic proportions.
The floor above is used as a house of convocation of the clergy of the diocese.   I cannot
describe the various minor chapels ; but a few
words must be said of that of Christian IV.   In
it is a sarcophagus of the king, richly decorated
with silver, Anna-Catharina his consort, and
also Frederik III. and his queen, Sophia-
Amelia.   In the north aisle is the tombstone
of the celebrated Saxo-Grammaticus, the last
of the legendary chroniclers, and the first of
Danish historians, who died in 1207.   This
eminent writer, who was prefect in the
cathedral of Roeskilde, wrote an elaborate

work entitled *The History of Denmark*, which I believe was first printed at Paris in 1514, and was followed by other editions, the best being that of Sora, in 1644, folio.

Altogether, the cathedral of Roeskilde is one of the most interesting monuments of the mediæval time. Its sculptures, tombs, paintings, frescoes, and relics of art of other kinds, form a rich museum; and, as it contains the tombs of nearly all the monarchs of Denmark for many generations past, it may be likened to our own Westminster Abbey, in this one respect only ; for Roeskilde, before the addition of the ugly chapels which surround it, must have been of grand and imposing appearance : our Abbey could never boast of much architectural grandeur. This remark, of course, applies to the exterior of the buildings only ; for they possess both architectural and monumental beauties of high excellence and interest within.

By way of varying these sketches, I will now draw again from Mrs. Ellis's MS. translation from the Norwegian.

On a promontory near Trondheim stand the church and parsonage of Trondenæs. The church is the oldest ecclesiastical structure, and one of the finest in that part of Norway. The story is not of the sensational kind; but has internal evidence of being true.

The church, in St. Olaf's time, was royal property. It is said to have been possessed in ancient times of two very singular adjuncts in the shape of towers, of which one was square, copper-roofed, and surmounted by a tall iron spire, and the other octangular. No traces of these towers now exist, and they were destroyed, probably, some ages ago. This church stood, at one time, the northern boundary-fortress of Christianity; and one might call to his imagination the time when the far-sounding tones of its bells, its lofty spires, and other marks of the first Christian period existed; nay, he might go further, and fancy a spiritual giant-bishop, and St. Olaf together, bringing in the holy Sacraments, while the enlightenment which Christianity always conveys with it was daily gaining ground among the hitherto pagans of the north, and the light of truth was successful in dispelling the darkness, and the witcheries of the old dwellers in Finmark.

Hither must have resorted the new converts from long distances to worship the only true God; since it was not until long afterwards that other churches sprang up nearer their own villages and homesteads. Could the baptismal font which stands in the choir proclaim the names there given, or could the altar tell of the Eucharist there partaken of, the Christian marriages there performed; and could the church relate what had passed within it since the time of its erection, should we not wonder to hear

P

their narratives and experiences! But, even before the Reformation, the spirit of sacrilege invaded the sacred building. Remnants of its ancient church-furniture were stolen, and some of the painted doors of its altars still remain in cottages, and serve the secular office of doors to cupboards! But now the work of destruction has been stayed, and the peasant would think it quite as bad to steal such things as to take away the communion plate itself. The sentiment of the Roman Catholic religion remains here to this day, in old traditions; and in the admiration of the mysterious vaults, and the mediæval paintings on the walls, and the many pictures of different ages, the poor mechanic and the day-labourer delight in rebuilding the old church in misty grandeur. There is, to speak the truth, not a little of the old leaven of the unreformed Church remaining amongst them; thus they would think it no harm to offer candles for the altars if they could thereby placate the Almighty, and be saved alive in times of danger; nor do they think there is anything wrong in praying to the Virgin Mary. They know that she has been dethroned indeed, but piously acknowledge her all the same. Thus, this class virtually seem to 'halt between two opinions,' and are practically only half Protestant.

The narrative I am about to give contains the experiences of the young gentleman of intelligence, David Holst, of whom mention has been made before, who was sent by his father to a kind of seminary here, he having previously studied in the University of Christiania. His delight was to ramble around and within the church, and there to ponder over its grand and time-honoured remains with a kind of sombre affection, not unmixed with awe. To use his own words : ' I was very much influenced by the impressions of the place upon my imagination. The ground, said to be hollowed beneath with vaults, was for me a closed abyss of secrets, and the church, whose quiet I often sought, had a sacred charm. It was close to the parsonage.

It generally stood open, that the seminarists might practise on the organ. The daylight sometimes threw shades on the aisles and niches, so that you could fancy that there were beings from another sphere moving stealthily about. I made great advances in my Latin and Greek, which I read with the learned and amiable clergyman in whose house I lived. The other branches I read with one of the teachers of the seminary; but in my leisure hours I sought these places, which had taken such hold on my imagination, and therefore Trondenæs was not the place to which I ought to have been sent.

My nervous excitability was the greatest at the change of the moon. At such times these weird haunts drew me irresistibly to them.

I stole thither alone, and would stay for hours together, giving way to all kinds of fancies, even believing I saw Susanne [his *affiancée*], thinking I saw her light figure gliding towards me, though I could never discern her face. It was at such a time, the second spring I was there, that as I was sitting near the altar, with Susanne's cross in my hand, I noticed a large dark picture, which I had often seen before, but had never examined until now. It was a full-length painting of a martyr, who had been thrown into a thorn-bush, the thorns being as long and sharp as so many daggers. They went through his flesh in many places. One in particular passed through his throat, so that he could not speak, or even groan. Now as my eyes fell on it, the expression seemed to me to become dreadful. He looked at me as if he knew that I was to become a fellow-sufferer, and should lie there when he was at rest. It was impossible for me to take my eyes off this frightful scene, and the picture seemed to approach me more and more nearly. In this dreadful representation the veil seemed to be drawn aside to show me a part of my own soul's secret story; and it was only through exerting my strength of will, and the fear of my being drawn too far by my imagination, that I could tear myself from the spot. Turning away from it, I saw a lady with a rose in her hand standing by the upper pew. Her expression was one of extreme pity, as if she knew the connexion between myself and the picture; and the thorny rose which she carried represented in miniature the thorn-bush on which the martyr lay. In the quietude of the empty church I felt a fear of invisible powers, and in a panic, hastily rushed out of it. As I stopped outside for a moment, I missed the cross that Susanne had formed for me with blue beads intertwined with her lovely hair. It must have fallen from my hand where I had been sitting. At this moment, with the dread still in my mind, nothing in the world would have induced me to go back into the church, except Susanne's cross, which was to me invaluable. As I was diligently looking about, I happily found it, and bore it off in a kind of transport.

The second year of my remaining at Trondenæs my nervous system showed its weakness. I was looking forward to my return home in a few weeks. On one of my subsequent visits to the church, in the meantime, I was again alarmed by a trivial cause. A peasant had led his horse, which was " wall-eyed," to the churchyard gate, and I stood still to look at it; but the dead glassy eye haunted me all day. It seemed to me that the animal saw the invisible rather than the visible world, and therefore, should the driver be careless of his reins, the horse would naturally turn from the common road into that where the departed spirits roam. In the afternoon, while sitting with the clergyman's family, and chatting on various subjects, I suddenly saw a face *from home.* It was pale and worn from exhaustion; and I could see that the man to whom it belonged was despairingly trying to climb up a rock to save himself from the surging waves; while it seemed to me that he was burdened by some object at his feet, which I could not see, but which was retarding his efforts to ascend. The man gazed at me with almost a glassy look. It appeared too, as if he wanted to speak to me, or to tell me something. Judge of my horror when I saw that it was our man *Anders !* The vision lasted only a moment, but a painful and unbearable feeling succeeded, that at that moment some misfortune was happening at home. This drove me out of the room, and caused me to wander uneasily about for the remainder of the day. When I at last returned, I was asked what it was that had made me go back to the church. However, I had not been there for some hours. Then they asked what made me look as pale as death, and rush out of the room, as I had done.

A fortnight later I received a letter from home—and a mournful one it was. My father's smack, " Hope," had been wrecked in a storm at Stalhavel. The boat had sprung a leak, and was obliged to be left on the shore. The lives of the crew were all saved, but poor Anders had had his legs badly crushed. The cargo consisted chiefly of fish, and as marine insurance did not exist in those days, both the smack and fish were my father's loss. This misfortune was succeeded, the following year, by the wreck of another boat, " the Unity;" and the third and finishing stroke was, the decision of the Government that the steamer should not, in future, touch at our place.'

———

I have said that there is a strong affinity between the three languages of Scandinavia, not differing more than do the dialects of some of our English counties—perhaps hardly so much. This is a strong proof of the common origin of the inhabitants of Denmark, Sweden, and Norway. I am sorry to say that I am not acquainted with the northern tongues, but I can give a few specimens. I think many people have been, deterred from getting at least a smattering of the language by the repulsive Gothic characters, resembling those of the German; though the Scandinavians, like the Germans, are gradually abandoning these forms, and introducing the Roman letter. For examples of the similarity of the three languages, I subjoin a table of the numerals :—

| ENGLISH. | DANISH AND NORWEGIAN. | SWEDISH. |
|---|---|---|
| One | Eeen | En |
| Two | To | Twa |
| Three | Tree | Tre |
| Four | Fire | Fyra |
| Five | Fem | Fem |
| Six | Sex | Sex |
| Seven | Syr | Sju |
| Eight | Otte | Atta |
| Nine | Ni | Nio |
| Ten | Ti | Tio |
| Eleven | Elleve | Elfwa |
| Twelve | Tolv | Tolf |
| Thirteen | Tretten | Tretton |
| Fourteen | Fjorten | Fjorton |
| Fifteen | Femten | Femton |
| Sixteen | Sexten | Sexton |
| Seventeen | Sytten | Sjutton |
| Eighteen | Atten | Aderton |
| Nineteen | Nitten | Nitton |
| Twenty | Tyve | Tjugu |

From this table it will be apparent that the English, Norwegian, Danish, and Swedish numerals have a common origin; and the same

similarity exists as to the names of the days of
the week and the months :—

| ENGLISH. | DANISH AND NORWEGIAN. | SWEDISH. |
| --- | --- | --- |
| Sunday | Sondag | Sondag |
| Monday | Mandag | Mandag |
| Tuesday | Tirsdag | Tisdag |
| Wednesday | Onsdag | Onsdag |
| Thursday | Thorsdag | Thorsdag |
| Friday | Fredag | Fredag |
| Saturday | Soverdag | Sordag |
| | | |
| January | Januar | Januari |
| February | Februar | Februari |
| March | Marts | Mars |
| April | April | April |
| May | Mai | Maj |
| June | Juni | Juni |
| July | Juli | Juli |
| August | August | Augusti |
| September | September | September |
| October | October | October |
| November | November | November |
| December | December | December |

There is the like similarity in conversational phrases. Thus 'Good morning' is in Norwegian *God morgen*, and in Swedish, *God morgon.* 'Good evening' is in Norwegian *God aften*, in Swedish, *God afton*, and so on; but as the object of these sketches is not to attempt to teach languages which I do not pretend to understand, I must refer my reader to the instructive pages of our friend of Albemarle Street; and should he desire a deeper acquaintance with the Scandinavian tongues, he can easily procure grammars and lexicons without sending to the North for the purpose; and if he is thoroughly grounded in his mother tongue and the German, he will not, as I believe, find much difficulty in *reading* the three : of course the *pronunciation* is quite another thing.

And now a few words concerning the nationalities of the North. We have been too much in the habit of believing that the Teutonic and Scandinavian peoples and languages differ widely; but it is not so. These nationalities have sprung from local and physical circumstances, and it would probably be no more difficult to prove the common origin of the peoples than it would be to prove that of a great noble family for the last seven or eight centuries. Slight differences of climate change not only the physical characteristics, making men shorter or taller, but also their voices, so that in the course of generations their languages become different. The old Teutonic appears to me to be the great mother of these races and tongues, and her influence, in the form of what we now call *German*, has been influential in forming both the physique and the language of all North-western Europe. We speak of the successive invasions of this country by the Anglo-Saxons, the Danes, and the Normans, as if they were of widely different origins—but they were all distant cousins of each other; all of the Gothic type. True it is, that the Normans had previously adopted the language of the country they had conquered, but their general characteristics were the same—a marauding, sea-going people, anxious of acquiring territory everywhere.

The influence of the Danish conquest of England is sufficiently proved by the local names, in the southern counties especially. The name Ring was a personal appellation in Denmark. Hence probably we get Ringwood in Hampshire, and Ringmer in Sussex. In the latter county we find Danegate, Danehill, Danny, and many other places upon which the Danes have impressed their name by conquest. I believe, too, that Hastings, Winchelsea, Seaford, Shoreham, and other sea-coast towns might be traced to a Danish etymology. It may be observed also, that a great number of our nautical words and phrases are from Denmark, and are pronounced alike in that country and in ours, though the orthography often differs. In some parts of Scandinavia, the word *skipper* is applied to the captain of a merchant-vessel, as .with us.

It seems strange that the people of one country cannot pronounce the local names of another. The French persist in calling our metropolis *Londres*, though the letter R was never an element in the word. The Germans too are great name-changers. In. Windek's History of the Emperor Sigismund, Canterbury is called *Kandeberg*, Rochester, *Rosschetter*, and Sittingbourne, *Sigenbos!* And we are perhaps as much in fault as others ; for we call Helsingor, *Elsinore*, and Kjobenhavn, *Copenhagen*.

By way of variety I will here introduce a portion of ' The Gallant Soldier,' the national war-song, ' Den tappre Landsoldat,' 1848.

> ' The time I marched away,
> The time I marched away,
> My girl would go with me,
> Yes, my girl would go with me.
> No, love, you can't do so,
> For to the war I go.

And if I do not fall, my dear, I'll soon return to you.
If danger were not near, why, I'd remain with thee ;
But all the girls of Denmark are trusting now to me,
And therefore will I fight like a gallant Soldier.
      Hurra, Hurra, Hurra !

      My mammy and my dad,
      My mammy and my dad,
      They thus to me did say,
      Yes, they thus to me did say :
      When those we trust upon
      Forth to the war are gone,
By whom shall all the fields be ploughed, by whom the grass
    be mown ?
Why, that's the very reason we all must march away ;
Or else will come the Germans, and for us make our hay ;
And therefore will I fight like a gallant Soldier.
      Hurra, Hurra, Hurra !

      Should the German us enthral,
      Should the German us enthral,
      Then woe be to us all,
      Yes, then woe be to us all.
      To *Pe'er* and to *Paul*,
      He bellows ' *Du bis faul,*'
And if in Danish he's abused, he tells you then: ' *Hols*
    *Maul !*'
To those who speak all languages, perhaps it matters none,
But a mighty deal of difference to him that speaks but one ;
And therefore will I fight like a gallant Soldier.
      Hurra, Hurra, Hurra !
      Q

. . . . . .

To the foe defiance fling,
To the foe defiance fling,
For with us is our King,
Yes, for with us is our King,
He stands with sabre drawn,
To cut the Germans down ;
For years no king so *Dansk* as he has worn the royal crown.
Now, they 'd have all the world believe that he 's no longer
free,
And yet themselves would keep him fast, in German slavery,
And therefore will I fight like a gallant Soldier.
Hurra, Hurra, Hurra !

For our girls and for our home,
For our girls and for our home,
We 'll fight 'gainst all who come,
Yes, we 'll fight 'gainst all who come ;
And woe the wretch betide,
Who his mother-tongue denied,
And would not give his life and blood for Dannébrog, our
pride.
But should I not return to my dad and mammy dear,
King Frederik with these faméd words their drooping hearts
will cheer :
" His loyalty he proved, did the gallant Soldier."
Hurra, Hurra, Hurra !"[1]

------

[1] *Danish Ditties done into English*, by R. S. E.

Here I may appropriately introduce the 'Capstan-song for the Danish Navy,' written in 1848, and somewhat expanded by R. S. E. It is entitled, 'Come all ye jolly Sailors bold.'

'Come all ye jolly sailors bold,
    Heave and go, my Nancy O!
Listen till my tale is told,
    Heave and go, my Nancy O!

King Frederik from his castle wall,
    Heave and go, my Nancy O!
Heard the German brag and bawl,
    Heave and go, my Nancy O!'

[The Scandinavian national songs abound in reiterations *usque ad nauseam.* I shall therefore omit the 'Heave and go,' and give only the real sentiments of the song.]

'He heard the German's empty scoff,
Which only made him louder laugh.

King Frederik, in his own quaint way,
Says he, "Lads, list to what I say.

If you'll to my assistance come,
We'll keep those Germans safe at home.

You know and all the world beside,
The Germans have a *jaw so wide,*

*Skin and bone they'd eat us quite,*
*To satisfy their appetite.*

Now let us see to give these chaps,
A nice dose for their morning's *snaps*.[1]

They say the Danish fleet they'll have,
To cruise upon the dashing wave.

And so they shall—to stop their trade,
Their ports and harbours to blockade.

If this won't do to raise their fears,
We'll knock their towns about their ears !

Of Denmark, too, they want a slice,
And say, they'll have it in a trice.

And they shall have the slice they crave,—
A prison *for the German knave.*

All this shall happen, as I say,
If, lads, your orders you'll obey."

Thus spoke our noble, gallant King,
And with his words the air shall ring.

For we will never cease to shout :
" South Jutland in—the German out !"

--- ---

[1] *Snaps*, a kind of liquor distilled from corn, and sometimes called corn-brandy. It has a peculiar flavour, and is drunk from liqueur glasses, not only at every meal among the well-to-do classes, but even by peasants and labourers. It is very cheap, costing only about 4½d. a bottle.

The King trusts to his sailors bold,
And he shall find them as of old—

A loyal, true, and noble Navy,
To send the Germans to Old Davy !

For Denmark's bright and fertile plains,
We 'll fight till not one man remains.

For Frederik, our King and Lord,
We 'll shed the last drop of our blood.

For father, mother, sisters, wives,
We 're ready now to risk our lives.

For Danish girls, with eyes so blue,
We 'll do all that can sailors do.

And *Dannebrog*[1] upon our masts,
Shall float as long as this world lasts.

And now for our brave captain, we
Will give three cheers right heartily.

And for our noble frigate, *Freia*,
Than heaven we 'll raise our cheering higher.

Until the German hears the cheer,
Which turns his swaggering into fear.

Then, up, mates, up, and blaze away,
　　Heave and go, my Nancy O !
With God for our King and Country ;
　　Heave and go, my Nancy O !'

---

[1] *Dannebrog*, the Danish standard.　See p. 32.

While on the subject of Danish poetry, I must remark, that from what I have been able to make out of it, it lacks the polish of southern national song, both as to rhyme and rhythm. Indeed, it seems to recall the times of our own Chaucer and Gower. It is rough and romantic, and not at all wanting in vigour and expressiveness. I have a notion that climate regulates poesy as it does the human constitution.

———

This seems to be a suitable place for the introduction of the 'Song of the Watchman,' which, down to the year 1863, was chanted in the streets of Copenhagen. The following is a literal translation by Mr. Ellis :—

### 8 o'clock.

When Day departs, and Darkness reigns on earth,
The scene reminds us of the gloomy grave!
Then let Thy light, O Lord, before us shine,
While to the silent tomb our steps we bend,
And grant a blessed Immortality.

### 9 o'clock.

The Day glides by, and sable Night appears—
For Jesus' sake, O God, our sins forgive.
     Preserve the Royal Family;
And guard the people which this land contains
     From danger of the Enemy!

### 10 o'clock.

Master, maid, and boy, would you the hour know?
It is the time that you to rest should go—
Trust in the Lord with faith—and careful be
Of fire and light;[1] for Ten o'clock has struck!

### 11 o'clock.

Almighty God protects both great and small;
His holy Angels guard us like a wall:,
The Lord himself our city watches o'er,
And keeps our bodies and our souls from harm.

### 12 o'clock.

At th' hour of midnight was our Saviour born—
Great blessing to a world which else was lost!
Then with unfeigned lips in prayer and praise
Commend yourselves to God.—Past Twelve o'clock.

---

[1] 'Of fire and light.' Oh that this warning were observed everywhere! Then would the disastrous fires, now so constantly occurring, be greatly diminished.

### 1 o'clock.

O Jesu Christ, we pray Thee send us help
To bear our Cross with patience in the world,
   For Thou art God alone!
And Thou, O Comforter, Thine hand stretch forth:
Then will the burthen light and easy be!
   The clock has stricken One!

### 2 o'clock.

O gracious Lord, whose love for us was such
That Thou shouldst deign in darkness[1] to be born:
   All glory's due to Thee!
Come, Holy Ghost, and pour into our hearts
Thy heavenly light, that we may see Thee now,
   And in Eternity.

### 3 o'clock.

Black Night departs, and Day begins to dawn—
Keep them far off, O God, who wish us harm!
   The clock has stricken Three!
Father, Thine aid we seek! and of Thy grace
   Give us abundantly!

### 4 o'clock.

Eternal God! who wouldst the Keeper be
   Of us who dwell below—
To Thee, surrounded by the Heavenly Host,
   Honour and praise are due!
For this good night give thanks unto the Lord!
Remember 'Four'—we're summoned from our guard.

---

[1] Figuratively, *obscurity*.

5 o'clock.

Jesu, Thou Morning Star! we now resign
To Thy protection, cheerfully, our King;
　　Be thou his Sun and Shield!
And thou, bright Orb of Day, begin thy course,
And, rising from the mercy-seat of God,
　　Thy radiant lustre yield!

The reason for the discontinuance of this old chant, so pious and devout, I did not learn. It has a special charm for the British mind, inasmuch as its composer was the son of a Scotchman. Mr. Ellis remarks, that 'the author of the original song was Thomas Kingo, Bishop of Fyen, born at Slangerup in Zealand, 15th December 1634, and son of John King, a native of Scotland, whose father, Thomas King, grandfather of the bishop, came over to Denmark with his son, and settled at Elsinore, as tapestry-weaver to Christian IV. John King was a poor but respectable and honest damask-weaver of Slangerup, as is impressively stated in some pious verses by his son; and a tablet to his memory still exists in Slangerup church, where he was buried.

'The Bishop, Thomas Kingo, is unquestionably the most admired psalmist ever known in Denmark, and his psalm-book, all of his own composition, is now the authorized Psalter of Christiania in Norway.

'The change of the name of King to *Kingo* is most naturally accounted for by the habit prevalent with students in the seventeenth century, of latinizing their names.'

————

The ancient capital of Norway was Bergen, but, that city having much fallen off, Christiania is now considered the metropolis. Bergen was founded about the year 1069, by King Olaf Kyrre. Soon after its erection, its fine harbour attracted the notice of the Hanseatic League, who erected a factory there, and it soon became the capital of the kingdom. The grand old castle, called the Bergenhuus, overlooking the city, gave the port additional importance. The trade is at this day greater than that of any other Norwegian port ; but the place has sadly fallen off since the disruption of Norway from Denmark, and the population at present does not exceed 27,000. Its commerce, however, is extensive, and exceeds that of Christiania, and, though its temperature is higher, and perhaps more healthy, it does not vie in fashion or respectability with the modern capital ; which has the advantages of a Court and a University.

Bergen possesses a romantic history. In 1135 King Magnus was taken prisoner here, and Harald Gille, one of the competitors for the crown, put out his eyes. Not long after this, the cruel tyrant was himself murdered. In 1164 Magnus Erlingson ascended the throne, and was crowned by the papal legate ; and in the following century King Hacon, and his son and successor, held the sovereignty. Norway suffered greatly at different times from the Plague, which first attacked Bergen ; and in the earlier part of the seventeenth century no less than four distinct visitations of that direful disease were experienced here, each carrying off thousands of unhappy victims. In the war between England and Holland in 1665, the great Sir Edward Montague, joint High-admiral of England, and Knight of the Garter, pursued Admiral Van Bitter and his fleet into Bergen harbour, but was compelled to retire, as the Dutch were defended by the fortifications of the city. Some reminders of this engagement are traceable in the English shot remaining affixed to the walls of the Cathedral, the fortress, and other conspicuous buildings.

The Norwegians carried on considerable trade with England, when the junior Hacon (Haconson) concluded a commercial treaty with this country in 1217. The English gained little by the interchange, and they were finally ousted by a monopoly granted to the Hanse Towns in

1435. The League, who had a large factory here, carried on an extensive trade until about 1750, when the monopoly was broken through, and commerce established with all nations.

At present the principal export trade of the city is 'stock-fish,' a term constantly occurring in the records of our English mediæval feasts, and meaning dried cod-fish, herrings, and cod oil. The annual *take* of codfish is enormous ; and the oil is said to amount to twenty thousand barrels annually. The fish is generally fat and oily when caught. The livers are thrown into casks, and the best of the oil, rising to the surface, is used for lamps, and, medicinally, for scrofulous and consumptive diseases.[1] The less refined portions are employed by curriers for dressing leather.

Besides the castle or fortress of Bergenhuus which commands the harbour, there is an ancient

---

[1] Few English people would take this medicine if they knew the nauseous mode of its production.

tower called Malhendorf.   It was considered im-
pregnable before the introduction of gunpowder.
Before  the  Reformation  the city possessed upwards  of  thirty churches and conventual estab-
lishments ; but  five  churches  now  supply  the
spiritual  needs  of  this  decaying  capital.   The
old  Cathedral  retains  in  its  services  much  of
what we call the *ritualistic*.   In fact, as before
observed,  Norway,  or  at  least  a  considerable
portion  of it, was  only  half  reformed  by  the
introduction  of  the  Lutheran  doctrines.   The
reformation  was  rather  political  than  religious.
The  double-towered  church  of  St.  Mary  is  the
most ancient ecclesiastical edifice in Bergen, and
is  mentioned  by  Snorro  Sturleson  as  being  in
existence so early as 1181.   The sculptures both
in  stone  and  wood  are  good of their kind.   The
font  is  odd  and  curious.   It  represents  a  flying
angel  of  life-size,  coloured,  and  holding  the
baptismal  basin  in  his  out-stretched  hands.
This grotesque piece of workmanship is ascribed,
I  know  not  on  what  grounds,  to  a  Dutch  artist.

Like all considerable towns in the North, Bergen has its Museum. It contains works good, bad, and indifferent. There is a kind of art-union exhibition within it, chiefly of Norwegian art, and one picture by Jansen, representing a Viking rescuing a Greek lady from her assailants, is sure to attract the notice of the visitor: the drawing and colouring are alike excellent, and the picture may perhaps be pronounced the best piece of art in the whole kingdom. The Museum also contains a number of Scandinavian antiquities, from barrows near Vosse, and a considerable cabinet of natural-history objects, a collection of 3000 Norwegian coins, dating from the tenth century, and various other interesting articles. Among the rest is 'a beautiful and elaborately carved oak bedstead of Dutch manufacture. Upwards of two hundred years ago, this bedstead was brought to Bergen by a young English couple, just married. They settled here. The husband was unfortunate in

trade, and soon afterwards died, leaving his
widow *enceinte* with her first child.   Norwegian
hearts warmed to the young mourner and her
fatherless infant, and when they at last sailed for
England the widow gave this only and valued
relic of her happy days to a family here, who
had shown her the greatest kindness.   Their
descendants presented it to the Museum, where
it remains a token of British gratitude for Norwegian generosity.'[1]   An object in the natural-
history department is sure to attract the notice
of the visitor.   It is the skeleton of a horse that
faithfully served one master for *forty years !*
In Scandinavia horses frequently attain an age
quite unusual in more favoured latitudes.

In the middle ages leprosy was a common
curse in Asia and Europe, and *lazar-houses* were
found in the vicinity of all great towns.   Though
nearly extinct in other countries, it unhappily

---

[1] Murray.

exists in Norway, and hence, like other towns, Bergen has its Hospital for Lepers.

A curious weapon, extinct elsewhere, still exists here. It is carried by the night-watchmen. It consists of a staff four or five feet long, to which is attached a ball furnished with spikes of iron about half an inch in length. This formidable weapon is called *the morning star*, and much resembles that which is held by Gog in our London Guildhall. I believe that our Cockney giants are derived from a Scandinavian parentage.

I may remark that some years ago, when the Marquis of Waterford visited this city, he received at the hands of one of the guardians of the night a blow from one of these *lucifers* which nearly deprived him of life.

The city is very quaint and picturesque, and the houses are of timber, and painted white and red. It has been visited by many conflagrations, and even at this time every house has at

R

the door a water-butt for use, in case of such a calamity. In the year 1488 great part of Bergen succumbed to a direful visitation of this kind, and most of the town, including no less than eleven parish churches, was destroyed. So lately as 1855 nearly 200 houses in the western quarter were burned, and the fire must have extended further, but for the open space called the market-place, which the flames could not cross. The streets are for the most part well paved, but very indirect and irregular, as indeed are those of most Scandinavian towns. The haven is the forum of Bergen, and thither do the inhabitants continually resort. On certain days of the week the fish-market is held, and as fish is the staple of Norwegian food, it is very much frequented. The price of the fish astonishes the stranger, as you can get one of the immense flat fish called the *halibut* for eighteenpence English, and three good mackerel for a penny! The port during summer is

crowded with merchant and fishing vessels—
the latter of peculiar and antique build, bearing
such names as the Orme or Serpent, the Drage
or Dragon, and other romantic appellations.
Along the north bank of the haven are the fish
warehouses, principally filled with stock-fish for
the southern markets. These stores formerly
belonged to the merchants of the Hanseatic
League; and it is noteworthy that Bergen still
contains a kind of independent colony, descend-
ed from the Leaguers, who yet adhere to the
customs and language of the Germans. Many
of the sea-going population have customs and
costumes differing from the rest of the Bergen-
ers, in this respect reminding one of the inhabitants of the Pollet, a suburb of Dieppe; of
the fisher class formerly residing at Brighton;
and of the Claddagh fishermen of Galway. In
all these cases the isolated tribe seems to be of
a different nationality from the general population. This is a subject worthy of consideration
and research by the ethnologist.

The environs of the city are beautiful, and in a high degree romantic. They abound with villas, which command extensive prospects. The great drawback is the rain, caused partly by the proximity of the lofty mountains, which at some points exceed two thousand feet in height. It rains, more or less, more than half the days in the year. We had not an opportunity of visiting these cloud-capped heights, and my physical strength was not such as to allow me to *clamber* up to such an elevation.

Our 'guide, philosopher, and (ubiquitous) friend' of Albemarle Street observes, that 'travellers should endeavour to assist at a Bergen Farmer's *wedding.*' We had not that opportunity. It is described as 'a highly picturesque and entertaining scene. Immediately the ceremony is over, the house is thrown open to all friends and neighbours, and feasting and dancing are kept up for several days. Each guest brings a present. The bride

remains dressed in her crown and ornaments during all the merry-making; the crown is so constructed that, by drawing a pin, it opens, and falls from the head. Immediately she does this, the music is hushed, and the guests depart.'
The inns of Bergen cannot be commended, as they are neither comfortable nor cheap.

Christiania, though now the acknowledged metropolis of Norway, contains a population of little more than 70,000, or considerably less than that of our fashionable town of Brighton. Its original name was Osloe, which was founded in 1058 by king Harold Haardrade, and, a few generations later, was accounted only the third city of the kingdom,—Trondheim (Nidaros) and Bergen having the precedence. When Norway became united with Denmark it was accounted the metropolis of the former kingdom, and two or three kings were crowned there. It possessed a noble Cathedral, in which our King James I. was married in 1589, to Anne, sister of Christian IV., king of Denmark. He was then only James VI. of Scotland. He had not yet written his ' Counterblast to Tobacco,' and I do not know whether the Norwegians of his day smoked as they do now. Next to the Germans, they are the greatest consumers of *the weed* in the world, though smoking in the streets is strictly prohibited by the police regulations.

Christiania has its real founder in Christian IV., who called it after his own name. Osloe, with the exception of a few houses and the Bishop's Palace, was burnt to the ground in 1624. Christian had been lucky enough to have discovered for him a rich silver mine at Kongsberg, and after visiting it he set to work with a will to found the new city. The town had previously consisted of what in England we call post-and-panel houses; but Christian laid the foundations on a much better scale, arranging the streets at right angles, and making the roadways broad and handsome. I wish our ancestors had followed his example after the great fire of London in 1666. All the cities and towns of Scandinavia were originally built of wood, and hence the numerous disasters by fire which they have experienced. Even so lately as 1858, a great conflagration took place here; but the mean 'messuages and tenements' have been replaced by well-built houses, some of which would adorn any city in the world. The fire alluded to occurred in the spring of 1858, and about a thousand people were rendered homeless by the destruction of sixty houses. The loss in buildings and furniture amounted to nearly a quarter of a million sterling.

A traveller has well observed that 'the city of Christiania is so lovely in position, floating on the waters, encircled by hills and islands, as to need little adornment from art.' The Norwegians are justly proud of their capital and their country. They are an energetic people, and overflow with patriotism, notwithstanding the many natural disadvantages to which they are subject, as to geographical position and climate. To their national cry of *Gamle Norge*, we must sympathetically exclaim 'God bless *Old Norway!*' I only wish they belonged to Denmark, and not to Sweden; but they seem to be bound up in their own nationality, to whatever foreign rule they may be subject. They remind us somewhat of the Roman *fasces* or 'bundle of sticks,' with an axe in the middle, representing the sovereign, who is harmless so long as they continue to remain bound together, in mutual self-defence.

Christiania contains the usual public buildings, a finely situated royal palace, a new Storthing or House of Parliament, and a curious octagonal church of brick, called Trinity Church (Trefoldigheds-Kirke). It looks more like a chapter-house than a church. It is covered by an immense dome of brick, and even the groining ribs are of the same material. At the University, five hundred students are educated gratis on payment of a trifling entrance fee. It contains a National Gallery, and an excellent library of 200,000 volumes.

I think the Scandinavians pay more attention to their national antiquities than the inhabitants of any other region in existence. It is true that their museums cannot vie with our own British Museum and the great collections in Germany and France; but their excellence consists in their strict *nationality*. The Museum of Northern Antiquities contains, among other notable objects, Runic inscriptions; a remarkable massive gold collar with numerous gold and silver ornaments found in 1834. They are perhaps somewhat fancifully believed to have originally adorned a statue of Woden, and to have been buried in the earth at the introduction of Christianity into Norway. We 'Southrons' should have known better, and turned the precious metals into current coins of the realm. And here I may remark, parenthetically, that, during our brief sojourn in Scandinavia we never saw a single gold coin except what we carried with us—the currency being small bank-notes, and silver and copper coins, the latter silvered over.

Duelling was common in Norway within the present century, especially among the lower classes. The antagonists commenced operations by driving their weapon, a knife, into a piece of wood. So much of the iron as was not buried in the wood was then bound round with slips of bullock's hide. Then the antagonists were tied face to face with each other by a strong girdle, so that neither of them could escape the terrible embrace. 'Then came the tug of war.' Each man, furnished by the bystanders with his deadly weapon, fought as long as human endurance would permit him. This curious duel was known as 'the battle of the girdle.'

Specimens of the girdle and duel-knives are. preserved in the Museum. But perhaps the objects most interesting to lady visitors in this collection are the crown, girdle, and frontlet, similar to those worn by the Norwegian brides at the present day. 'A virtuous woman is a *crown* to her husband;' and those women whose previous lives have been unchaste dare not don the emblem at the marriage ceremony. This is a sad disgrace to the bride; but, happily, comparatively few cases of this kind are found in the Bergen district, where I believe the morals of the people are as good as those of the inhabitants of any country of Europe. The collection contains many specimens of mediæval wood-carving, and ornaments in flint, silver, gold and bronze, old pieces of armour, swords, etc. There are also many statuettes of the Scandinavian gods and heroes, horses, and other objects in bronze.

I have elsewhere said that parts of Norway

were but half-Protestantized at the Reformation;
and I might have said not even Christianized;
for, to this day, if a peasant finds one of these
little bronze statuettes, he will not willingly part
with it, because forsooth he thinks that it
possesses some magical healing powers, and
literally makes it *a household god!* In fact the
Norsemen of the higher latitudes are nearly as
idolatrous as the Ashantees or the inhabitants
of Central Africa. Superstition, rather than
Religion, has its hold on the uncultivated mind
of these ignorant people.

-----

On a previous page I have alluded to
Scandinavian names in England, both local
and surnomical, which have been borrowed
from the Scandinavian nations. I now proceed to give a few more instances. *By* is a
very common termination to place-names in
England, and nearly all of them have given
surnames to our families. Appleby, Rugby,

Whitby, Newby, Saxby, Frisby, *Danby*, Swainby, Brandsby, and a host of others, are not only local, but family names. '*By*' itself exists as a surname, and is the shortest one in our language. The word primarily signified a farm-house or country-dwelling; afterwards it came to mean a village, town, or borough (see Worsaæ's *Danes in England*). I should have observed that in Lincolnshire alone there are no less than 212 places which have this termination.

To proceed with other names, I may remark that our Swain, Swayne, etc., are derived from Sven, a well-known name in Scandinavia. Our name Holden is the Danish for *wealthy*, like Rich, etc. Scrase, again, is pure Danish Skraas, which means non-erect, or, as we say, 'lop-sided,' probably a nickname given to the first bearer from his personal deformity. The family of Scrase is believed to be the oldest in England, having held good lands in Sussex at

and before the date of the Norman Conquest.
Our name Holman (in Danish *Holmen*) signi-
fies the inhabitant of a 'holm,' or little island,
whence therefore our Holmes.  Gurre is a
place in Norway, whence our family name of
Gurr.

The name Thorvald (whence Thorvaldsen)
has become in England Tyrrel, Torel, Turl,
Tourle, etc.  Sigurd of Denmark is our Segar.
We derive our Harrild from Harald, our Foster
from Fostre, our Anderson from Andersen,
our Earle from Jarl (pronounced Iarl), our
Olive from Olaf, our Eager from Ægir, our
Lye from Lie, our Wickens from Wikin (originally Viking), our Berners from Berner, our
Kettel and Catell from the Norwegian Kitil,
our Gill from Gillie, our Warner from Werner,
our Winter from Winther, and our Geere from
Geer.  The Scandinavian Bright is our Bright,
Lumbye our Lumby, Isgar our Isgar, Strange
our Strange, and Kaaré our Carey.

It may be objected that some of the names cited come from Normandy. Granted ; but it must be remembered that many hundreds of Norman names came originally from Scandinavia. See a recent work called *The Norman People*, passim. We are in want of a book which might be called *The Common Origin of Nations*, to show how all mankind have sprung from one stock.

———

I had not much opportunity, in my short visit, to look into the state of Education in Scandinavia, but I believe there are few parts of it where all classes are not better educated than in England. A 'national school' in England is generally superintended by a person —often pretentious—who can teach the 'three R's,' and a little besides. He is usually, so far as my observation goes, nothing of a scholar. In Scandinavia, however, the case is different, and the national schoolmaster is a graduate of

one or the other of the Universities.   I could
not help laughing when I was informed that a
common barber, before he could open shop,
was obliged to pass an examination in Cornelius
Nepos !  What connexion there was between
easy shaving and cutting hair and that good
old classic I did not understand at first ; but I
afterwards recollected that the barber of the
present age represents the ' barber-chirurgeon '
of bygone days, whose functions were not
limited to the trimming of the facial ornament,
but extended to blood-letting and other surgical
operations ; so that he was really a professional
man.   I wonder how many London barbers
now-a-days could construe and parse ten words
of simple old Nepos, or even parse the Ten
Commandments in English.

*Apropos* of barbers, I heard a good story
at Copenhagen.   A very fashionable Countess,
highly distinguished for her musical abilities,
was once at an evening party, and playing the

piano. At length she opened her portfolio on a piece which required a violin accompaniment. She inquired if any gentleman present played that instrument. Unluckily no one could play; but the lady of the house said she could easily obtain an excellent violinist in a few minutes. Accordingly, shortly afterwards, a sprucely-dressed young man entered the room, fiddle in hand. The Countess, not noticing him, commenced her piece, which, with the assistance of the violin, went off admirably, and was *encored.* When the piece was over, her ladyship turned round to thank the gentleman for his able assistance, when, horror of horrors! she found that he was her own hair-dresser. A woman's anger may be conceived, but in this case it cannot be described.

Music is much cultivated in these regions, and is considered almost an integral part of education. I may mention as a curious fact that bagpipes were invented in Norway, and thence imported into Scotland during the period when a portion of that country fell into Scandinavian hands.

———

We were preparing for a journey to Stockholm, when I again relapsed, and was obliged to call in a physician, who carefully attended to my ailments, and directed me to return to England by the next steamer, for which, however, we had several days to wait. I soon got strong enough to walk about the streets, and to look at some things which I had not seen before, and to have conversation with the people of several nations at our glorious *table-d'hôte*, so that the time was not wholly lost ; especially as our kind friends were constantly near us, to render us every possible assistance in our inquiries.

We might have steamed on the following Friday ; but no—it was an unlucky day to commence a voyage. I do not know how this superstition arose, but it seems to be a common one throughout all Christendom—so we were obliged to wait for Sunday, when we left Copenhagen, 'the Haven of Ships' as local etymologists call it. The weather was beautiful, but we left the harbour with much regret, after the great kindness we had received, with only a partially fulfilled object. Several of our friends 'accompanied us to the ship.' The ship, this time, was the ' Phœnix,' a less vessel than the 'Valdemar,' but equally comfortable, and we found good accommodation. We had eleven biped passengers, and twenty oxen on board. We were almost six days on the voyage, and a truly miserable one it was. Neptune brandished his great trident with frightful majesty; Thetis was grinning with her big white teeth; while Auster did his very best to impede our progress. Indeed it was, though in summer, the most uncomfortable voyage I ever experienced. Everybody, except the captain, his wife, the crew, and

myself, was sick. I fortunately escaped that
direful malady, and, on going one morning to the
breakfast-table in the saloon, I found that I was
the only passenger who could eat. My 'sea-
legs' failed me, however, but the kind-hearted
steward was always ready to render his assistance. Besides the delay occasioned by the
stormy weather, we had to remain some hours
outside the Thames, and for a shorter time at
Thames Haven for the discharge of our
bovine passengers. Glad enough those poor
creatures must have been to set their trembling
legs once more on *terra firma*, for they were
as sick all the passage as the human voyagers.
It is no wonder that we see such poor emaciated
animals arrive on our shores, as we almost daily
do, when we consider the sufferings they have
undergone in a sea-voyage, especially such a
one as we suffered.

At length we reached Wapping, and were
glad enough to find ourselves in our snug little

home a few miles distant, rather the worse for wear and tear, but full of agreeable reminiscences of the pleasant scenes and new-made friendships in Scandinavia.

FINIS.

# INDEX.

PRINTED BY T. AND A. CONSTABLE, PRINTERS TO HER MAJESTY,
AT THE EDINBURGH UNIVERSITY PRESS.

# A CLASSIFIED CATALOGUE OF

# HENRY S. KING & CO.'S PUBLICATIONS.

## CONTENTS.

## HISTORY AND BIOGRAPHY.

**AUTOBIOGRAPHY AND OTHER MEMORIALS OF MRS. GILBERT, FORMERLY ANN TAYLOR.** By **Josiah Gilbert,** Author of "The Titian and Cadore Country," &c. In 2 vols. Post 8vo. With Steel Portraits, and several Wood Engravings. [*Preparing.*]

**AUTOBIOGRAPHY OF DR. A. B. GRANVILLE, M.D., F.R.S., &c.** Edited, with a brief account of his concluding years, by his youngest Daughter. 2 vols. Demy 8vo. With a Portrait. [*Preparing.*]

**SAMUEL LOVER, THE LIFE AND UNPUBLISHED WORKS OF.** By **Bayle Bernard.** In 2 vols. Post 8vo. With a Steel Portrait. [*Preparing.*]

**A MEMOIR OF THE REV. DR. ROWLAND WILLIAMS,** with selections from his Note-books and Correspondence. Edited by **Mrs. Rowland Williams.** With a Photographic Portrait. In 2 vols. Large post 8vo. [*Shortly.*]

**POLITICAL WOMEN.** By **Sutherland Menzies.** 2 vols. Post 8vo. Price 24s.

"Has all the information of history, with all the interest that attaches to biography." —*Scotsman.*

"A graceful contribution to the lighter record of history."—*English Churchman.*

65, *Cornhill;* & 12, *Paternoster Row, London.*

HISTORY AND BIOGRAPHY—*continued.*

**SARA COLERIDGE, MEMOIR AND LETTERS OF.** Edited by her **Daughter.** 2 vols. Crown 8vo. With 2 Portraits. Price 24s. Third Edition, Revised and Corrected. With Index.

"Sara Coleridge, as she is revealed, or rather reveals herself, in the correspondence, makes a brilliant addition to a brilliant family reputation."—*Saturday Review.*

"These charming volumes are attractive as a memorial of a most amiable woman of high intellectual mark."—*Athenæum.*
"We have read these two volumes with genuine gratification."—*Hour.*

**THE LATE REV. F. W. ROBERTSON, M.A., LIFE AND LETTERS OF.** Edited by **Stopford Brooke, M.A.,** Chaplain in Ordinary to the Queen.

I. In 2 vols., uniform with the Sermons. Price 7s. 6d.
II. Library Edition, in demy 8vo, with Two Steel Portraits. Price 12s.
III. A Popular Edition, in 1 vol. Price 6s.

**NATHANIEL HAWTHORNE, A MEMOIR OF,** with Stories now first published in this country. By **H. A. Page.** Large post 8vo. 7s. 6d.

"Seldom has it been our lot to meet with a more appreciative delineation of character than this Memoir of Hawthorne."—*Morning Post.*

"Exhibits a discriminating enthusiasm for one of the most fascinating of novelists."—*Saturday Review.*

**LEONORA CHRISTINA, MEMOIRS OF,** Daughter of Christian IV. of Denmark: Written during her Imprisonment in the Blue Tower of the Royal Palace at Copenhagen, 1663—1685. Translated by **F. E. Bunnett.** With an Autotype Portrait of the Princess. Medium 8vo. 12s. 6d.

"A valuable addition to history."—*Daily News.*

"A valuable addition to the tragic romance of history."—*Spectator.*

**LIVES OF ENGLISH POPULAR LEADERS.** No. 1.—STEPHEN LANGTON. By **C. Edmund Maurice.** Crown 8vo. 7s. 6d.

**CABINET PORTRAITS.** BIOGRAPHICAL SKETCHES OF STATESMEN OF THE DAY. By **T. Wemyss Reid.** 1 vol. Crown 8vo. 7s. 6d.

"We have never met with a work which we can more unreservedly praise. The sketches are absolutely impartial."—*Athenæum.*

"We can heartily commend this work."—*Standard.*
"Drawn with a master hand."—*Yorkshire Post.*

**THE CHURCH AND THE EMPIRES:** Historical Periods. By the late **Henry W. Wilberforce.** Preceded by a Memoir of the Author by the **Rev. John Henry Newman, D.D.** 1 vol. Post 8vo. With a Portrait. Price 10s. 6d.

**HISTORY OF THE ENGLISH REVOLUTION OF 1688.** By **C. D. Yonge,** Regius Professor, Queen's Coll., Belfast. 1 vol. Crown 8vo. Price 6s.

**ALEXIS DE TOCQUEVILLE.** Correspondence and Conversations with NASSAU W. SENIOR, from 1833 to 1859. Edited by **Mrs. M. C. M. Simpson.** In 2 vols. Large post 8vo. 21s.

"A book replete with knowledge and thought."—*Quarterly Review.*

"An extremely interesting book."—*Saturday Review.*

**JOURNALS KEPT IN FRANCE AND ITALY.** From 1848 to 1852. With a Sketch of the Revolution of 1848. By the late **Nassau William Senior.** Edited by his Daughter, **M. C. M. Simpson.** In 2 vols. Post 8vo. **24s.**

"The book has a genuine historical value."—*Saturday Review.*
"No better, more honest, and more read-

able view of the state of political society during the existence of the second Republic could well be looked for."—*Examiner.*

**PERSIA; ANCIENT AND MODERN.** By **John Piggot, F.S.A.** Post 8vo. Price 10s. 6d.

**THE HISTORY OF JAPAN.** From the Earliest Period to the Present Time. By **Francis Ottiwell Adams,** H.B.M.'s Secretary of Embassy at Berlin, formerly H.B.M.'s Chargé d'Affaires, and Secretary of Legation at Yedo. Demy 8vo. With Map and Plans. Price 21s.

**THE NORMAN PEOPLE,** AND THEIR EXISTING DESCENDANTS IN THE BRITISH DOMINIONS AND THE UNITED STATES OF AMERICA. One handsome vol. 8vo. Price 21s.

**THE RUSSIANS IN CENTRAL ASIA.** A Critical Examination, down to the present time, of the Geography and History of Central Asia. By **Baron F. von Hellwald.** Translated by **Lieut.-Col. Theodore Wirgman, LL.B.** In 1 vol. Large post 8vo, with Map. Price 12s.

**BOKHARA : ITS HISTORY AND CONQUEST.** By **Professor Arminius Vâmbèry,** of the University of Pesth, Author of "Travels in Central Asia," &c. Demy 8vo. Price 18s.

"We conclude with a cordial recommendation of this valuable book."—*Saturday Review.*

"Almost every page abounds with composition of peculiar merit." — *Morning Post.*

**THE RELIGIOUS HISTORY OF IRELAND :** PRIMITIVE, PAPAL, AND PROTESTANT; including the Evangelical Missions, Catholic Agitations, and Church Progress of the last half Century. By **James Godkin,** Author of "Ireland : her Churches," &c. 1 vol. 8vo. Price 12s.

"These latter chapters on the statistics of the various religious denominations will be welcomed."—*Evening Standard.*
"Mr. Godkin writes with evident honesty,

and the topic on which he writes is one about which an honest book is greatly wanted."—*Examiner.*

**THE GOVERNMENT OF THE NATIONAL DEFENCE.** From the 30th June to the 31st October, 1870. The Plain Statement of a Member. By **Mons. Jules Favre.** 1 vol. Demy 8vo. 10s. 6d.

"Of all the contributions to the history of the late war, we have found none more fascinating and, perhaps, none more valuable than the 'apology,' by M.

Jules Favre, for the unsuccessful Government of the National Defence."—*Times.*
"A work of the highest interest. The book is most valuable."—*Athenæum.*

**ECHOES OF A FAMOUS YEAR.** By **Harriet Parr,** Author of "The Life of Jeanne d'Arc," "In the Silver Age," &c. Crown 8vo. 8s. 6d.

"Miss Parr has the great gift of charming simplicity of style ; and if children are not interested in her book, many of their

seniors will be."—*British Quarterly Review.*

# *VOYAGES AND TRAVEL.*

**SOME TIME IN IRELAND**; A Recollection. 1 vol. Crown Svo.
[*Preparing.*

**WAYSIDE NOTES IN SCANDINAVIA.** Being Notes of Travel in the North of Europe. By **Mark Antony Lower, M.A.** 1 vol. Crown Svo.
[*Preparing.*

**ON THE ROAD TO KHIVA.** By **David Ker**, late Khivan Correspondent of the *Daily Telegraph*. Illustrated with Photographs of the Country and its Inhabitants, and a copy of the Official Map in use during the Campaign, from the Survey of CAPTAIN LEUSILIN. 1 vol. Post Svo. 12s.

**VIZCAYA**; or, Life in the land of the Carlists at the outbreak of the Insurrection, with some account of the Iron Mines and other characteristics of the country. With a Map and 8 Illustrations. Crown Svo. [*Just ready.*

**ROUGH NOTES OF A VISIT TO BELGIUM, SEDAN, AND PARIS**, in September, 1870-71. By **John Ashton.** Crown Svo, bevelled boards. Price 3s. 6d.

"The author does not attempt to deal with military subjects, but writes sensibly of what he saw in 1870-71."—*John Bull.*
"Possesses a certain freshness from the straightforward simplicity with which it is written."—*Graphic.*
"An interesting work by a highly intelligent observer."—*Standard.*

**THE ALPS OF ARABIA**; or, Travels through Egypt, Sinai, Arabia, and the Holy Land. By **William Charles Maughan.** 1 vol. Demy Svo, with Map. Price 12s.

"Deeply interesting and valuable."—*Edinburgh Review.*
"He writes freshly and with competent knowledge."—*Standard*
"Very readable and instructive. . . . A work far above the average of such publications."—*John Bull.*

**THE MISHMEE HILLS**: an Account of a Journey made in an Attempt to Penetrate Thibet from Assam, to open New Routes for Commerce. By **T. T. Cooper**, Author of "The Travels of a Pioneer of Commerce." Demy Svo. With Four Illustrations and Map. Price 10s. 6d.

"The volume, which will be of great use in India and among Indian merchants here, contains a good deal of matter that will interest ordinary readers. It is especially rich in sporting incidents."—*Standard.*

**GOODMAN'S CUBA, THE PEARL OF THE ANTILLES.** By **Walter Goodman.** Crown Svo. Price 7s. 6d.

"A series of vivid and miscellaneous sketches. We can recommend this whole volume as very amusing reading."—*Pall Mall Gazette.*
"The whole book deserves the heartiest commendation. . . . Sparkling and amusing from beginning to end."—*Spectator.*

**FIELD AND FOREST RAMBLES OF A NATURALIST IN NEW BRUNSWICK.** With Notes and Observations on the Natural History of Eastern Canada. By **A. Leith Adams, M.A.** In Svo, cloth. Illustrated. Price 14s.

"Both sportsmen and naturalists will find this work replete with anecdote and carefully-recorded observation, which will entertain them."—*Nature.*
"Will be found interesting by those who take a pleasure either in sport or natural history."—*Athenæum.*
"To the naturalist the book will be most valuable. . . To the general reader most interesting."—*Evening Standard.*

**ROUND THE WORLD IN** 1870. A Volume of Travels, with Maps. By **A. D. Carlisle, B.A.**, Trin. Coll., Camb. Demy Svo. Price 16s.

"We can only commend, which we do very heartily, an eminently sensible and readable book." *British Quarterly Review.*

65, *Cornhill;* & 12, *Paternoster Row, London.*

**TENT LIFE WITH ENGLISH GIPSIES IN NORWAY.** By
**Hubert Smith.** In 8vo, cloth. Five full-page Engravings, and 31
smaller Illustrations, with Map of the Country showing Routes. Second
Edition. Revised and Corrected. Price 21s.

" Written in a very lively style, and has throughout a smack of dry humour and satiric reflection which shows the writer to be a keen observer of men and things. We hope that many will read it and find in it the same amusement as ourselves."—*Times.*

**FAYOUM ; OR, ARTISTS IN EGYPT.** A Tour with M. Gérôme and others.
By **J. Lenoir.** Crown 8vo, cloth. Illustrated. Price 7s. 6d.

"A pleasantly written and very readable book."—*Examiner.*
" The book is very amusing. . . . Who- ever may take it up will find he has with him a bright and pleasant companion."—*Spectator.*

**SPITZBERGEN THE GATEWAY TO THE POLYNIA; OR, A**
VOYAGE TO SPITZBERGEN. By **Captain John C. Wells, R.N.**
In 8vo, cloth. Profusely Illustrated. Price 21s.

"A charming book, remarkably well written and well illustrated."—*Standard.*
" Straightforward and clear in style, securing our confidence by its unaffected simplicity and good sense."—*Saturday Review.*

**AN AUTUMN TOUR IN THE UNITED STATES AND**
**CANADA.** By **Lieut.-Col. J. G. Medley.** Crown 8vo. Price 5s.

"Colonel Medley's little volume is a pleasantly written account of a two-months' visit to America."—*Hour.*
"May be recommended as manly, sensible, and pleasantly written."—*Globe.*

**THE NILE WITHOUT A DRAGOMAN.** By **Frederic Eden.**
Second Edition. In 1 vol. Crown 8vo, cloth. Price 7s. 6d.

"Should any of our readers care to imitate Mr. Eden's example, and wish to see things with their own eyes, and shift for themselves, next winter in Upper Egypt, they will find this book a very agreeable guide."—*Times.*
" It is a book to read during an autumn holiday."—*Spectator.*

**IRELAND IN 1872.** A Tour of Observation, with Remarks on Irish Public
Questions. By **Dr. James Macaulay.** Crown 8vo. Price 7s. 6d.

"A careful and instructive book. Full of facts, full of information, and full of interest."—*Literary Churchman.*
" We have rarely met a book on Ireland which for impartiality of criticism and general accuracy of information could be so well recommended to the fair-minded Irish reader."—*Evening Standard.*

**OVER THE DOVREFJELDS.** By **J. S. Shepard,** Author of " A
Ramble through Norway," &c. Crown 8vo. Illustrated. Price 4s. 6d.

"We have read many books of Norwegian travel, but . . . we have seen none so pleasantly narrative in its style, and so varied in its subject."—*Spectator.*
" As interesting a little volume as could be written on the subject. So interesting and shortly written that it will commend itself to all intending tourists."—*Examiner.*

**A WINTER IN MOROCCO.** By **Amelia Perrier.** Large crown 8vo.
Illustrated. Price 10s. 6d.

"Well worth reading, and contains several excellent illustrations."—*Hour.*
" Miss Perrier is a very amusing writer. She has a good deal of humour, sees the oddity and quaintness of Oriental life with a quick observant eye, and evidently turned her opportunities of sarcastic examination to account."—*Daily News.*

SCIENCE—*continued.*

A New Edition.

**CHANGE OF AIR AND SCENE.** A Physician's Hints about Doctors, Patients, Hygiène, and Society; with Notes of Excursions for health in the Pyrenees, and amongst the Watering-places of France (Inland and Seaward), Switzerland, Corsica, and the Mediterranean. By **Dr. Alphonse Donné.** Large post 8vo. Price 9s.

"A very readable and serviceable book. . . . The real value of it is to be found in the accurate and minute information given with regard to a large number of places which have gained a reputation on the continent for their mineral waters."—*Pall Mall Gazette.*
"A singularly pleasant and chatty as well as instructive book about health."—*Guardian.*

**MISS YOUMANS' FIRST BOOK OF BOTANY.** Designed to cultivate the observing powers of Children. From the Author's latest Stereotyped Edition. New and Enlarged Edition, with 300 Engravings. Crown 8vo. Price 5s.

"It is but rarely that a school-book appears which is at once so novel in plan, so successful in execution, and so suited to the general want, as to command universal and unqualified approbation, but such has been the case with Miss Youmans' First Book of Botany. . . . It has been everywhere welcomed as a timely and invaluable contribution to the improvement of primary education."—*Pall Mall Gazette.*

**AN ARABIC AND ENGLISH DICTIONARY OF THE KORAN.** By **Major J. Penrice, B.A.** 4to. Price 21s.

**MODERN GOTHIC ARCHITECTURE.** By **T. G. Jackson.** Crown 8vo. Price 5s.

"This thoughtful little book is worthy of the perusal of all interested in art or architecture."—*Standard.*
"The reader will find some of the most important doctrines of eminent art teachers practically applied in this little book, which is well written and popular in style."—*Manchester Examiner.*

**A TREATISE ON RELAPSING FEVER.** By **R. T. Lyons,** Assistant-Surgeon, Bengal Army. Small post 8vo. Price 7s. 6d.

"A practical work, thoroughly supported in its views by a series of remarkable cases."—*Standard.*

### FOUR WORKS BY DR. EDWARD SMITH.

I. HEALTH AND DISEASE, as influenced by the Daily, Seasonal, and other Cyclical Changes in the Human System. A New Edition. Price 7s. 6d.
II. FOODS. Second Edition. Profusely Illustrated. Price 5s.
III. PRACTICAL DIETARY FOR FAMILIES, SCHOOLS, AND THE LABOURING CLASSES. A New Edition. Price 3s. 6d.
IV. CONSUMPTION IN ITS EARLY AND REMEDIABLE STAGES. A New Edition. Price 7s. 6d.

**CHOLERA: HOW TO AVOID AND TREAT IT.** Popular and Practical Notes by **Henry Blanc, M.D.** Crown 8vo. Price 4s. 6d.

"A very practical manual, based on experience and careful observation, full of excellent hints on a most dangerous disease."—*Standard.*

SCIENCE—*continued.*

## THE INTERNATIONAL SCIENTIFIC SERIES.

Fourth Edition.

I. THE FORMS OF WATER IN RAIN AND RIVERS, ICE AND GLACIERS. By **J. Tyndall, LL.D., F.R.S.** With 26 Illustrations. Crown 8vo. Price 5s.

Second Edition.

II. PHYSICS AND POLITICS; OR, THOUGHTS ON THE APPLICATION OF THE PRINCIPLES OF "NATURAL SELECTION" AND "INHERITANCE" TO POLITICAL SOCIETY. By **Walter Bagehot.** Crown 8vo. Price 4s.

Third Edition.

III. FOODS. By **Dr. Edward Smith.** Profusely Illustrated. Price 5s.

Third Edition.

IV. MIND AND BODY: THE THEORIES OF THEIR RELATIONS. By **Alexander Bain, LL.D.,** Professor of Logic at the University of Aberdeen. Four Illustrations. Price 4s.

Third Edition.

V. THE STUDY OF SOCIOLOGY. By **Herbert Spencer.** Crown 8vo. Price 5s.

Second Edition.

VI. ON THE CONSERVATION OF ENERGY. By **Professor Balfour Stewart.** Fourteen Engravings. Price 5s.

Second Edition.

VII. ANIMAL LOCOMOTION; or, Walking, Swimming, and Flying. By **Dr. J. B. Pettigrew, M.D., F.R.S.** 119 Illustrations. Price 5s.

Second Edition.

VIII. RESPONSIBILITY IN MENTAL DISEASE. By **Dr. Henry Maudsley.** Price 5s.

Second Edition.

IX. THE NEW CHEMISTRY. By **Professor Josiah P. Cooke,** of the Harvard University. Illustrated. Price 5s.

X. THE SCIENCE OF LAW. By **Professor Sheldon Amos.**

[*Just ready.*

65, *Cornhill;* & 12, *Paternoster Row, London.*

# FORTHCOMING VOLUMES.

**Prof. E. J. MAREY.**
The Animal Frame. [*In the Press.*

**Prof. OSCAR SCHMIDT** (Strasburg Univ.).
The Theory of Descent and Darwinism. [*In the Press.*

**Prof. VOGEL** (Polytechnic Acad. of Berlin).
The Chemical Effects of Light. [*In the Press.*

**Prof. LONMEL** (University of Erlangen).
Optics. [*In the Press.*

{ **Rev. M. J. BERKELEY, M.A., F.L.S.,**
and **M. COOKE, M.A., LL.D.**
Fungi ; their Nature, Influences, and Uses.

**Prof. W. KINGDOM CLIFFORD, M.A.**
The First Principles of the Exact Sciences explained to the non-mathematical.

**Prof. T. H. HUXLEY, LL.D., F.R.S.**
Bodily Motion and Consciousness.

**Dr. W. B. CARPENTER, LL.D., F.R.S.**
The Physical Geography of the Sea.

**Prof. WILLIAM ODLING, F.R.S.**
The Old Chemistry viewed from the new Standpoint.

**W. LAUDER LINDSAY, M.D., F.R.S.E.**
Mind in the Lower Animals.

**Sir JOHN LUBBOCK, Bart., F.R.S.**
The Antiquity of Man.

**Prof. W. T. THISELTON DYER, B.A., B.SC.**
Form and Habit in Flowering Plants.

**Mr. J. N. LOCKYER, F.R.S.**
Spectrum Analysis.

**Prof. MICHAEL FOSTER, M.D.**
Protoplasm and the Cell Theory.

**Prof. W. STANLEY JEVONS.**
Money : and the Mechanism of Exchange.

**Dr. H. CHARLTON BASTIAN, M.D., F.R.S.**
The Brain as an Organ of Mind.

**Prof. A. C. RAMSAY, LL.D., F.R.S.**
Earth Sculpture : Hills, Valleys, Mountains, Plains, Rivers, Lakes ; how they were Produced, and how they have been Destroyed.

**Prof. RUDOLPH VIRCHOW** (Berlin Univ.)
Morbid Physiological Action.

**Prof. CLAUDE BERNARD.**
Physical and Metaphysical Phenomena of Life.

**Prof. H. SAINTE-CLAIRE DEVILLE.**
An Introduction to General Chemistry.

**Prof. WURTZ.**
Atoms and the Atomic Theory.

**Prof. DE QUATREFAGES.**
The Negro Races.

**Prof. LACAZE-DUTHIERS.**
Zoology since Cuvier.

**Prof. BERTHELOT.**
Chemical Synthesis.

**Prof. J. ROSENTHAL.**
General Physiology of Muscles and Nerves.

**Prof. JAMES D. DANA, M.A., LL.D.**
On Cephalization : or, Head-Characters in the Gradation and Progress of Life.

**Prof. S. W. JOHNSON, M.A.**
On the Nutrition of Plants.

**Prof. AUSTIN FLINT, Jr. M.D.**
The Nervous System and its Relation to the Bodily Functions.

**Prof. W. D. WHITNEY.**
Modern Linguistic Science.

**Prof. BERNSTEIN** (University of Halle).
Physiology of the Senses.

**Prof. FERDINAND COHN** (Breslau Univ.).
Thallophytes (Algæ, Lichens, Fungi).

**Prof. HERMANN** (University of Zurich).
Respiration.

**Prof. LEUCKART** (University of Leipsic).
Outlines of Animal Organization.

**Prof. LIEBREICH** (University of Berlin).
Outlines of Toxicology.

**Prof. KUNDT** (University of Strasburg).
On Sound.

**Prof. REES** (University of Erlangen).
On Parasitic Plants.

**Prof. STEINTHAL** (University of Berlin).
Outlines of the Science of Language.

# ESSAYS, LECTURES, AND COLLECTED PAPERS.

**IN STRANGE COMPANY**; or, The Note Book of a Roving Correspondent. By **James Greenwood,** "The Amateur Casual." Second Edition. Crown 8vo. 6s.

"A bright, lively book."—*Standard.*
"Has all the interest of romance."—*Queen.*

"Some of the papers remind us of Charles Lamb on beggars and chimney sweeps."—*Echo.*

**MASTER-SPIRITS.** By **Robert Buchanan.** Post 8vo. 10s. 6d.

" Good Books are the precious life-blood of Master-Spirits."—*Milton.*

" Full of fresh and vigorous writing, such as can only be produced by a man of keen and independent intellect."—*Saturday Review.*
"A very pleasant and readable book."—*Examiner.*

" Written with a beauty of language and a spirit of vigorous enthusiasm rare even in our best living word-painters." *Standard.*
" Mr. Buchanan is a writer whose books the critics may always open with satisfaction . . . both manly and artistic."—*Hour.*

**THEOLOGY IN THE ENGLISH POETS**; COWPER, COLERIDGE, WORDSWORTH, and BURNS. Being Lectures delivered by the **Rev. Stopford A. Brooke,** Chaplain in Ordinary to Her Majesty the Queen. Crown 8vo. 9s.

**SHORT LECTURES ON THE LAND LAWS.** Delivered before the Working Men's College. By **T. Lean Wilkinson.** Crown 8vo, limp cloth. 2s.

"A very handy and intelligible epitome of the general principles of existing land laws."—*Standard.*

**AN ESSAY ON THE CULTURE OF THE OBSERVING POWERS OF CHILDREN,** especially in connection with the Study of Botany. By **Eliza A. Youmans.** Edited, with Notes and a Supplement, by **Joseph Payne, F.C.P.,** Author of "Lectures on the Science and Art of Education," &c. Crown 8vo. 2s. 6d.

"This study, according to her just notions on the subject, is to be fundamentally based on the exercise of the pupil's own powers of observation. He is to see and

examine the properties of plants and flowers at first hand, not merely to be informed of what others have seen and examined."—*Pall Mall Gazette.*

**THE GENIUS OF CHRISTIANITY UNVEILED.** Being Essays by **William Godwin,** Author of "Political Justice," &c. Never before published. 1 vol. Crown 8vo. 7s. 6d.

"Few have thought more clearly and directly than William Godwin, or expressed their reflections with more simplicity and unreserve." *Examiner.*

"The deliberate thoughts of Godwin deserve to be put before the world for reading and consideration."—*Athenæum.*

## MILITARY WORKS.

— • —

**RUSSIA'S ADVANCE EASTWARD**; Translated from the German of LIEUT. STUMM. By **Lt. C. E. H. Vincent.** 1 vol. Crown 8vo. With a Map.

**THE VOLUNTEER, THE MILITIAMAN, AND THE REGULAR SOLDIER**; a Conservative View of the Armies of England, Past, Present, and Future, as Seen in January, 1874. By **A Public School Boy.** 1 vol. Crown 8vo.

**THE OPERATIONS OF THE FIRST ARMY, UNDER STEIN-METZ.** By **Major von Schell.** Translated by **Captain E. O. Hollist.** Demy 8vo. Uniform with the other volumes in the Series. Price 10s. 6d.

**THE OPERATIONS OF THE FIRST ARMY UNDER GEN. VON GOEBEN.** By **Major von Schell.** Translated by **Col. C. H. von Wright.** Four Maps. Demy 8vo. Price 9s.

**THE OPERATIONS OF THE FIRST ARMY IN NORTHERN FRANCE AGAINST FAIDHERBE.** By **Colonel Count Hermann von Wartensleben,** Chief of the Staff of the First Army. Translated by **Colonel C. H. von Wright.** In demy 8vo. Uniform with the above. Price 9s.

"Very clear, simple, yet eminently instructive, is this history. It is not overladen with useless details, is written in good taste, and possesses the inestimable value of being in great measure the record of operations actually witnessed by the author, supplemented by official documents."—*Athenæum.*

**THE GERMAN ARTILLERY IN THE BATTLES NEAR METZ.** Based on the official reports of the German Artillery. By **Captain Hoffbauer,** Instructor in the German Artillery and Engineer School. Translated by **Capt. E. O. Hollist.**     [*Preparing.*

**THE OPERATIONS OF THE BAVARIAN ARMY CORPS.** By **Captain Hugo Helvig.** Translated by **Captain G. S. Schwabe.** With 5 large Maps. Demy 8vo. In 2 vols. Price 24s. Uniform with the other Books in the Series.

**AUSTRIAN CAVALRY EXERCISE.** From an Abridged Edition compiled by CAPTAIN ILLIA WOINOVITS, of the General Staff, on the Tactical Regulations of the Austrian Army, and prefaced by a General Sketch of the Organisation, &c., of the Country. Translated by **Captain W. S. Cooke.** Crown 8vo, cloth. Price 7s.

*History of the Organisation, Equipment, and War Services of*

**THE REGIMENT OF BENGAL ARTILLERY.** Compiled from Published Official and other Records, and various private sources, by **Major Francis W. Stubbs,** Royal (late Bengal) Artillery. Vol. I. will contain WAR SERVICES. The Second Volume will be published separately, and will contain the HISTORY OF THE ORGANISATION AND EQUIPMENT OF THE REGIMENT. In 2 vols. 8vo. With Maps and Plans.     [*Preparing.*

**VICTORIES AND DEFEATS.** An Attempt to explain the Causes which have led to them. An Officer's Manual. By **Col. R. P. Anderson.** Demy 8vo. Price 14s.

"The present book proves that he is a diligent student of military history, his illustrations ranging over a wide field, and including ancient and modern Indian and European warfare." *Standard.*

"The young officer should have it al-

ways at hand to open anywhere and read a bit, and we warrant him that let that bit be ever so small it will give him material for an hour's thinking."—*United Service Gazette.*

**THE FRONTAL ATTACK OF INFANTRY.** By **Capt. Laymann,** Instructor of Tactics at the Military College, Neisse. Translated by **Colonel Edward Newdigate.** Crown 8vo, limp cloth. Price 2s. 6d.

"An exceedingly useful kind of book. A valuable acquisition to the military student's library. It recounts, in the first place, the opinions and tactical formations which regulated the German army during the early battles of the late war; explains

how these were modified in the course of the campaign by the terrible and unanticipated effect of the fire; and how, accordingly, troops should be trained to attack in future wars." *Naval and Military Gazette.*

**ELEMENTARY MILITARY GEOGRAPHY, RECONNOITRING, AND SKETCHING.** Compiled for Non-Commissioned Officers and Soldiers of all Arms. By **Lieut. C. E. H. Vincent,** Royal Welsh Fusiliers. Small crown 8vo. Price 2s. 6d.

"This manual takes into view the necessity of every soldier knowing how to read a military map, in order to know to what points in an enemy's country to direct his attention; and provides for this necessity

by giving, in terse and sensible language, definitions of varieties of ground and the advantages they present in warfare, together with a number of useful hints in military sketching."—*Naval and Military Gazette.*

**THREE WORKS BY LIEUT.-COL. THE HON. A. ANSON, V.C., M.P.**

THE ABOLITION OF PURCHASE AND THE ARMY REGULATION BILL OF 1871. Crown 8vo. Price One Shilling.

ARMY RESERVES AND MILITIA REFORMS. Crown 8vo. Sewed. Price One Shilling. THE STORY OF THE SUPERSESSIONS. Crown 8vo. Price Sixpence.

**STUDIES IN THE NEW INFANTRY TACTICS.** Parts I. & II. By **Major W. von Scheref.** Translated from the German by **Col. Lumley Graham.** Price 7s. 6d.

"The subject of the respective advantages of attack and defence, and of the methods in which each form of battle should be carried out under the fire of modern arms, is exhaustively and admir-

ably treated; indeed, we cannot but consider it to be decidedly superior to any work which has hitherto appeared in English upon this all-important subject."— *Standard.*

Second Edition. Revised and Corrected.

**TACTICAL DEDUCTIONS FROM THE WAR OF 1870—71.** By **Captain A. von Boguslawski.** Translated by **Colonel Lumley Graham,** late 18th (Royal Irish) Regiment. Demy 8vo. Uniform with the above. Price 7s.

"We must, without delay, impress brain and forethought into the British Service; and we cannot commence the good work too soon, or better, than by placing the two books 'The Operations of

the German Armies' and 'Tactical Deductions') we have here criticised, in every military library, and introducing them as class books in every tactical school."— *United Service Gazette.*

**THE OPERATIONS OF THE SOUTH ARMY IN JANUARY AND FEBRUARY, 1871.** Compiled from the Official War Documents of the Head-quarters of the Southern Army. By **Count Hermann von Wartensleben,** Colonel in the Prussian General Staff. Translated by **Colonel C. H. von Wright.** Demy 8vo, with Maps. Uniform with the above. Price 6s.

## THE ARMY OF THE NORTH-GERMAN CONFEDERATION.

A Brief Description of its Organisation, of the different Branches of the Service and their "Rôle" in War, of its Mode of Fighting, &c. By a **Prussian General.** Translated from the German by **Col. Edward Newdigate.** Demy 8vo. Price 5s.

" The work is quite essential to the full use of the other volumes of the ' German Military Series,' which Messrs. King are now producing in handsome uniform style." —*United Service Magazine.*

" Every page of the book deserves at-

tentive study . . . . The information given on mobilisation, garrison troops, keeping up establishment during war, and on the employment of the different branches of the service, is of great value."—*Standard.*

## THE OPERATIONS OF THE GERMAN ARMIES IN FRANCE, FROM SEDAN TO THE END OF THE WAR OF 1870-71.

With Large Official Map. From the Journals of the Head-quarters Staff, by **Major Wm. Blume.** Translated by **E. M. Jones,** Major 20th Foot, late Professor of Military History, Sandhurst. Demy 8vo. Price 9s.

" The book is of absolute necessity to the military student. . . . The work is one of high merit."—*United Service Gazette.*

" The work of Major von Blume in its English dress forms the most valuable addition to our stock of works upon

the war that our press has put forth. Our space forbids our doing more than commending it earnestly as the most authentic and instructive narrative of the second section of the war that has yet appeared."—*Saturday Review.*

## HASTY INTRENCHMENTS. By Colonel A. Brialmont. Translated by **Lieutenant Charles A. Empson, R.A.** Demy 8vo. Nine Plates. Price 6s.

" A valuable contribution to military literature."—*Athenæum.*

" In seven short chapters it gives plain directions for forming shelter-trenches, with the best method of carrying the necessary tools, and it offers practical illustrations of the use of hasty intrenchments on the field of battle."—*United Service Magazine.*

" It supplies that which our own text-books give but imperfectly, viz., hints as to how a position can best be strengthened by means . . . of such extemporised intrenchments and batteries as can be thrown up by infantry in the space of four or five hours . . . deserves to become a standard military work."—*Standard.*

## STUDIES IN LEADING TROOPS. By Colonel von Verdy Du Vernois. An authorised and accurate Translation by **Lieutenant H. J. T. Hildyard,** 71st Foot. Parts I. and II. Demy 8vo. Price 7s.

*.* General BEAUCHAMP WALKER says of this work:—" I recommend the first two numbers of Colonel von Verdy's ' Studies ' to the attentive perusal of my brother officers. They supply a want which I have often felt during my service in this country, namely, a minuter tactical detail of the minor operations of war than any but the most observant and for-

tunately-placed staff-officer is in a position to give. I have read and re-read them very carefully, I hope with profit, certainly with great interest, and believe that practice, in the sense of these ' Studies,' would be a valuable preparation for manœuvres on a more extended scale."—*Berlin, June, 1872.*

## CAVALRY FIELD DUTY. By **Major-General von Mirus.** Translated by **Captain Frank S. Russell,** 14th (King's) Hussars. Crown 8vo. limp cloth. Price 7s. 6d.

## DISCIPLINE AND DRILL. Four Lectures delivered to the London Scottish Rifle Volunteers. By **Captain S. Flood Page.** A New and Cheaper Edition. Price 1s.

" An admirable collection of lectures." —*Times.*

" The very useful and interesting work." —*Volunteer Service Gazette.*

# INDIA AND THE EAST.

**THE THREATENED FAMINE IN BENGAL;** How IT MAY BE MET, AND THE RECURRENCE OF FAMINES IN INDIA PREVENTED. Being No. 1 of "Occasional Notes on Indian Affairs." By **Sir H. Bartle E. Frere, G.C.B., G.C.S.I.,** &c. &c. Crown 8vo. With 3 Maps. Price 5s.

**THE ORIENTAL SPORTING MAGAZINE.** A Reprint of the first 5 Volumes, in 2 Volumes, demy 8vo. Price 28s.

"Lovers of sport will find ample amusement in the varied contents of these two volumes."—*Allen's Indian Mail.*
"Full of interest for the sportsman and naturalist. Full of thrilling adventures of sportsmen who have attacked the fiercest and most gigantic specimens of the animal world in their native jungle. It is seldom we get so many exciting incidents in a similar amount of space ... Well suited to the libraries of country gentlemen and all those who are interested in sporting matters."—*Civil Service Gazette.*

**THE EUROPEAN IN INDIA.** A Hand-book of Practical Information for those proceeding to, or residing in, the East Indies, relating to Outfits, Routes, Time for Departure, Indian Climate, &c. By **Edmund C. P. Hull.** With a MEDICAL GUIDE FOR ANGLO-INDIANS. Being a Compendium of Advice to Europeans in India, relating to the Preservation and Regulation of Health. By **R. S. Mair, M.D., F.R.C.S.E.,** late Deputy Coroner of Madras. In 1 vol. Post 8vo. Price 6s.

"Full of all sorts of useful information to the English settler or traveller in India."—*Standard.*
"One of the most valuable books ever published in India—valuable for its sound information, its careful array of pertinent facts, and its sterling common sense. It supplies a want which few persons may have discovered, but which everybody will at once recognise when once the contents of the book have been mastered. The medical part of the work is invaluable."—*Calcutta Guardian.*

**THE MEDICAL GUIDE FOR ANGLO-INDIANS.** Being a Compendium of advice to Europeans in India, relating to the Preservation and Regulation of Health. By **R. S. Mair, F.R.C.S.E.,** late Deputy Coroner of Madras. Reprinted, with numerous additions and corrections, from "The European in India."

**EASTERN EXPERIENCES.** By **L. Bowring, C.S.I.,** Lord Canning's Private Secretary, and for many years the Chief Commissioner of Mysore and Coorg. In 1 vol. Demy 8vo. Price 16s. Illustrated with Maps and Diagrams.

"An admirable and exhaustive geographical, political, and industrial survey."—*Athenæum.*
"This compact and methodical summary of the most authentic information relating to countries whose welfare is intimately connected with our own."—*Daily News.*
"Interesting even to the general reader, but more especially so to those who may have a special concern in that portion of our Indian Empire."—*Post.*

INDIA AND THE EAST—*continued.*

## TAS-HĪL UL KALĀM; OR, HINDUSTANI MADE EASY. By **Captain W. R. M. Holroyd,** Bengal Staff Corps, Director of Public Instruction, Punjab. Crown 8vo. Price 5s.

"As clear and as instructive as possible." —*Standard.*

"Contains a great deal of most necessary

information, that is not to be found in any other work on the subject that has crossed our path."—*Homeward Mail.*

Second Edition.

## WESTERN INDIA BEFORE AND DURING THE MUTINIES. Pictures drawn from Life. By **Major-Gen. Sir George Le Grand Jacob, K.C.S.I., C.B.** In 1 vol. Crown 8vo. Price 7s. 6d.

"The most important contribution to the history of Western India during the Mutinies which has yet, in a popular form, been made public."—*Athenæum.*

"Few men more competent than himself to speak authoritatively concerning Indian affairs."—*Standard.*

## EDUCATIONAL COURSE OF SECULAR SCHOOL BOOKS FOR INDIA. Edited by **J. S. Laurie,** of the Inner Temple, Barrister-at-Law; formerly H.M. Inspector of Schools, England; Assistant Royal Commissioner, Ireland; Special Commissioner, African Settlements; Director of Public Instruction, Ceylon.

"These valuable little works will prove of real service to many of our readers, especially to those who intend entering the

Civil Service of India." — *Civil Service Gazette.*

*The following Works are now ready:—*

|  | s. d. |  | s. d. |
|---|---|---|---|
| THE FIRST HINDUSTANI READER, stiff linen wrapper | 0 6 | GEOGRAPHY OF INDIA, with Maps and Historical Appendix, | |
| Ditto ditto strongly bound in cloth | 0 9 | tracing the growth of the British | |
| THE SECOND HINDUSTANI READER, stiff linen wrapper | 0 6 | Empire in Hindustan. 128 pp. | |
| Ditto ditto strongly bound in cloth | 0 9 | Cloth | 1 6 |

*In the Press.*

| | |
|---|---|
| ELEMENTARY GEOGRAPHY OF INDIA. | FACTS AND FEATURES OF INDIAN HISTORY, in a series of alternating Reading Lessons and Memory Exercises. |

## EXCHANGE TABLES OF STERLING AND INDIAN RUPEE CURRENCY, UPON A NEW AND EXTENDED SYSTEM, embracing Values from One Farthing to One Hundred Thousand Pounds, and at rates progressing, in Sixteenths of a Penny, from 1s. 9d. to 2s. 3d. per Rupee. By **Donald Fraser,** Accountant to the British Indian Steam Navigation Co. Limited. Royal 8vo. Price 10s. 6d.

"The calculations must have entailed great labour on the author, but the work is one which we fancy must become a standard one in all business houses which

have dealings with any country where the rupee and the English pound are standard coins of currency."—*Inverness Courier.*

# BOOKS FOR THE YOUNG AND FOR LENDING LIBRARIES.

**AUNT MARY'S BRAN PIE.** By the Author of "St. Olave's," "When I was a Little Girl," &c. *[In the Press.*

**BY STILL WATERS.** A Story in One Volume. By **Edward Garrett.** *[Preparing.*

**WAKING AND WORKING; OR, FROM GIRLHOOD TO WOMANHOOD.** By **Mrs. G. S. Reaney.** 1 vol. Crown 8vo. Illustrated. *[Preparing.*

**PRETTY LESSONS IN VERSE FOR GOOD CHILDREN,** with some Lessons in Latin, in Easy Rhyme. By **Sara Coleridge.** A New Edition. *[Preparing.*

## NEW WORKS BY HESBA STRETTON.

**CASSY.** A New Story, by **Hesba Stretton.** Square crown 8vo, Illustrated, uniform with "Lost Gip." Price 1s. 6d.

**THE KING'S SERVANTS.** By **Hesba Stretton,** Author of "Lost Gip." Square crown 8vo, uniform with "Lost Gip." 8 Illustrations. Price 1s. 6d.

Part I.—Faithful in Little. Part II.—Unfaithful. Part III.—Faithful in Much.

**LOST GIP.** By **Hesba Stretton,** Author of "Little Meg," "Alone in London." Square crown 8vo. Six Illustrations. Price 1s. 6d.

\*\* *A HANDSOMELY BOUND EDITION, WITH TWELVE ILLUSTRA-TIONS, PRICE HALF-A-CROWN.*

**DADDY'S PET.** By **Mrs. Ellen Ross (Nelsie Brook).** Square crown 8vo, uniform with "Lost Gip." 6 Illustrations. Price 1s.

" We have been more than pleased with this simple bit of writing." — *Christian World.* | " Full of deep feeling and true and noble sentiment."--*Brighton Gazette.*

**SEEKING HIS FORTUNE, AND OTHER STORIES.** Crown 8vo. Four Illustrations. Price 3s. 6d.

Contents.—Seeking his Fortune.—Oluf and Stephanoff.—What's in a Name?—Contrast.—Onesta.

### Three Works by MARTHA FARQUHARSON.

**I. ELSIE DINSMORE.** Crown 8vo. 3s. 6d.

**II. ELSIE'S GIRLHOOD.** Crown 8vo. 3s. 6d.

**III. ELSIE'S HOLIDAYS AT ROSELANDS.** Crown 8vo. 3s. 6d.

Each Story is independent and complete in itself. They are published in uniform size and price, and are elegantly bound and illustrated.

**THE AFRICAN CRUISER.** A Midshipman's Adventures on the West Coast. A Book for Boys. By S. **Whitchurch Sadler, R.N.,** Author of "Marshall Vavasour." Illustrations. Crown 8vo. 3s. 6d.

" A capital story of youthful adventure. . . . Sea loving boys will find few pleasanter gift books this season than 'The African Cruiser.'"—*Hour.* | " Sea yarns have always been in favour with boys, but this, written in a brisk style by a thorough sailor, is crammed full of adventures."—*Times.*

**THE LITTLE WONDER-HORN.** By **Jean Ingelow.** A Second Series of "*Stories told to a Child.*" Fifteen Illustrations. Cloth, gilt. 3*s.* 6*d.*

"We like all the contents of the 'Little Wonder-Horn' very much."—*Athenæum.*
"We recommend it with confidence."—*Pall Mall Gazette.*

"Full of fresh and vigorous fancy : it is worthy of the author of some of the best of our modern verse."—*Standard.*

**BRAVE MEN'S FOOTSTEPS.** A Book of Example and Anecdote for Young People. Second Edition. By the Editor of "**Men who have Risen.**" With Four Illustrations, by **C. Doyle.** 3*s.* 6*d.*

"A readable and instructive volume."—*Examiner.*
"The little volume is precisely of the stamp to win the favour of those who, in

choosing a gift for a boy, would consult his moral development as well as his temporary pleasure."—*Daily Telegraph.*

**PLUCKY FELLOWS.** A Book for Boys. By **Stephen J. Mac Kenna.** With Six Illustrations. Second Edition. Crown 8vo. 3*s.* 6*d.*

"This is one of the very best 'Books for Boys' which have been issued this year."—*Morning Advertiser.*
"A thorough book for boys . . . written

throughout in a manly straightforward manner that is sure to win the hearts of the children."—*London Society.*

**GUTTA-PERCHA WILLIE, THE WORKING GENIUS.** By **George Macdonald.** With Illustrations by **Arthur Hughes.** Crown 8vo. Second Edition. 3*s.* 6*d.*

"The cleverest child we know assures us she has read this story through five times. Mr. Macdonald will, we are convinced,

accept that verdict upon his little work as final."—*Spectator.*

**THE TRAVELLING MENAGERIE.** By **Charles Camden,** Author of "Hoity Toity." Illustrated by **J. Mahoney.** Crown 8vo. 3*s.* 6*d.*

"A capital little book . . . . deserves a wide circulation among our boys and girls."—*Hour.*

"A very attractive story." — *Public Opinion.*

**THE DESERT PASTOR, JEAN JAROUSSEAU.** Translated from the French of **Eugene Pelletan.** By **Colonel E. P. De L'Hoste.** In fcap. 8vo, with an Engraved Frontispiece. New Edition. 3*s.* 6*d.*

"A touching record of the struggles in the cause of religious liberty of a real man."—*Graphic.*
"There is a poetical simplicity and picturesqueness ; the noblest heroism ; unpre-

tentious religion : pure love, and the spectacle of a household brought up in the fear of the Lord. . . . ."—*Illustrated London News.*

**THE DESERTED SHIP.** A Real Story of the Atlantic. By **Cupples Howe,** Master Mariner. Illustrated by **Townley Green.** Crown 8vo. 3*s.* 6*d.*

"Curious adventures with bears, seals, and other Arctic animals, and with scarcely more human Esquimaux, form the mass of

material with which the story deals, and will much interest boys who have a spice of romance in their composition."—*Courant.*

**HOITY TOITY, THE GOOD LITTLE FELLOW.** By **Charles Camden.** Illustrated. Crown 8vo. 3*s.* 6*d.*

"Relates very pleasantly the history of a charming little fellow who meddles always with a kindly disposition with other people's

affairs and helps them to do right. There are many shrewd lessons to be picked up in this clever little story."—*Public Opinion.*

BOOKS FOR THE YOUNG, ETC.—*continued.*

**SLAVONIC FAIRY TALES.** From Russian, Servian, Polish, and Bohemian Sources. Translated by **John T. Naaké.** Crown 8vo. Illustrated. Price 5s.

**AT SCHOOL WITH AN OLD DRAGOON.** By **Stephen J. Mac Kenna.** Crown 8vo. Six Illustrations. Price 5s.

"Consisting almost entirely of startling stories of military adventure . . . Boys will find them sufficiently exciting reading."—*Times.*

"These yarns give some very spirited and interesting descriptions of soldiering in various parts of the world."—*Spectator.*

"Mr. Mac Kenna's former work, 'Plucky Fellows,' is already a general favourite, and those who read the stories of the Old Dragoon will find that he has still plenty of materials at hand for pleasant tales, and has lost none of his power in telling them well."—*Standard.*

**FANTASTIC STORIES.** Translated from the German of **Richard Leander,** by **Paulina B. Granville.** Crown 8vo. Eight full-page Illustrations, by **M. E. Fraser-Tytler.** Price 5s.

"Short, quaint, and, as they are fitly called, fantastic, they deal with all manner of subjects."—*Guardian.*

"'Fantastic' is certainly the right epithet to apply to some of these strange tales."—*Examiner*

Third Edition.
**STORIES IN PRECIOUS STONES.** By **Helen Zimmern.** With Six Illustrations. Crown 8vo. Price 5s.

"A pretty little book which fanciful young persons will appreciate, and which will remind its readers of many a legend, and many an imaginary virtue attached to the gems they are so fond of wearing."—*Post.*

"A series of pretty tales which are half fantastic, half natural, and pleasantly quaint, as befits stories intended for the young."—*Daily Telegraph.*

**THE GREAT DUTCH ADMIRALS.** By **Jacob de Liefde.** Crown 8vo. Illustrated. Price 5s.

"May be recommended as a wholesome present for boys. They will find in it numerous tales of adventure."—*Athenæum.*

"A really good book."—*Standard.*
"A really excellent book."—*Spectator.*

**PHANTASMION.** A Fairy Romance. A new Edition. By **Sara Coleridge.** With an Introductory Preface by the **Right Hon. Lord Coleridge of Ottery S. Mary.** In 1 vol. Crown 8vo. Price 7s. 6d.

**LAYS OF A KNIGHT ERRANT IN MANY LANDS.** By **Major-General Sir Vincent Eyre, C.B., G.C.S.I., &c.** Square crown 8vo. Six Illustrations. Price 7s. 6d.

Pharaoh Land.
Home Land.
Wonder Land.
Rhine Land.

**BEATRICE AYLMER AND OTHER TALES.** By the Author of "Brompton Rectory." 1 vol. Crown 8vo. [*Preparing.*

**THE TASMANIAN LILY.** By **James Bonwick.** Crown 8vo. Illustrated. Price 5s.

"An interesting and useful work."—*Hour.*
"The characters of the story are capitally

conceived, and are full of those touches which give them a natural appearance."—*Public Opinion.*

**MIKE HOWE, THE BUSHRANGER OF VAN DIEMEN'S LAND.** By **James Bonwick,** Author of "The Tasmanian Lily," &c. Crown 8vo. With a Frontispiece.

"He illustrates the career of the bushranger half a century ago; and this he does in a highly creditable manner; his delineations of life in the bush are, to say

the least, exquisite, and his representations of character are very marked."—*Edinburgh Courant.*

# WORKS BY ALFRED TENNYSON, D.C.L.,

### POET LAUREATE.

## THE CABINET EDITION.

Messrs. HENRY S. KING & Co. have the pleasure to announce that they will immediately issue an Edition of the Laureate's works, in *Ten Monthly Volumes*, foolscap 8vo, to be entitled " The Cabinet Edition," at *Half-a-Crown each*, which will contain the whole of Mr. Tennyson's works. The first volume will be illustrated by a beautiful Photographic Portrait, and subsequent Volumes will each contain a Frontispiece. They will be tastefully bound in Crimson Cloth, and will be issued in the following order :—

| Vol. | | Vol. | |
|---|---|---|---|
| 1. | EARLY POEMS. | 6. | IDYLLS OF THE KING. |
| 2. | ENGLISH IDYLLS & OTHER POEMS. | 7. | IDYLL OF THE KING. |
| 3. | LOCKSLEY HALL & OTHER POEMS. | 8. | THE PRINCESS. |
| 4. | AYLMER'S FIELD & OTHER POEMS. | 9. | MAUD AND ENOCH ARDEN. |
| 5. | IDYLLS OF THE KING. | 10. | IN MEMORIAM. |

Subscribers' names received by all Booksellers.

| | PRICE. | |
|---|---|---|
| | *s.* | *d.* |
| POEMS. Small 8vo. . . . . . . | 9 | 0 |
| MAUD AND OTHER POEMS. Small 8vo. . . | 5 | 0 |
| THE PRINCESS. Small 8vo. . . . . | 5 | 0 |
| IDYLLS OF THE KING. Small 8vo. . . | 7 | 0 |
| „ „ Collected. Small 8vo. . | 12 | 0 |
| ENOCH ARDEN, &c. Small 8vo. . . . . | 6 | 0 |
| THE HOLY GRAIL, AND OTHER POEMS. Small 8vo. . | 7 | 0 |
| GARETH AND LYNETTE. Small 8vo. . . . | 5 | 0 |
| SELECTIONS FROM THE ABOVE WORKS. Square 8vo, cloth extra . | 5 | 0 |
| SONGS FROM THE ABOVE WORKS. Square 8vo, cloth extra . | 5 | 0 |
| IN MEMORIAM. Small 8vo. . . . . | 6 | 0 |
| LIBRARY EDITION OF MR. TENNYSON'S WORKS. 6 vols. Post 8vo, each | 10 | 6 |
| POCKET VOLUME EDITION OF MR. TENNYSON'S WORKS. 10 vols., in | | |
| neat case . . . . . . . | 45 | 0 |
| „ gilt edges . . . . . . . | 50 | 0 |
| THE WINDOW ; OR, THE SONGS OF THE WRENS. A Series of Songs. | | |
| By ALFRED TENNYSON. With Music by ARTHUR SULLIVAN. 4to, cloth, gilt extra | 21 | 0 |

## POETRY.

**LYRICS OF LOVE**, Selected and arranged from Shakspeare to Tennyson, by **W. Davenport Adams**. Fcap. 8vo. Price 3s. 6d.

"We cannot too highly commend this work, delightful in its contents and so pretty in its outward adornings."—*Standard.*

"Carefully selected and elegantly got up . . It is particularly rich in poems from living writers."—*John Bull.*

**WILLIAM CULLEN BRYANT'S POEMS.** Red-line Edition. Handsomely bound. With Illustrations and Portrait of the Author. Price 7s. 6d. A Cheaper Edition is also published. Price 3s. 6d.

*These are the only complete English Editions sanctioned by the Author.*

**ENGLISH SONNETS.** Collected and Arranged by **John Dennis**. Small crown 8vo. Elegantly bound. Price 3s. 6d.

"An exquisite selection, a selection which every lover of poetry will consult again and again with delight. The notes are very useful. . . . The volume is one for which

English literature owes Mr. Dennis the heartiest thanks."—*Spectator.*

"Mr. Dennis has shown great judgment in this selection."—*Saturday Review.*

Second Edition.

**HOME-SONGS FOR QUIET HOURS.** By the **Rev. Canon R. H. Baynes**, Editor of "English Lyrics" and "Lyra Anglicana." Handsomely printed and bound. Price 3s. 6d.

**POEMS.** By **Annette F. C. Knight**. Fcap. 8vo. [*Preparing.*

**POEMS.** By the **Rev. J. W. A. Taylor.** Fcap. 8vo. [*In the Press.*

**ALEXANDER THE GREAT.** A Dramatic Poem. By **Aubrey de Vere**, Author of "The Legends of St. Patrick," &c. Crown 8vo. [*Nearly ready.*

**THE DISCIPLES. A New Poem.** By **Harriet Eleanor Hamilton King**. Crown 8vo. Price 7s. 6d.

**ASPROMONTE, AND OTHER POEMS.** Second Edition. Cloth, 4s. 6d.

"The volume is anonymous, but there is no reason for the author to be ashamed of it. The 'Poems of Italy' are evidently inspired by genuine enthusiasm in the cause espoused ; and one of them, 'The

Execution of Felice Orsini,' has much poetic merit, the event celebrated being told with dramatic force."—*Athenæum.*

"The verse is fluent and free."—*Spectator.*

**SONGS FOR MUSIC.** By **Four Friends.** Square crown 8vo. Price 5s.

CONTAINING SONGS BY

Reginald A. Gatty.            Stephen H. Gatty.
Greville J. Chester.         Juliana H. Ewing.

"A charming gift-book, which will be very popular with lovers of poetry." *John Bull.*

**ROBERT BUCHANAN, THE POETICAL AND PROSE WORKS OF.** Collected Edition, in 5 Vols. Vol. I. contains,—"Ballads and Romances ;" "Ballads and Poems of Life," and a Portrait of the Author.

Vol. II. "Ballads and Poems of Life ;" "Allegories and Sonnets."

Vol. III. "Cruiskeen Sonnets ;" "Book of Orm ;" "Political Mystics."

*The Contents of the remaining Volumes will be duly announced.*

**THOUGHTS IN VERSE.** Small crown 8vo. Price 1s. 6d.

This is a Collection of Verses expressive of religious feeling, written from a Theistic stand-point.

POETRY—*continued.*

**COSMOS. A Poem.** Small crown 8vo. Price 3s. 6d.

SUBJECT.— Nature in the Past and in the Present.— Man in the Past and in the Present.—The Future.

**NARCISSUS AND OTHER POEMS.** By E. Carpenter. Small crown 8vo. Price 5s.

"Displays considerable poetic force."— *Queen.*

**A TALE OF THE SEA, SONNETS, AND OTHER POEMS.** By James Howell. Crown 8vo. Cloth, 5s.

"Mr. Howell has a keen perception of the beauties of nature, and a just appreciation of the charities of life. . . . Mr. Howell's book deserves, and will probably receive, a warm reception."—*Pall Mall Gazette.*

**IMITATIONS FROM THE GERMAN OF SPITTA AND TERSTEGEN.** By Lady Durand. Crown 8vo. 4s.

"A charming little volume. . . . Will be a very valuable assistance to peaceful, meditative souls."—*Church Herald.*

Second Edition.

**VIGNETTES IN RHYME.** Collected Verses. By Austin Dobson. Crown 8vo. Price 5s.

"Clever, clear-cut, and careful."—*Athenæum.*

"As a writer of Vers de Société, Mr. Dobson is almost, if not quite, unrivalled."—*Examiner.*

"Lively, innocent, elegant in expression, and graceful in fancy."—*Morning Post.*

**ON VIOL AND FLUTE.** A New Volume of Poems, by Edmund W. Gosse. With a Frontispiece by W. B. Scott. Crown 8vo. 5s.

"A careful perusal of his verses will show that he is a poet. . . . His song has the grateful, murmuring sound which reminds one of the softness and deliciousness of summer time. . . . There is much that is good in the volume."—*Spectator.*

**METRICAL TRANSLATIONS FROM THE GREEK AND LATIN POETS, AND OTHER POEMS.** By R. B. Boswell, M.A. Oxon. Crown 8vo. 5s.

**EASTERN LEGENDS AND STORIES IN ENGLISH VERSE.** By Lieutenant Norton Powlett, Royal Artillery. Crown 8vo. 5s.

"There is a rollicking sense of fun about the stories, joined to marvellous power of rhyming, and plenty of swing, which irresistibly reminds us of our old favourite."—*Graphic.*

**EDITH ; OR, LOVE AND LIFE IN CHESHIRE.** By T. Ashe, Author of the "Sorrows of Hypsipyle," etc. Sewed. Price 6d.

"A really fine poem, full of tender, subtle touches of feeling."—*Manchester News.*

"Pregnant from beginning to end with the results of careful observation and imaginative power."—*Chester Chronicle.*

**THE GALLERY OF PIGEONS, AND OTHER POEMS.** By Theo. Marzials. Crown 8vo. 4s. 6d.

"A conceit abounding in prettiness."— *Examiner.*

"The rush of fresh, sparkling fancies is too rapid, too sustained, too abundant, not to be spontaneous."—*Academy.*

**THE INN OF STRANGE MEETINGS, AND OTHER POEMS.** By Mortimer Collins. Crown 8vo. 5s.

"Abounding in quiet humour, in bright fancy, in sweetness and melody of expression, and, at times, in the tenderest touches of pathos."—*Graphic.*

"Mr. Collins has an undercurrent of chivalry and romance beneath the trifling vein of good-humoured banter which is the special characteristic of his verse."— *Athenæum.*

**EROS AGONISTES.** By E. B. D. Crown 8vo. 3s. 6d.

"It is not the least merit of these pages that they are everywhere illumined with moral and religious sentiment suggested, not paraded, of the brightest, purest character."—*Standard.*

**CALDERON'S DRAMAS.** Translated from the Spanish. By Denis Florence MacCarthy. 10s.

"The lambent verse flows with an ease, spirit, and music perfectly natural, liberal, and harmonious."—*Spectator.*

"It is impossible to speak too highly of this beautiful work."—*Month.*

**SONGS FOR SAILORS.** By Dr. W. C. Bennett. Dedicated by Special Request to H. R. H. the Duke of Edinburgh. Crown 8vo. 3s. 6d. With Steel Portrait and Illustrations.

An Edition in Illustrated paper Covers. Price 1s.

**WALLED IN, AND OTHER POEMS.** By the Rev. Henry J. Bulkeley. Crown 8vo. 5s.

"A remarkable book of genuine poetry." —*Evening Standard.*

"Genuine power displayed."— *Examiner.*

"Poetical feeling is manifest here, and the diction of the poem is unimpeachable." —*Pall Mall Gazette.*

## POETRY—*continued.*

**SONGS OF LIFE AND DEATH.** By John Payne, Author of "Intaglios," "Sonnets," "The Masque of Shadows," etc. Crown 8vo. 5s.

"The art of ballad-writing has long been lost in England, and Mr. Payne may claim to be its restorer. It is a perfect delight to meet with such a ballad as ' May Margaret' in the present volume." — *Westminster Review.*

**A NEW VOLUME OF SONNETS.** By the Rev. C. Tennyson Turner. Crown 8vo. 4s. 6d.

"Mr. Turner is a genuine poet : his song is sweet and pure, beautiful in expression, and often subtle in thought."—*Pall Mall Gazette.*

"The light of a devout, gentle, and kindly spirit, a delicate and graceful fancy, a keen intelligence irradiates these thoughts." - *Contemporary Review.*

**THE DREAM AND THE DEED, AND OTHER POEMS.** By Patrick Scott, Author of " Footpaths between Two Worlds," etc. Fcap. 8vo. Cloth, 5s.

"A bitter and able satire on the vice and follies of the day, literary, social, and political."—*Standard.*

"Shows real poetic power coupled with evidences of satirical energy."—*Edinburgh Daily Review.*

**GOETHE'S FAUST.** A New Translation in Rime. By the Rev. C. Kegan Paul. Crown 8vo. 6s.

"His translation is the most minutely accurate that has yet been produced. . . " —*Examiner.*

"Mr. Paul is a zealous and a faithful interpreter."—*Saturday Review.*

**SONGS OF TWO WORLDS.** First Series. By a New Writer. Fcap. 8vo, cloth. 5s. Second Edition.

"These poems will assuredly take high rank among the class to which they belong." —*British Quarterly Review, April 1st.*

"No extracts could do justice to the exquisite tones, the felicitous phrasing and delicately wrought harmonies of some of these poems." — *Nonconformist.*

"A purity and delicacy of feeling like morning air."—*Graphic.*

**SONGS OF TWO WORLDS.** Second Series. By the Author of " Songs of Two Worlds." Crown 8vo. [*In the Press.*

**THE LEGENDS OF ST. PATRICK AND OTHER POEMS.** By Aubrey de Vere. Crown 8vo. 5s.

"Mr. De Vere's versification in his earlier poems is characterised by great sweetness and simplicity. He is master of his instrument, and rarely offends the ear with false notes." -*Pall Mall Gazette.*

"We have but space to commend the varied structure of his verse, the carefulness of his grammar, and his excellent English."—*Saturday Review.*

# FICTION.

**AILEEN FERRERS.** By Susan Morley. In 2 vols. Crown 8vo, cloth. [*Immediately.*

**IDOLATRY.** A Romance. By Julian Hawthorne. Author of " Bressant." 2 vols. Crown 8vo, cloth.

**VANESSA.** By the Author of " Thomasina," " Dorothy," etc. 2 vols. Crown 8vo.

**CIVIL SERVICE.** By J. P. Listado. Author of " Maurice Rhynhart." 2 vols. Crown 8vo.

**JUDITH GWYNNE.** By Lisle Carr. In 3 vols. Crown 8vo, cloth.

**TOO LATE.** By Mrs. Newman. 2 vols. Crown 8vo.

**LADY MORETOUN'S DAUGHTER.** By Mrs. Eiloart. In 3 vols. Crown 8vo, cloth.

**MARGARET AND ELIZABETH.** A Story of the Sea. By Katherine Saunders, Author of " Gideon's Rock," etc. In 1 vol. Cloth, crown 8vo.

"Simply yet powerfully told. . . . This opening picture is so exquisitely drawn as to be a fit introduction to a story of such simple pathos and power. . . . A very beautiful story closes as it began, in a tender and touching picture of homely happiness." *Pall Mall Gazette.*

FICTION—*continued.*

**MR. CARINGTON.** A Tale of Love and Conspiracy. By **Robert Turner Cotton.** In 3 vols. Cloth, crown 8vo.

"A novel in so many ways good, as in a fresh and elastic diction, stout unconventionality, and happy boldness of conception and execution. His novels, though free spoken, will be some of the healthiest of our day."—*Examiner.*

**TWO GIRLS.** By **Frederick Wedmore,** Author of "A Snapt Gold Ring." In 2 vols. Cloth, crown 8vo. [*Just out.*]

"A carefully-written novel of character, contrasting the two heroines of one love tale, an English lady and a French actress. Cicely is charming; the introductory description of her is a good specimen of the well-balanced sketches in which the author shines."—*Athenæum.*

**HEATHERGATE.** In 2 vols. Crown 8vo, cloth. A Story of Scottish Life and Character. By a new Author.

"Its merit lies in the marked antithesis of strongly developed characters, in different ranks of life, and resembling each other in nothing but their marked nationality."—*Athenæum.*

**THE QUEEN'S SHILLING.** By Captain **Arthur Griffiths,** Author of "Peccavi." 2 vols.

"Every scene, character, and incident of the book are so life-like that they seem drawn from life direct."—*Pall Mall Gazette.*

**MIRANDA.** A Midsummer Madness. By **Mortimer Collins.** 3 vols.

"Not a dull page in the whole three volumes."—*Standard.*

"The work of a man who is at once a thinker and a poet."—*Hour.*

**SQUIRE SILCHESTER'S WHIM.** By **Mortimer Collins,** Author of "Marquis and Merchant," "The Princess Clarice," etc. 3 vols. Crown 8vo.

"We think it the best (story) Mr. Collins has yet written. Full of incident and adventure."—*Pall Mall Gazette.*

"So clever, so irritating, and so charming a story."—*Standard.*

**THE PRINCESS CLARICE.** A Story of 1871. By **Mortimer Collins.** 2 vols. Crown 8vo.

"Mr. Collins has produced a readable book, amusingly characteristic."—*Athenæum.*

"A bright, fresh, and original book."—*Standard.*

**REGINALD BRAMBLE.** A Cynic of the 19th Century. An Autobiography. 1 vol.

"There is plenty of vivacity in Mr. Bramble's narrative."—*Athenæum.*

"Written in a lively and readable style."—*Hour.*

**EFFIE'S GAME;** How she Lost and how she Won. By **Cecil Clayton.** 2 vols.

"Well written. The characters move, and act, and, above all, talk like human beings, and we have liked reading about them."—*Spectator.*

**CHESTERLEIGH.** By **Ansley Conyers.** 3 vols. Crown 8vo.

"We have gained much enjoyment from the book."—*Spectator.*

**BRESSANT.** A Romance. By **Julian Hawthorne.** 2 vols. Crown 8vo.

"One of the most powerful with which we are acquainted."—*Times.*

"We shall once more have reason to rejoice whenever we hear that a new work is coming out written by one who bears the honoured name of Hawthorne."—*Saturday Review.*

**HONOR BLAKE:** The Story of a Plain Woman. By **Mrs. Keatinge,** Author of "English Homes in India," etc. 2 vols. Crown 8vo.

"One of the best novels we have met with for some time."—*Morning Post.*

"A story which must do good to all, young and old, who read it."—*Daily News.*

**OFF THE SKELLIGS.** By **Jean Ingelow.** (Her First Romance.) In 4 vols. Crown 8vo.

"Clever and sparkling."—*Standard.*

"We read each succeeding volume with increasing interest, going almost to the point of wishing there was a fifth."—*Athenæum.*

**SEETA.** By **Colonel Meadows Taylor,** Author of "Tara," "Ralph Darnell," etc. 3 vols. Crown 8vo.

"Well told, native life is admirably described, and the petty intrigues of native rulers, and their hatred of the English mingled with fear lest the latter should eventually prove the victors, are cleverly depicted."—*Athenæum.*

"Thoroughly interesting and enjoyable reading."—*Examiner.*

**WHAT 'TIS TO LOVE.** By the Author of "Flora Adair," "The Value of Fosterstown." 3 vols.

FICTION—*continued.*

**HESTER MORLEY'S PROMISE.** By Hesba Stretton. 3 vols.

" Much better than the average novels of the day ; has much more claim to critical consideration as a piece of literary work.—very clever."—*Spectator.*

" All the characters stand out clearly and are well sustained, and the interest of the story never flags."—*Observer.*

**THE DOCTOR'S DILEMMA.** By Hesba Stretton. Author of " Little Meg," &c. &c. 3 vols. Crown 8vo.

" A fascinating story which scarcely flags in interest from the first page to the last."—*British Quarterly Review.*

**THE ROMANTIC ANNALS OF A NAVAL FAMILY.** By Mrs. Arthur Traherne. Crown 8vo. 10s. 6d.

" Some interesting letters are introduced : amongst others, several from the late King William IV."—*Spectator.*

" Well and pleasantly told."—*Evening Standard.*

**THOMASINA.** By the Author of " Dorothy," " De Cressy," &c. 2 vols. Crown 8vo.

" A finished and delicate cabinet picture ; no line is without its purpose."—*Athenæum.*

**JOHANNES OLAF.** By E. de Wille. Translated by F. E. Bunnett. 3 vols. Crown 8vo.

" The art of description is fully exhibited ; perception of character and capacity for delineating it are obvious ; while there is great breadth and comprehensiveness in the plan of the story."—*Morning Post.*

**THE STORY OF SIR EDWARD'S WIFE.** By Hamilton Marshall, Author of " For Very Life." 1 vol. Crown 8vo.

" A quiet, graceful little story."—*Spectator.*

" Mr. Hamilton Marshall can tell a story closely and pleasantly."—*Pall Mall Gaz.*

**HERMANN AGHA.** An Eastern Narrative. By W. Gifford Palgrave. 2 vols. Crown 8vo, cloth, extra gilt. 18s.

" There is a positive fragrance as of newly-mown hay about it, as compared with the artificially perfumed passions which are detailed to us with such gusto by our ordinary novel-writers in their endless volumes."—*Observer.*

**A GOOD MATCH.** By Amelia Perrier, Author of " Mea Culpa." 2 vols.

" Racy and lively."—*Athenæum.*

" This clever and amusing novel."—*Pall Mall Gazette.*

**LINKED AT LAST.** By F. E. Bunnett. 1 vol. Crown 8vo.

" The reader who once takes it up will not be inclined to relinquish it without concluding the volume."—*Morning Post.*

" A very charming story."—*John Bull.*

**THE SPINSTERS OF BLATCH-INGTON.** By Mar. Travers. 2 vols. Crown 8vo.

" A pretty story. Deserving of a favourable reception."—*Graphic.*

" A book of more than average merits."—*Examiner.*

**PERPLEXITY.** By Sydney Mostyn. 3 vols. Crown 8vo.

" Written with very considerable power, great cleverness, and sustained interest."—*Standard.*

" The literary workmanship is good, and the story forcibly and graphically told."—*Daily News.*

**MEMOIRS OF MRS. LÆTITIA BOOTHBY.** By William Clark Russell. Author of " The Book of Authors." Crown 8vo. 7s. 6d.

" Clever and ingenious." — *Saturday Review.*

" Very clever book."—*Guardian.*

**CRUEL AS THE GRAVE.** By the Countess Von Bothmer. 3 vols. Crown 8vo.

" *Jealousy is cruel as the Grave.*"

" Interesting, though somewhat tragic."—*Athenæum.*

"Agreeable, unaffected, and eminently readable."—*Daily News.*

**HER TITLE OF HONOUR.** By Holme Lee. Second Edition. 1 vol. Crown 8vo.

" With the interest of a pathetic story is united the value of a definite and high purpose."—*Spectator.*

" A most exquisitely written story."—*Literary Churchman.*

**SEPTIMIUS.** A Romance. By Nathaniel Hawthorne. Second Edition. 1 vol. Crown 8vo, cloth, extra gilt. 9s.

The *Athenæum* says that " the book is full of Hawthorne's most characteristic writing."

## COL. MEADOWS TAYLOR'S INDIAN TALES.

### THE CONFESSIONS OF A THUG

Is now ready, and is the Volume of A New and Cheaper Edition, in 1 vol. each, Illustrated, price 6s. It will be followed by " TARA " (now in the press) " RALPH DARNELL," and " TIPPOO SULTAN."

*65, Cornhill ; and 12, Paternoster Row, London.*

# THE CORNHILL LIBRARY OF FICTION.
## 3s. 6d. per Volume.

IT is intended in this Series to produce books of such merit that readers will care to preserve them on their shelves. They are well printed on good paper, handsomely bound, with a Frontispiece, and are sold at the moderate price of 3s. 6d. each.

## THE HOUSE OF RABY. By **Mrs. G. Hooper.**

## A FIGHT FOR LIFE. By **Moy Thomas.**

## ROBIN GRAY. By **Charles Gibbon.**

"Pure in sentiment, well written, and cleverly constructed."—*British Quarterly Review.*

"A pretty tale, prettily told."—*Athenæum.*

"A novel of tender and pathetic interest."—*Globe.*

"An unassuming, characteristic, and entertaining novel."—*John Bull.*

## KITTY. By **Miss M. Betham-Edwards.**

"Lively and clever ... There is a certain dash in every description ; the dialogue is bright and sparkling."—*Athenæum.*

"Very pleasant and amusing."—*Globe.*

"A charming novel."—*John Bull.*

## HIRELL. By **John Saunders.**

"A powerful novel ... a tale written by a poet."—*Spectator.*

"A novel of extraordinary merit."—*Morning Post.*

"We have nothing but words of praise to offer for its style and composition."—*Examiner.*

## ONE OF TWO; or, The left-handed Bride. By **J. H. Friswell.**

"Told with spirit ... the plot is skilfully made."—*Spectator.*

"Admirably narrated, and intensely interesting."—*Public Opinion.*

## READY–MONEY MORTIBOY. A Matter-of-Fact Story.

"There is not a dull page in the whole story."—*Standard.*

"A very interesting and uncommon story." *Vanity Fair.*

"One of the most remarkable novels which has appeared of late."—*Pall Mall Gazette.*

## GOD'S PROVIDENCE HOUSE. By **Mrs. G. L. Banks.**

"Far above the run of common three-volume novels, evincing much literary power in not a few graphic descriptions of manners and local customs. .... A genuine sketch."—*Spectator.*

"Possesses the merit of care, industry, and local knowledge."—*Athenæum.*

"Wonderfully readable. The style is very simple and natural."—*Morning Post.*

## FOR LACK OF GOLD. By **Charles Gibbon.**

"A powerfully written nervous story."—*Athenæum.*

"A piece of very genuine workmanship."—*British Quarterly Review.*

"There are few recent novels more powerful and engrossing."—*Examiner.*

## ABEL DRAKE'S WIFE. By **John Saunders.**

"A striking book, clever, interesting, and original. We have seldom met with a book so thoroughly true to life, so deeply

interesting in its detail, and so touching in its simple pathos."—*Athenæum.*

*OTHER STANDARD NOVELS TO FOLLOW.*

# THEOLOGICAL.

**WORDS OF TRUTH AND CHEER.** A Mission of Instruction and Suggestion. By the **Rev. Archer P. Gurney.** 1 vol. Crown 8vo. Price 6s. *[In the Press.*

**THE GOSPEL ITS OWN WITNESS.** Being the Hulsean Lectures for 1873. By the **Rev. Stanley Leathes.** 1 vol. Crown 8vo.

**THE CHURCH AND THE EMPIRES:** Historical Periods. By **Henry W. Wilberforce.** Preceded by a Memoir of the Author, by J. H. Newman, D.D. 1 vol. Post 8vo. Price 10s. 6d.

**THE HIGHER LIFE.** A New Volume by the **Rev. J. Baldwin Brown,** Author of "The Soul's Exodus," etc. 1 vol. Crown 8vo. Price 7s. 6d.

**HARTHAM CONFERENCES; OR, DISCUSSIONS UPON SOME OF THE RELIGIOUS TOPICS OF THE DAY.** By the **Rev. F. W. Kingsford, M.A.,** Vicar of S. Thomas's, Stamford Hill; late Chaplain H. E. I. C. (Bengal Presidency). "Audi alteram partem." Crown 8vo. Price 3s. 6d.

**STUDIES IN MODERN PROBLEMS.** A Series of Essays by various Writers. Edited by the **Rev. Orby Shipley, M.A.** Vol. I. Cr. 8vo. Price 5s.

### CONTENTS.

Sacramental Confession. A. H. WARD, B.A.
Abolition of the 39 Articles.
    NICHOLAS POCOCK, M.A.
The Sanctity of Marriage.
    JOHN WALTER LEA, B.A.
Creation and Modern Science.
    GEORGE GREENWOOD, M.A.

Retreats for Persons Living in the World.
    T. T. CARTER, M.A.
Catholic and Protestant.
    EDWARD L. BLENKINSOPP, M.A.
The Bishops on Confession. THE EDITOR.

A Second Series is being published, price 6d. each part.

**UNTIL THE DAY DAWN.** Four Advent Lectures delivered in the Episcopal Chapel, Milverton, Warwickshire, on the Sunday Evenings during Advent, 1870. By the **Rev. Marmaduke E. Browne.** Crown 8vo. Price 2s. 6d.

"Four really original and stirring sermons." *John Bull.*

**A SCOTCH COMMUNION SUNDAY.** To which are added Discourses from a Certain University City. Second Edition. By **A. K. H. B.,** Author of "The Recreations of a Country Parson." Crown 8vo. Second Edition. Price 5s.

"Some discourses are added, which are couched in language of rare power." *John Bull.*
"Exceedingly fresh and readable."— *Glasgow News.*

"We commend this volume as full of interest to all our readers. It is written with much ability and good feeling, with excellent taste and marvellous tact." *Church Herald.*

**EVERY DAY A PORTION:** Adapted from the Bible and the Prayer Book, for the Private Devotions of those living in Widowhood. Collected and Edited by the **Lady Mary Vyner.** Square crown 8vo, printed on good paper, elegantly bound. Price 5s.

"Now she that is a widow indeed, and desolate, trusteth in God."

**CHURCH THOUGHT AND CHURCH WORK.** Edited by the **Rev. Chas. Anderson, M.A.**, Editor of "Words and Works in a London Parish." Demy 8vo. Pp. 250. 7s. 6d. Containing Articles by the Rev. J. LL. DAVIES, J. M. CAPES, HARRY JONES, BROOKE LAMBERT, A. J. ROSS, Professor CHEETHAM, the EDITOR, and others.

Second Edition.

**WORDS AND WORKS IN A LONDON PARISH.** Edited by the **Rev. Charles Anderson, M.A.** Demy 8vo. 6s.

"It has an interest of its own for not a few minds, to whom the question 'Is the National Church worth preserving as such, and if so, how best increase its vital power?' is of deep and grave importance."—*Spectator.*

**ESSAYS ON RELIGION AND LITERATURE.** By Various Writers. Edited by the **Most Reverend Archbishop Manning.** Demy 8vo. 10s. 6d.

CONTENTS:—The Philosophy of Christianity.—Mystical Elements of Religion.—Controversy with the Agnostics.—A Reasoning Thought.—Darwinism brought to Book.—Mr. Mill on Liberty of the Press.—Christianity in relation to Society.—The Religious Condition of Germany.—The Philosophy of Bacon.—Catholic Laymen and Scholastic Philosophy.

**WHY AM I A CHRISTIAN?** By **Viscount Stratford de Redcliffe, P.C., K.G., G.C.B.** Crown 8vo. 3s. Third Edition.

"Has a peculiar interest, as exhibiting the convictions of an earnest, intelligent, and practical man."—*Contemporary Review.*

**THEOLOGY AND MORALITY.** Being Essays by the **Rev. J. Llewellyn Davies.** 1 vol. 8vo. Price 7s. 6d.

"The position taken up by Mr. Llewellyn Davies is well worth a careful survey on the part of philosophical students, for it represents the closest approximation of any theological system yet formulated to the religion of philosophy. . . We have not space to do more with regard to the social essays of the work before us, than to testify to the kindliness of spirit, sobriety, and earnest thought by which they are uniformly characterised."—*Examiner.*

**THE RECONCILIATION OF RELIGION AND SCIENCE.** Being Essays by the **Rev. T. W. Fowle, M.A.** 1 vol. 8vo. 10s. 6d.

"A book which requires and deserves the respectful attention of all reflecting Churchmen. It is earnest, reverent, thoughtful, and courageous. . . . There is scarcely a page in the book which is not equally worthy of a thoughtful pause."—*Literary Churchman.*

**HYMNS AND SACRED LYRICS.** By the **Rev. Godfrey Thring, B.A.** 1 vol. Crown 8vo.

**HYMNS AND VERSES,** Original and Translated. By the **Rev. Henry Downton.** Small crown 8vo. 3s. 6d.

"Considerable force and beauty characterise some of these verses."—*Watchman.* "Mr. Downton's 'Hymns and Verses' are worthy of all praise."—*English Churchman.* "Will, we do not doubt, be welcome as a permanent possession to those for whom they have been composed or to whom they have been originally addressed."—*Church Herald.*

THEOLOGICAL—*continued.*

**MISSIONARY ENTERPRISE IN THE EAST.** By the **Rev. Richard Collins.** Illustrated. Crown 8vo. 6s.

"A very graphic story told in lucid, simple, and modest style." — *English Churchman.*
"A readable and very interesting volume."—*Church Review.*

"We may judge from our own experience, no one who takes up this charming little volume will lay it down again till he has got to the last word."—*John Bull.*

**MISSIONARY LIFE IN THE SOUTH SEAS.** By **James Hutton.** 1 vol. Crown 8vo.        [*In the Press.*

**THE ETERNAL LIFE.** Being Fourteen Sermons. By the **Rev. Jas. Noble Bennie, M.A.** Crown 8vo. 6s.

"The whole volume is replete with matter for thought and study."—*John Bull.*
"Mr. Bennie preaches earnestly and well."—*Literary Churchman.*

"We recommend these sermons as wholesome Sunday reading."—*English Churchman.*

**THE REALM OF TRUTH.** By **Miss E. T. Carne.** Crown 8vo. 5s. 6d.

"A singularly calm, thoughtful, and philosophical inquiry into what Truth is, and what its authority."—*Leeds Mercury.*
"It tells the world what it does not like to hear, but what it cannot be told too often,

that Truth is something stronger and more enduring than our little doings, and speakings, and actings." — *Literary Churchman.*

**LIFE**: Conferences delivered at Toulouse. By the **Rev. Père Lacordaire.** Crown 8vo. 6s.

"Let the serious reader cast his eye upon any single page in this volume, and he will find there words which will arrest his attention and give him a desire to know

more of the teachings of this worthy follower of the saintly St. Dominick."—*Morning Post.*

Second Edition.

**CATHOLICISM AND THE VATICAN.** With a Narrative of the Old Catholic Congress at Munich. By **J. Lowry Whittle, A.M.,** Trin. Coll., Dublin. Crown 8vo. 4s. 6d.

"We may cordially recommend his book to all who wish to follow the course of the

Old Catholic movement." — *Saturday Review.*

**SIX PRIVY COUNCIL JUDGMENTS**—1850-1872. Annotated by **W. G. Brooke, M.A.,** Barrister-at-Law. Crown 8vo. 9s.

"The volume is a valuable record of cases forming precedents for the future."—*Athenæum.*
"A very timely and important publication. It brings into one view the great

judgments of the last twenty years, which will constitute the unwritten law of the English Establishment."—*British Quarterly Review.*

THE MOST COMPLETE HYMN BOOK PUBLISHED.

**HYMNS FOR THE CHURCH AND HOME.** Selected and Edited by the **Rev. W. Fleming Stevenson,** Author of "Praying and Working."

*The Hymn-book consists of Three Parts:*—I. For Public Worship. II. For Family and Private Worship. III. For Children; and contains Biographical Notices of nearly 300 Hymn-writers, with Notes upon their Hymns.

*⁎⁎ Published in various forms and prices, the latter ranging from 8d. to 6s. Lists and full particulars will be furnished on application to the Publisher.*

THEOLOGICAL—*continued.*

## WORKS BY THE REV. H. R. HAWEIS, M.A.
Sixth Edition.

**THOUGHTS FOR THE TIMES.** By the **Rev. H. R. Haweis, M.A.,** "Author of Music and Morals," etc. Crown 8vo. Price 7s. 6d.

"Bears marks of much originality of thought and individuality of expression."—*Pall Mall Gazette.*
"Mr. Haweis writes not only fearlessly,

but with remarkable freshness and vigour. In all that he says we perceive a transparent honesty and singleness of purpose."—*Saturday Review.*

**SPEECH IN SEASON.** A New Volume of Sermons. By the **Rev. H. R. Haweis.** Crown 8vo. Price 9s.

**UNSECTARIAN FAMILY PRAYERS,** for Morning and Evening for a Week, with short selected passages from the Bible. By the **Rev. H. R. Haweis, M.A.** Square crown 8vo. Price 3s. 6d.

## WORKS BY THE REV. C. J. VAUGHAN, D.D.
Fourth Edition.

**THE SOLIDITY OF TRUE RELIGION.** [*In the Press.*

**FORGET THINE OWN PEOPLE.** An Appeal for Missions. Small Crown 8vo. Price 3s. 6d.

**WORDS OF HOPE FROM THE PULPIT OF THE TEMPLE CHURCH.** Crown 8vo. Price 5s.

**THE YOUNG LIFE EQUIPPING IT-SELF FOR GOD'S SERVICE.** Being Four Sermons Preached before the University of Cambridge, in November, 1872. Crown 8vo. Price 3s. 6d.
"Has all the writer's characteristics of devotedness, purity, and high moral tone."—*London Quarterly Review.*
"As earnest, eloquent, and as liberal as everything else that he writes."—*Examiner.*

## WORKS BY THE REV. G. S. DREW, M.A.,
VICAR OF TRINITY, LAMBETH.

Second Edition.

**SCRIPTURE LANDS IN CONNECTION WITH THEIR HISTORY.** Bevelled Boards, 8vo. Price 10s. 6d.

"Mr. Drew has invented a new method of illustrating Scripture history—from observation of the countries. Instead of narrating his travels, and referring from time to time to the facts of sacred history belonging to the different countries, he writes an outline history of the Hebrew nation from Abraham downwards, with special reference to the various points in which the geography illustrates the history. . . He is very successful in picturing to his readers the scenes before his own mind."—*Saturday Review.*

Second Edition.

**NAZARETH: ITS LIFE AND LES-SONS.** Second Edition. In small 8vo, cloth. Price 5s.
"We have read the volume with great interest. It is at once succinct and suggestive, reverent and ingenious, observant of small details, and yet not forgetful of great principles."—*British Quarterly Review.*
"A very reverent attempt to elicit and develop Scripture intimations respecting our Lord's thirty years' sojourn at Nazareth. The author has wrought well at the unworked mine, and has produced a very valuable series of Scripture lessons, which will be found both profitable and singularly interesting."—*Guardian.*

**THE DIVINE KINGDOM ON EARTH AS IT IS IN HEAVEN.** In demy 8vo, bound in cloth. Price 10s. 6d.

"Entirely valuable and satisfactory. . . . . . . . . There is no living divine to whom the authorship would not be a credit."—*Literary Churchman.*

"Thoughtful and eloquent. . . . Full of original thinking admirably expressed."—*British Quarterly Review.*

## THEOLOGICAL—*continued.*

# WORKS OF THE LATE REV. F. W. ROBERTSON.

### NEW AND CHEAPER EDITIONS.

**SERMONS.**

Vol. I. Small crown 8vo. Price 3s. 6d.
Vol. II. Small crown 8vo. Price 3s. 6d.
Vol. III. Small crown 8vo. Price 3s. 6d.
Vol. IV. Small crown 8vo. Price 3s. 6d.

**EXPOSITORY LECTURES ON ST. PAUL'S EPISTLE TO THE CORINTHIANS.** Small crown 8vo. 5s.

**AN ANALYSIS OF MR. TENNYSON'S "IN MEMORIAM."** (Dedicated by permission to the Poet-Laureate.) Fcap. 8vo. 2s.

**THE EDUCATION OF THE HUMAN RACE.** Translated from the German of **Gotthold Ephraim Lessing.** Fcap. 8vo. 2s. 6d.

**LECTURES AND ADDRESSES, WITH OTHER LITERARY REMAINS.** A New Edition. With Introduction by the Rev. Stopford A. Brooke, M.A. In One Vol. Uniform with the Sermons. 5s. [*Preparing.*

**A LECTURE ON FRED. W. ROBERTSON, M.A.** By the Rev. F. A. Noble. Delivered before the Young Men's Christian Association of Pittsburgh, U.S. 1s. 6d.

---

# WORKS BY THE REV. STOPFORD A. BROOKE, M.A.

### Chaplain in Ordinary to Her Majesty the Queen.

**THE LATE REV. F. W. ROBERTSON, M.A., LIFE AND LETTERS OF.** Edited by **Stopford Brooke, M.A.**

I. In 2 vols., uniform with the Sermons. 7s. 6d.

II. Library Edition, in demy 8vo, with Two Steel Portraits. 12s.

III. A Popular Edition, in 1 vol. 6s.

**THEOLOGY IN THE ENGLISH POETS.** Being Lectures delivered by the Rev. Stopford A. Brooke. 9s.

Seventh Edition.

**CHRIST IN MODERN LIFE.** Sermons Preached in St. James's Chapel, York Street, London. Crown 8vo. 7s. 6d.

"Nobly fearless, and singularly strong. . . . carries our admiration throughout."—*British Quarterly Review.*

Second Edition.

**FREEDOM IN THE CHURCH OF ENGLAND.** Six Sermons suggested by the Voysey Judgment. In 1 vol. Crown 8vo, cloth. 3s. 6d.

"A very fair statement of the views in respect to freedom of thought held by the liberal party in the Church of England."—*Blackwood's Magazine.*

"Interesting and readable, and characterised by great clearness of thought, frankness of statement, and moderation of tone."—*Church Opinion.*

Seventh Edition.

**SERMONS** Preached in St. James's Chapel, York Street, London. Crown 8vo. 6s.

"No one who reads these sermons will wonder that Mr Brooke is a great power in London, that his chapel is thronged, and his followers large and enthusiastic. They are fiery, energetic, impetuous sermons, rich with the treasures of a cultivated imagination."—*Guardian.*

**THE LIFE AND WORK OF FREDERICK DENISON MAURICE: A** Memorial Sermon. Crown 8vo, sewed. 1s.

A NEW VOLUME OF SERMONS IS IN THE PRESS.

---

*65, Cornhill; & 12, Paternoster Row, London.*

## MISCELLANEOUS.

— ✦ —

VILLAGE HEALTH. By **Horace Swete, M.D.** [*In the Press.*

THE POPULAR EDITION OF THE DAILY NEWS' NARRA-
TIVE OF THE ASHANTEE WAR. 1 vol. Crown 8vo.
[*In the Press.*

HAKAYET ABDULLA. A Tale of the early British Settlement in the
Malaccas. By a **Native.** Translated by **John T. Thompson.** 1 vol.
Post 8vo.

THE SHAKESPEARE ARGOSY : containing much of the wealth of
Shakespeare's Wisdom and Wit, alphabetically arranged by **Captain A.
Harcourt.** Crown 8vo. [*In the Press.*

SOCIALISM : its Nature, its Dangers, and its Remedies considered by the
**Rev. M. Kaufman, B.A.** 1 vol. Crown 8vo. [*In the Press.*

CHARACTERISTICS FROM THE WRITINGS OF Dr. J. H.
NEWMAN : being Selections Personal, Historical, Philosophical, and
Religious ; from his various Works. Arranged with the Author's personal
approval. 1 vol. With a Portrait.

Second Edition.
CREMATION ; THE TREATMENT OF THE BODY AFTER
DEATH : with a Description of the Process and necessary Apparatus.
Crown 8vo, sewed. 1s.

'ILAM ÉN NAS. Historical Tales and Anecdotes of the Times of the Early
Khalifahs. Translated from the Arabic Originals. By **Mrs. Godfrey
Clerk,** Author of "The Antipodes and Round the World." Crown 8vo.
Price 7s.

"As full of valuable information as it is of amusing incident."—*Evening Standard.* "Those who like stories full of the genuine colour and fragrance of the East should by all means read Mrs. Godfrey Clerk's volume."—*Spectator.*

THE PLACE OF THE PHYSICIAN. Being the Introductory Lecture at
Guy's Hospital, 1873-74 ; to which is added
ESSAYS ON THE LAW OF HUMAN LIFE AND ON THE RELATION
BETWEEN ORGANIC AND INORGANIC WORLDS.

By **James Hinton,** Author of "Man and His Dwelling-Place." Crown
8vo, cloth. Price 3s. 6d.

Third Edition.
LITTLE DINNERS ; HOW TO SERVE THEM WITH ELE-
GANCE AND ECONOMY. By **Mary Hooper,** Author of "The
Handbook of the Breakfast Table." 1 vol. Crown 8vo. Price 5s.

THE PORT OF REFUGE ; OR, COUNSEL AND AID TO SHIPMASTERS
IN DIFFICULTY, DOUBT, OR DISTRESS. By **Manley Hopkins,** Author
of "A Handbook of Average," "A Manual of Insurance," &c. Cr. 8vo.
Price 6s.

SUBJECTS :—The Shipmaster's Position and Duties.—Agents and Agency.—Average.—Bottomry, and other Means of Raising Money.—The Charter-Party, and Bill-of-Lading. Stoppage in Transitu ; and the Shipowner's Lien.—Collision.

MISCELLANEOUS—*continued.*

**LOMBARD STREET.** A Description of the Money Market. By **Walter Bagehot.** Large crown 8vo. Fourth Edition. 7*s.* 6*d.*

"Mr. Bagehot touches incidentally a hundred points connected with his subject, and pours serene white light upon them all."—*Spectator.*
"Anybody who wishes to have a clear idea of the workings of what is called the Money Market should procure a little

volume which Mr. Bagehot has just published, and he will there find the whole thing in a nut-shell." —*Saturday Review.*
"Full of the most interesting economic history."—*Athenæum.*

**THE ENGLISH CONSTITUTION.** By **Walter Bagehot.** A New Edition, revised and corrected, with an Introductory Dissertation on recent Changes and Events. Crown 8vo. 7*s.* 6*d.*

"A pleasing and clever study on the department of higher politics."—*Guardian.*
"No writer before him had set out so

clearly what the efficient part of the English Constitution really is."—*Pall Mall Gazette.*

**NEWMARKET AND ARABIA; AN EXAMINATION OF THE DESCENT OF RACERS AND COURSERS.** By **Roger D. Upton,** Captain late 9th Royal Lancers. Post 8vo. With Pedigrees and Coloured Frontispiece. 9*s.*

"It contains a good deal of truth, and it abounds with valuable suggestions."—*Saturday Review.*
"A remarkable volume. The breeder can well ponder over its pages."—*Bell's Life.*

"A thoughtful and intelligent book. . . A contribution to the history of the horse of remarkable interest and importance."—*Baily's Magazine.*

**MOUNTAIN, MEADOW, AND MERE:** a Series of Outdoor Sketches of Sport, Scenery, Adventures, and Natural History. By **G. Christopher Davies.** With 16 Illustrations by W. HARCOURT. Crown 8vo. Price 6*s.*

"Mr. Davies writes pleasantly, graphically, with the pen of a lover of nature, a naturalist, and a sportsman."—*Field.*
"Pervaded throughout by the graceful

melody of a natural idyl, and the details of sport are subordinated to a dominating sense of the beautiful and picturesque."
*Saturday Review.*

**HOW TO AMUSE AND EMPLOY OUR INVALIDS.** By **Harriet Power.** Fcap. 8vo. 2*s.* 6*d.*

"A very useful little brochure . . . Will become a universal favourite with the class for whom it is intended, while it will afford

many a useful hint to those who live with them."—*John Bull.*

**REPUBLICAN SUPERSTITIONS.** Illustrated by the Political History of the United States. Including a Correspondence with M. Louis Blanc. By **Moncure D. Conway.** Crown 8vo. 5*s.*

"A very able exposure of the most plausible fallacies of Republicanism, by a writer of remarkable vigour and purity of style."—*Standard.*

"Mr. Conway writes with ardent sincerity. He gives us some good anecdotes, and he is occasionally almost eloquent."—*Guardian.*

**STREAMS FROM HIDDEN SOURCES.** By **B. Montgomerie Ranking.** Crown 8vo. 6*s.*

"We doubt not that Mr. Ranking's enthusiasm will communicate itself to many of his readers, and induce them in like manner to follow back these streamlets to their parent river." *Graphic.*

"The effect of reading the seven tales he presents to us is to make us wish for some seven more of the same kind." *Pall Mall Gazette.*

**GLANCES AT INNER ENGLAND.** A Lecture delivered in the United States and Canada. By **Edward Jenkins, M.P.,** Author of "Ginx's Baby," &c. Crown 8vo. 5*s.*

Thirty-Second Edition.

## GINX'S BABY: HIS BIRTH AND OTHER MISFORTUNES.
By **Edward Jenkins.** Crown Svo. Price 2s.

Fourteenth Thousand.

## LITTLE HODGE. A Christmas Country Carol. By **Edward Jenkins,**
Author of "Ginx's Baby," &c. Illustrated. Crown Svo. 5s.
A Cheap Edition in paper covers, price 1s.

Sixth Edition.

## LORD BANTAM. By **Edward Jenkins,** Author of "Ginx's Baby."
Crown Svo. Price 2s. 6d.

## LUCHMEE AND DILLOO. A Story of West Indian Life. By **Edward Jenkins,** Author of "Ginx's Baby," "Little Hodge," &c. 2 vols. Demy Svo. Illustrated. [*Preparing.*

## TALES OF THE ZENANA, OR A NUWAB'S LEISURE HOURS.
In 2 Vols. Crown Svo. [*Preparing.*

## PANDURANG HARI; or, MEMOIRS OF A HINDOO. A Tale of Mahratta Life sixty years ago. With a Preface by **Sir H. Bartle E. Frere, G.C.S.I.,** &c. 2 vols. Crown Svo. Price 21s.

"There is a quaintness and simplicity in the roguery of the hero that makes his life as attractive as that of Guzman d'Alfarache or Gil Blas, and so we advise our readers not to be dismayed at the length of Pandurang Hari, but to read it resolutely through. If they do this they cannot, we think, fail to be both amused and interested."—*Times.*

## GIDEON'S ROCK, and other Stories. By **Katherine Saunders.** In 1 vol. Crown Svo. Price 6s. [*Just out.*

CONTENTS.—Gideon's Rock.—Old Matthew's Puzzle.—Gentle Jack.—Uncle Ned.—The Retired Apothecary.

## JOAN MERRYWEATHER, and other Stories. By **Katherine Saunders.** In 1 vol. Crown Svo.

CONTENTS.—The Haunted Crust.—The Flower-Girl.—Joan Merryweather.—The Watchman's Story.—An Old Letter.

## MODERN PARISH CHURCHES; THEIR PLAN, DESIGN, AND FURNITURE. By **J. T. Micklethwaite.** Crown Svo. Price 7s. 6d.

## LONGEVITY; THE MEANS OF PROLONGING LIFE AFTER MIDDLE AGE. By **Dr. John Gardner,** Author of "A Handbook of Domestic Medicine," &c. Small Crown Svo.

## STUDIES AND ROMANCES. By **H. Schutz Wilson.** 1 vol. Crown Svo. Price 7s. 6d.

"Open the book, however, at what page the reader may, he will find something to amuse and instruct, and he must be very hard to please if he finds nothing to suit him, either grave or gay, stirring or romantic, in the capital stories collected in this well-got-up volume."—*John Bull.*

## THE PELICAN PAPERS. Reminiscences and Remains of a Dweller in the Wilderness. By **James Ashcroft Noble.** Crown Svo. 6s.

"Written somewhat after the fashion of Mr. Helps's 'Friends in Council.'"—*Examiner.*

"Will well repay perusal by all thoughtful and intelligent readers."—*Liverpool Leader.*

MISCELLANEOUS—*continued.*

**BRIEFS AND PAPERS.** Being Sketches of the Bar and the Press. By **Two Idle Apprentices.** Crown 8vo. 7s. 6d.

"Written with spirit and knowledge, and give some curious glimpses into what the majority will regard as strange and unknown territories."—*Daily News.*

"This is one of the best books to while away an hour and cause a generous laugh that we have come across for a long time." —*John Bull.*

**THE SECRET OF LONG LIFE.** Dedicated by Special Permission to Lord St. Leonards. Third Edition. Large crown 8vo. 5s.

"A charming little volume."—*Times.* "A very pleasant little book, cheerful, genial, scholarly."—*Spectator.*

"Entitled to the warmest admiration."— *Pall Mall Gazette.*

**SOLDIERING AND SCRIBBLING.** By **Archibald Forbes,** of the *Daily News,* Author of "My Experience of the War between France and Germany." Crown 8vo. 7s. 6d.

"All who open it will be inclined to read through for the varied entertainment which it affords."—*Daily News.*

"There is a good deal of instruction to outsiders touching military life, in this volume."—*Evening Standard.*

www.ingramcontent.com/pod-product-compliance
Lightning Source LLC
Chambersburg PA
CBHW060523030726
47498CB00004B/1049